# Dangerous

## An Anthology

Rainbows Publishing

The rights of Rosemarie Ford, Patricia Golledge, Peter Goodsall, Elspeth Green, Deborah Grice, Alyson Heap, Sarah Maguire, Martin Mickleburgh, Peter Owen, David Mills, Stephen Rigby and Peter Roberts to be identified as Authors of the Work has been asserted by them in accordance with the Copyright, Designs and Patents Act 1988.

First published in Great Britain by Rainbows Publishing in 2006

All rights reserved. No part of this publication may be reproduced, stored in a retrieval system, or transmitted, in any form or by any means without the prior written permission of the copyright owners.

A catalogue record is available for this title from the British Library
ISBN 0 954823 53 2

Published in Great Britain by
Rainbows Publishing
Weston-Super-Mare
Somerset

www.rainbows-publishing.co.uk
Copyright © 2006

# Contents

1. Acknowledgements — vi
2. Foreword — vii
3. "Rekishika (The Historian)" by Martin Mickleburgh — 9
4. "The Dam" by Deborah Grice — 19
5. "Healing" by Alyson Heap — 29
6. "Greed" by Peter Goodsall — 33
7. "The Rock of Death" by Elspeth Green — 39
8. "One For The Kiddies" by Peter Owen — 43
9. "Mary" by Alyson Heap — 51
10. "Killing Nigel" by Sarah Maguire — 59
11. "Power of Persuasion" by Patricia Golledge — 65
12. "Amnesia" by Stephen Rigby — 71
13. "The First Spots of Blood" by Peter Roberts — 85
14. "Reunion" by David Mills — 93
15. "A Bit of a Do" by Peter Owen — 105

# Contents

| | | |
|---|---|---|
| 16. | "Going Shopping" by Elspeth Green | 107 |
| 17. | "The Rugby Pitch …" a poem by Patricia Golledge | 115 |
| 18. | "Omar Kandala" by Peter Goodsall | 117 |
| 19. | "Nothing But The Truth" by Alyson Heap & Rose Ford | 125 |
| 20. | "Just a Normal Day!" by Elspeth Green | 137 |
| 21. | "The White Crow" by Martin Mickleburgh | 143 |
| 22. | "Doing It For Uncle Arthur" by Peter Owen | 149 |
| 23. | "Memories" by Rosemarie Ford | 153 |
| 24. | "It's Cool" by Peter Goodsall | 163 |
| 25. | "Rimes Last Case" by Cynthia Grimm | 169 |
| 26. | "The Other World" by Martin Mickleburgh | 175 |
| 27. | "Consequences" by Deborah Grice | 179 |
| 28. | "Rest" by Patricia Golledge | 183 |
| 29. | "Tone" by Peter Goodsall | 187 |
| 30. | "Mrs. Throttleback" by Peter Owen | 191 |

# Contents

| | |
|---|---|
| 31. "Passing Trade" by Martin Mickleburgh | 195 |
| 32. "The Life Model" by Alyson Heap | 199 |
| 33. "I Have Trapped An Angel" a poem by Peter Goodsall | 205 |
| 34. "The Artist" by Elspeth Green | 207 |
| 35. "Resurrection" by Deborah Grice | 215 |
| 36. "The Cave" a poem by Deborah Grice | 219 |
| 37. "The Dauber" by Martin Mickleburgh | 221 |
| 38. "Thirteen Minutes" by Peter Goodsall | 231 |
| 39. "Café des Amis" by Patricia Golledge | 235 |
| 40. "Traitors!" a poem by Alyson Heap | 241 |
| 41. "Crossing Point" by David Mills | 243 |
| 42. "Sir Willoughby" by Peter Owen | 249 |
| 43. "Enoch & Claude" by Martin Mickleburgh | 253 |
| 44. "A Love Story" by Sarah Maguire | 263 |

# Acknowledgements

We are once again greatly indebted to Stephen Troth for the excellent cover illustration and for the superbly executed Pier Group logo.

Thanks go to our wonderful and inspiring mentor: more than one of us have undergone an epiphany!

Many thanks must also go to the Clevedon Pier Trust for allowing us to use their photograph and to Hilary Semmens for her help with publishing the book and negotiating the minutiae of handling unexpected bureaucracy! And thank you also to Stephanie Goodsall for much proof-reading and coffee!

The Pier Group

# Foreword

Welcome to Dangerous Cocktail, the third collection of writing by the Pier Group.

After last year's individual successes in the Weston Short Story Competition we entered the entire collection, Disappeared, in a national competition and carried off first prize. Suitably enthused, we set about this year's anthology. What you hold is the result of nine months' writing, criticism and preparation, and reflects the wildly divergent interests and obsessions of our members; we have stories for most eventualities, from queens awaiting execution to old salts besotted with the sea. We hope you find much to enjoy and something to give you pause for thought and pleasure.

In our last collection, we ran a competition to write a story whose theme would be Reappeared. In the event, we couldn't choose between two fine potential winners so we have decided to print them both. The writers are Peter Roberts from Clevedon and Steve Rigby from Bath. Congratulations to both of you.

This year we thought we would do something rather different: we have decided to give £1 from the sale of every copy to the Babe Appeal. This is an appeal run by Children's Hospice South West, with the aim of building equipping and endowing a new hospice for children at Charlton Farm near Bristol. You can find out more about it at www.chsw.org.uk.

Finally, we must pay tribute once more to Stephen Troth, the artist responsible for the cover illustration and the Pier Group logo. We think he has excelled himself this year!

# 歴史家

## (The Historian)

### Martin Mickleburgh

We met on the long sweep of beach which lies to the south of what used to be the naval dockyard. What used to be. Of course, even now, even if I still had the power of speech, in law I would not be permitted to use such an expression. The authorities, or at least what then passed for them, decreed, two years after the last great war, that we must forget all. I was barely three years old at the time so that I have no distinct memory of the announcement, made via whole-page advertisements in the few remaining newspapers, by crude posters pasted to walls on every street, and by criers, bellowing in the squares and from temple porches. If we do not remember it, the past does not exist, and so we may start again, unstained by longing, guilt or regret. That was the decree, and in its name, men were decapitated for daring to speak of the days before the war. I do not think that the authorities any longer command sufficient respect to have a man put to death, but the habit has taken: our people have lost their past and regained a kind of innocence.

I said that I have no distinct memory of the day of the proclamation of forgetfulness, and this, as far as it goes, is true. But I can remember a before and an after. Before, my father and his three brothers would gather around the kitchen table after a day's work and talk and laugh and drink sake late into the night. I can remember being woken by their laughter and coming into the kitchen from my bedroom and being swept up onto my father's knee and being hugged and kissed and chucked under the chin - the only son, the beloved. After, there was

## Dangerous Cocktail

silence. Not the silence of a winter morning, but the silence of a held breath; the silence, as I came to understand after my mother's funeral, of loss sustained and borne. We took to looking at the ground at our feet: the sky had lost its beauty.

When I was seven years old, and so legally responsible for my actions, my father took me with him one day to the hives. We both donned smocks and veils and my father set about the business of tending his bees. For a while he said nothing to me and in the silence I watched his hands, moving with slow precision, no gesture wasted. They were tanned to a dark woody brown by the sun and had veins which ran like cords immediately below the skin.

After some time he stopped, took me by the elbow and led me to a corner of the field where there was an ancient maple, and, standing beneath its branches, he told me the little that I would know for the next thirty-seven years about what had befallen Japan. I cannot now remember his exact words, but I recall with pristine clarity one image that he used: China and America as hammer and anvil, with Japan caught in between. We were crushed, smashed, obliterated.

He gave me no idea of what the world before the war – the world of his own childhood and early marriage – had been like. But the weight in his voice, the long pauses between words, gave me to understand that it must have been a world filled with delight. He told me, clearly, that that was all he would ever say about the past and that it must be sufficient to explain the present - there could be no questions. By such means we are formed and fixed into a life; with such meagre fare we feed our souls.

After my father died, his brothers - my uncles - would have had me take over the hives, but I would not do it. I was beset by a kind of restlessness, that same restlessness that made women reject me; one said 'You have too much distance in your eyes.' And so I never married; and so I became a fisherman.

It is about three day's walk from our small town to the sea. I had never been there before, but my cousin - on my mother's side - lived in

## The Historian

a shack close by the beach and had come to visit the summer that I was nineteen. He said little - I have since learned that fishermen are by nature taciturn; the endless dialogue with the sea is all the conversation they can bear - but his few words, the space, the light, the wind, set a resonance ringing in me so that, the winter after my father's funeral, I packed my few belongings and made my way to the sea. I was twenty-nine years old.

For half a year I shared my cousin's shack and he taught me what I needed to know about fishing and the handling of a boat. He never asked for payment or compensation; that is another thing I learned about fishermen: their generosity, born of a profound sense of their mortality at the hands of the sea.

Then, during the first summer, I built a shack of my own, scavenging drift wood from the foreshore. Some of the wood bore strange marks which I came to know, much later, were the signs of life before the war. Even as we would forget, the world remembers for us.

In the second summer I built a boat, the first of three that I have owned. Until then I had accompanied my cousin and shared with him the repairing of nets, the mending of sails and the gutting and smoking of fish. If he was glad of my company, he never showed it; after the last trip I made with him, he shook my hand, looking down at the sand as he did so. We did not speak.

Six years later his boat was washed ashore, half full of water, the nets hopelessly tangled, the sails shredded by slatting in the wind. There was no sign of my cousin. I never found his body.

Soon afterwards I moved my shack to the long beach and so began my seven years' silence.

It was not that I made any singular decision to spare the world my voice; it was, so I think now, rather that the wind took from me any desire for speech. And besides, no-one ever passed. If I had wanted to speak, to whom would it have been?

Silence, as I came to understand it then, is more that the absence of one kind of noise; rather it is the suspension of the soul's commerce

## Dangerous Cocktail

with the outer world, and of the marking of days in some imagined pursuit of an end for a life. I inhabited the present, looking neither forwards or back.

In the spring of the eighth year, in the early morning of a cool day with flying cloud and rain threatening, I came upon you on the beach, an hour's walk south of my shack. As I had taken my morning's reconnaissance along to the black boulder, I had seen your footprints; they simply started, as if you had descended on wings and then begun walking. I knew immediately that it must be a woman because of the narrowness of the foot and the way the heel marks were almost in line, with the toes turning out.

I saw you from half a kilometre away, a dark lump against the silvery light. You were sitting with your knees drawn up and your head gathered in your arms.

I remember that I stopped momentarily, unsure what to do, unsure of whether to welcome your invasion. I shrugged - I see that clearly - and pressed on.

Eventually I came to you and stood over you. I saw that your fingers were stroking your forearms in tiny, barely-perceptible movements. I knew that I must wait. I cannot say - I mean that I can no longer remember - for how long I stood thus, listening to my heart and the rustling of blood in my ears and the rubbing of the sea on the beach. Later, when I tried to recall some sense of the time passing, it occurred to me that if I had come across you on the very first day of my seven years' silence, it would all have been as one.

Quite suddenly you looked up, your head facing directly towards me, your eyes closed.

It began to rain.

You opened your eyes and I fell through, out of this world. (As I remember it now there was a sound like a struck gong, heard at incalculable distance, but surely that cannot have been so.) I think that I must have looked backwards at my vanishing life, but I do not recall it now.

# The Historian

You asked What do you want? There was no hint of reproach or accusation; it was just a question, as if you were really saying What do you want of your life? My silence betrayed me: I could find no words. Instead I reached down with my hand; you took it and pulled yourself to your feet, all the time fixing me with your eye. I remember my surprise as you unfolded into the air before me, for you were barely shorter than me, your eyes almost level with mine. I cannot recall exactly your face as it was then - later, yes, but you had the capacity to fix yourself into time only at certain moments - but I remember that your hair was braided into a glossy plait which hung over your shoulder and between your breasts, almost to your waist. Your clothes - a skirt and a thin shirt - were damp and clung to you; you were all ribs, hips and elbows and blue-shadowed collar bones. You continued to hold my hand; I felt suddenly foolish.

You put your free hand behind the back of my neck and laid your cheek against mine and said, quietly, Feed me.

At first - for an hour? A day? A week? - you did not talk much, but I remember that you grunted with pleasure while eating the fish and rice which I prepared for you on the first morning. And you smiled at me. I remember the sense of that smile touching the nape of my neck. Light, cool, rain to my parched seven-years' drought.
You watched me mend a net. You watched me cut and re-braid a frayed rope. You watched me push my boat to the water's edge and jump aboard and scull it through the first wave or two before setting the sail and leaving you standing among the salt-ribbons and shells on the beach. And you watched me return. Again and again.
I watched you. I was baffled by you: you did not fit into my imagination. Your bones, your black river of hair, your eyes that followed me, slightly starting as if you had caught the moon's reflection in them. At night when I could not sleep, I sat and watched you breathing, and counted your dreams by the twitching of your

## Dangerous Cocktail

fingers. Was it desire? Even then? Yes, I see it now: you came and you brought hunger with you.

That was all before, because in the middle of the before-you-and-after-you there was another edge, another afterwards with its unwitting wilderness of before.

In the shadows of a late summer's evening, I had come back to the beach, riding the surf as I dropped the sail and made ready to jump into the shallows, bare of any catch, knowing we would go hungry that night. As I stood in the bows of my boat I looked up and saw you examining minutely the patchwork wooden shell of the shack. Did I feel a sudden cold gust of wind that blew my hair into my eyes and set the flesh on my forearms creeping? My memory says yes, but perhaps it is one of those elaborations with which we decorate life so as to mark more clearly its inflections.

I walked up to you and shook my head. You said nothing, only held me in your moon-gaze. The fingers of your right hand still rested on the wooden plank wall. And then the day blinked, the world changed and I took hold of your upper arms, jamming my mouth against yours and forcing your head back, as if my hunger could deflect what was coming.

You returned my kiss, violence for violence, biting and tearing at me; I tasted my own blood in my mouth. We stumbled into the shack, locked about each other, and fell onto the bed. Then oblivion.

Afterwards, as you slept, sprawled on your back, your breasts and belly still glazed with sweat, I watched you. I sat with my back against the wall and watched and remembered your skin, your heat, your taste. I was night-bound, erect and aching again, watching you and sucking on the memory of your flesh and your desolate ecstasy. Feed me. Feed me.

In the first light of the next morning you woke me and said I have waited to tell you. Now the time is right. Come. Look. You took me outside and you pointed at the wooden wall of the shack. This, you said, indicating a spray-greyed and smeary mark on one plank, this

# The Historian

says 'Mitsubishi'. Before the war they were a great company, one of the biggest in the world. And this - pointing to another mark – says 'Coca-Cola', which was a kind of drink made by the Americans, and this is the name of a Chinese bank, and this is the name of a ship, 'SS Meredith' - you mispronounced the central r - and this, underneath it, is, I think, the name of its destination, 'Yokohama'. You see, this is history, you said, right here, written into your walls. This is the faint glimmer of the past which bore you, of the world as it was.

When I turned away from you, I remembered my father's hands. Was it then a betrayal? How blithely I yielded to you, seizing your past so as to hold on to our present. Yes, just so, an easy betrayal.

I never knew where or how you had gorged yourself on memories, how you had trawled among the living and set your nets among the dead. You never told me. But you regurgitated it all for me, starting that night, on and on as the summer waned and winter overtook us. Then we would huddle together under a blanket, sometimes too cold even to make love, while you murmured all your known pasts into my ear and my heart. There were emperors, warriors, cities made entirely of glass, machines that could float among the clouds, great battles between ships and men, dynasties rising and falling, enmities and friendships, Americans, Chinese, British, Australians...and scattered amongst, the stories of ordinary people like your great-great-grandmother who died when a second sun bloomed one summer day in the sky over her city. You never knew how these things connected; they were like a litter of lights strewn across your sky: there was no sense of order, of what happened first and what later, but causation hummed through it all like a hidden principle. And slowly I began to understand the immensity of the past; all that unreckoned, unspoken sequence, all those threads snaking out of the dark to connect to you and to me in our shack by the sea. Sometimes, while you slept, I cried with the weight of it.

## Dangerous Cocktail

I became a creature of time.

Then, when I sat awake at night, looking at you sleeping, I could no longer sate myself on the memory of your flesh, for that was the past, even if only by an hour or two, and only the present could hold me still and quieted. And so I would contemplate your body, with such tenderness as I could summon, letting my eyes possess you, millimetre by millimetre, shadow, line, mass, relation, proportion. I discovered that you were beautiful. It was as much as I could bear.

In the spring of the following year you announced you were pregnant and I became, suddenly, a man with a future as well as a past. For a month, even to breathe was an exercise in joy. The vast beach seemed inexplicably intimate as if the world would fold itself about us like a protective arm. The fish gave themselves to us and we ate and grew sleek.

And then, on the first warm night of summer, as we lay at peace in each other's arms you said Only the past is real. Only the past is worth our love. You can only truly love what you no longer possess.

If I had understood, would I have tried to stop you? I cannot say.

In the half-light when I awoke I already knew you were gone. On the beach your footprints led to where the boat had been, and then there were the marks of the boat being pushed towards the water; but they stopped short of the sea's edge - you left as you had come, as if you had simply stepped out of the world.

I stumbled back into the shack to begin to remember you and to love you.

Seven years I was silent before you. Now it has been three times seven years since you left. Another twenty-one wordless years with no future and scarcely a present. What of our child? Our beloved? We should have grown old together.

Every day - many times each day! - I have thought of your last words and tried to wring the truth from them. But I have failed.

## The Historian

Sometimes I even wonder if you were wrong - but I could not live in a world where that was so.

What was it that you took from me? Was it any more than our history?

Now I am an old man and still I know nothing, still I understand nothing, save only these two things: all love is unbearable; all memory is loss.

# The Dam

Deborah Grice

Love beat inside Miss Avery's heart like a slow burning fuse. It was not love for anyone or anything in particular, but Love itself, unused and unclaimed by any man in the last forty or so years that had passed since Miss Avery had reached adolescence. Not *entirely* unused, as it is not the nature of love to lie confined and idle, but it must find some end or object to flow towards and around. Therefore, over the years, Miss Avery's pets have known an abundance of affection well beyond their own deserving. Even the most selfish of her cats basked in the sunshine of her adoration; and her canaries, not in themselves naturally affectionate, were nevertheless the recipients of much cooing and the blowing of mock kisses.

But love, fermenting slowly within the heart of an affectionate woman, is a powerful force, and, like a river that gradually rises against the wall of the dam, will, at some point, burst out in a great torrent, breaking through or over it.

The love in Miss Avery's heart, for which there was no sufficiently large outlet, had reached that point. Like a ripe seed pod ready to pop open at the lightest touch of a finger, her generous organ was barely restraining a veritable explosion of emotion. So true was this, that perhaps it would not have mattered who came within Miss Avery's purview that particular spring morning, though whether matters would have turned out better or worse with another, who can say? So, putting speculation aside and returning to matters of fact, let us follow our amiable character's journey on this particular morning, along her usual route and then into the unknown.

# Dangerous Cocktail

A stroll along Acacia Avenue had never previously led anywhere other than to Victoria Park, Miss Avery's favourite destination for her morning constitutional. However, on this morning, it led to a veritable helter-skelter of events, at least by the standards of genteel suburbia.

The unusual departure from routine began where Acacia Avenue turns into Laurel Drive. Scarcely had Miss Avery turned the corner when she was thrown off her feet by a violent collision. With what, she had initially no idea, but upon raising her head from the ground, she perceived a boy of ten or so wrapped round a lamppost and a skateboard upside down in the gutter, its wheels still slowly revolving. Feeling no bones broken, and concerned for the child, Miss Avery pulled herself onto her hands and knees and enquired after his well-being. Whereupon she is assaulted with such a torrent of invective and colourful abuse that our good lady bursts into tears of shock and distress, and sits back down on the pavement. The boy, well satisfied with this reaction, reclaims his board and trundles noisily off.

By another, co-incidental, departure from routine the whole incident was witnessed by a certain Mr. Pugh, a conventional and reticent man of sixty-four, who would have normally been in his office but, unusually, was still seated at his breakfast table at nine-thirty. His instinctive reaction is to shun the unusual and certainly to retreat from any form of unplanned encounter. However, on this occasion, his retiring nature is defeated by his upbringing, during which he was taught to come to the aid of any women, children or dogs in distress. Therefore, despite being half-way through a lightly-boiled egg (the perfect achievement of which is not to be taken lightly) he leaps up from the table and sprints (as far as a mature, portly gentleman *can* sprint) across the road. Thus Miss Avery, by then at the subsiding, gulping and sniffing stage of tears, sees suddenly in front of her a moustachioed gentleman bending solicitously over her and extending an arm. After the quick employment of her pocket handkerchief Miss

## The Dam

Avery grasps the arm and rises as gracefully as she can to her feet. Her neat recovery does not reflect, however, the sudden, chaotic confusion in her heart. For the visage of Mr. Pugh, unremarkable though it is, now represents for her the very epitome of chivalry and masculine succour, and so it is that the dam, under the force of a sudden surge of emotion, breaks, and the full force of Miss Avery's Love is released.

Mr. Pugh, of course, is entirely unaware of the beneficence that has fallen upon him, and asks politely if Miss Avery has sustained any injuries. Privately he is thinking of his egg, which is going cold, and regretting the fact that this incident is disrupting his timetable for the morning, for he has an appointment with the dentist.

Miss Avery, inexperienced in matters of love and courtship as she is, nevertheless has the Woman's innate instincts for entrapment. Suddenly she feels sure her ankle must be sprained, necessitating a reliance on the strong arm of Mr. Pugh as she attempts to walk. She speaks dismissively of the pain, but affects a strong limp as she takes a few steps along the pavement. "Oh dear," she muses, "however will I get home?"

Mr. Pugh is in a quandary. On the one hand, offering her a lift home will make him late for the dentist, and he prides himself on his punctuality. On the other hand, he possesses a delicacy that forbids him to enquire if the lady has the means to procure a taxi. Twenty-eight years in the bank, however, has given him a certain decisiveness, and he resolves the dilemma in an instant.

"I would be honoured, ma'am, to offer you a lift home, if you are able to permit a detour en-route to an appointment of previous standing, which will mean something of a wait for you in my motor vehicle."

## Dangerous Cocktail

Miss Avery, delighted that her unplanned, instinctive strategy has worked, replied that she was most grateful for the offer.

Thus it was that Miss Avery, for the first time in her life, rode in the front passenger seat of a rather grand car driven by a man wearing a well-tailored suit. She found the experience most pleasing, noting the comfortable leather seats, the polished wooden dashboard and the competent manoeuvres of her chauffeur. She felt shy to begin a conversation, so was relieved when her rescuer initiated a most appropriate discussion on the manners of today's youth and the regrettable lack of discipline in the modern home. The failings of parents and the inadequacies of the law enforcement agencies carried them safely to the door of the dentist, whereupon Mr. Pugh left her with the Light Classical channel on the car radio to entertain her until his return.

Closing her eyes to the sound of Prokofiev's Wedding March, Miss Avery allowed herself to drift along on the tide of a pleasing day-dream involving the elevation of Mr. Pugh onto a white charger and her own transformation into a dragon-beleaguered princess. She was still lost in this reverie when her knight returned, with the addition of a new amalgam filling in his right incisor. On the second half of the journey, due to the effect of the local anaesthetic, Mr. Pugh was disinclined to conversation, but the numbing sensation meant that his smile, normally of a cursory and minimal nature, was distorted into a wide, one-sided grin that distorted his expression into one of great satisfaction, even perhaps one of conspiratorial happiness. Miss Avery, the recipient of this lop-sided beaming, saw in it the desire to cement their expected new friendship and began to build new fantasies of extravagant proportions.

Following her womanly instincts however, she forbore from inviting him in for a cup of tea, knowing that Pursuit is the territory of the male sex, but she commented more than once upon her fortunate position on the corner of the street, overlooking the churchyard, so that he should remember the exact house. She planned, in the new certainty of her feelings being reciprocated, to leave nothing to chance. She passed the remainder of the day in that excited, fluttery state of those newly in love, lost in the re-living of each of the Beloved's expressions, words and gestures. To their great disgust she even forgot to feed the cats.

The next morning she woke early, with a feeling of nervous excitement in her stomach. Paying more than usual attention to her dress, she prepared for her morning walk. Her feet veritably danced along the pavement, drawing her irrevocably towards Laurel Drive. Having ascertained the previous day that her hero held a prestigious position at the Bank, she calculated that it would be safest to be in the vicinity of Laurel Drive before eight, not knowing his exact time of departure for work. By a happy co-incidence, or by the assistance of the gods that oversee the conduct of human love, our heroine turned the corner just as Mr. Pugh came through his garden gate. Remembering to lean heavily on her father's horse's-head walking cane, Miss Avery advanced, pronounced her ankle much improved already, and thanked him warmly for his chivalry of the day before. "I shall never forget your kindness," she concluded. Mr. Pugh, anxious to be punctual, dismissed her thanks in a self-deprecating manner, with a modest (and now more moderate) smile and set his course for the Bank, thinking no more of the encounter during the day. He was therefore all the more surprised to meet Miss Avery again, on his return journey.

"What a co-incidence," she exclaimed, laughing gaily. "Our paths seem destined to cross!"

What hand Destiny was playing, after the initial accident, was unclear, as Miss Avery was managing matters without relying on anything so unpredictable as fate. Each morning and evening of the

## Dangerous Cocktail

following week found her crossing Laurel Drive just as Mr. Pugh left and returned to his house. Good manners dictated an exchange of civilities, and so a pattern of a brief conversation was established. From having previously been unaware this lady's existence, Mr. Pugh now found himself, while he was in the bath on Friday evening, wondering what took his new acquaintances past his door with such regularity and what her movements were on a Saturday. The next morning he found himself glancing down from his bedroom window before descending to breakfast and for some reason did not feel great surprise when he saw Miss Avery lurking (yes that was the only word for it) on the corner of the two streets. An hour later she was still there. Clearly, his house was under siege.

Mr. Pugh was a rational man. He prided himself upon his powers of logic and mathematical deduction. As he toyed with the kipper he permitted himself on a Saturday, he strove to find a reason why a seemingly pleasant, well-educated, well-dressed lady of mature years should be stalking him. Briefly he wondered if she might be a burglar's accomplice, reporting on his movements, but dismissed the idea as too fanciful. Try as he might, he could think of no rational explanation for this behaviour. That he was the object of an excessive quantity of stored-up love did not occur to him. He was not a man of great Imagination and this was definitely outside its limits. He was, quite simply, baffled. He was also at a loss at to how he could explain this new development to his wife, when she returned from the Women's Institute 'Great Cathedrals of our Nation' coach tour in a week's time.

By Sunday, Miss Avery was equally at a loss. She had provided ample opportunities for Pursuit, but Pursuit had not occurred. After deep thought, she concluded that she must be too old-fashioned in her outlook. Things had moved on since she was a girl. In this day and age, women were supposed to be more encouraging, more overt in revealing their preferences. Sitting on her little camp stool in Victoria Park (from

## The Dam

where, with her grandfather's telescope, she could keep an eye on Mr. Pugh's comings and goings) she got out a notebook and began planning a new strategy. From now on, she would take the Initiative.

Mr. Pugh, having left his house on Monday morning rather nervously, was vastly relieved to find that he had reached the corner of the street without interception. His relief was short-lived, however, when his clerk showed in his first client of the day. He retreated back to the safety of his swivel chair behind the large desk as Miss Avery advanced.

In line with her strategy, she was not overtly or remotely flirtatious, but she let Mr. Pugh know that her wish to transfer her money to his Bank was on account of the fact that she liked to leave her savings in the care of someone she could clearly trust and whose personal integrity and character was above reproach. At this point she leaned forward across the mahogany desk and patted him gently on the arm. "Someone I know personally." Drawing on her gloves in a manner she had seen film stars use, she rose. "I look forward to seeing you again soon, Mr. Pugh, to discuss the details."

Mr. Pugh could see the logic behind this renewed contact, but on Tuesday things took a more perplexing aspect. As he pursued his accounts, he was interrupted by his clerk, who seemed to be greatly amused by something.

"Excuse me, Mr. Pugh, but there's a delivery for you."

Trying to recall if he had ordered new stationery or office equipment Mr. Pugh came out of his office to be presented, in front of all the counter staff, with a huge bouquet of red roses by a grinning delivery man. Retreating rapidly into his room, he then read the attached card. "From your grateful friend and admirer, Miss Rachel Avery." Mr. Pugh

## Dangerous Cocktail

groaned. An explanation for the strange nature of the last week was dawning on him, irrational, but possible. Wednesday's and Thursday's deliveries (an engraved fountain pen, with the words 'yours always' and a single red rose) confirmed his suspicions. He felt a rising sense of panic, albeit mingled with just the smallest trace of vanity.

His public school and National Service background had trained him to tackle problems 'head on.' Although he knew neither an honest-to-goodness wrestling match nor a bayonet charge could serve him here, he stuck to the principle and sent, via a young clerk, a politely worded request that Miss Avery attend his office at noon on the Friday.

How Miss Avery's heart leapt when the cream envelope with the Bank's crest on it was delivered to her door. Although the invitation was formally worded, she knew Mr. Pugh was a man of great discretion and restraint and would clearly not declare himself in missive that could have been opened by the messenger boy. The following morning she dressed with exceptional care, brought her mother's pearls out of storage and opened a new bottle of Rosewater. There was a strange perturbation in her breast that only one thing could assuage. She felt as though she were being carried along on a great torrent of water and that soon, soon, she would reach the vast open sea.

She could scarcely conceal her nervous excitement when ushered into Mr. Pugh's office the next day. Lowering her eyes modestly, she studied the desk, with its neat, orderly stationery and the engraved nameplate, 'Mr. Reginald Pugh, Accounts Manager'. Reginald. What a splendid name; so majestic. She would have to learn to call him Reginald.

There was a short burst of preparatory coughing from the other side of the desk.

# The Dam

"Ahem, Miss Avery, ah....um....now, well, I have asked you here this morning to...um, well." Mr. Pugh was floundering. He had launched into the attack without sufficient preparation, without marshalling his words first. He began again.

"Miss Avery, I have recently had the pleasure, ah, of being of some assistance to you; assistance I was glad, as a good citizen, to offer. And in return you have bestowed on me your, ah, um, thanks, and ah, your regard, a ......a.......gift not unappreciated. Not to mention your, ah, savings, bestowed upon the Bank of course, not myself." He stopped, fearing this latter remark could be misconstrued, but Miss Avery smiling, nodded him on, bobbing her head in a manner that reminded him of a canary.

"What I am trying to express, but not very adequately, is that I am not unaware of your....your...regard for me. That is why I feel I must now take the step of asking you, asking you..."

"Oh yes, yes, yes!" interrupted Miss Avery. "Oh Mr. Pugh, *Reginald,* you need not be so formal. Your feelings are returned. Of course I will marry you!" and with that she ran round the desk and embraced him, knowing off his gold-rimmed spectacles in the process. What would have ensued at that moment had the door not opened we must (once again) consign to the realm of speculation. What did happen is of more import, namely that the clerk, with a look of mingled fear and glee, ushered in *Mrs.* Pugh, returned early from her 'Great Cathedrals' tour. To say that her face was a picture would be an understatement. Her face was a canvas across which the whole gamut of human emotions passed in rapid succession. Confusion, astonishment, fury, sorrow, pensiveness, calculation, relief and jubilation are perhaps the nearest one could come to it. To discover her husband in the arms of a strange woman was so unexpected that she had to rapidly take stock and recalculate her position. For the fact was that she had returned early to

Dangerous Cocktail

confess to her husband an equally unexpected and overwhelming passion for the widowed clergyman leading the 'Great Cathedrals' tour and to beg for her release. Now, riding the unexpected tide of events, she launched into a tirade of horrified indignation, deep sorrow and irrevocably injured feelings, ending with the dramatic line (also culled from the silver screen), "You will never see me again!" With that she flounced from the room, whilst quickly trying to calculate how long it would take her to retrieve her clothes and jewellery from the house in Laurel Drive and install it in the well-appointed Rectory in Upper Ridthorpe owned by the Reverend Rutwell.

Mr. Pugh, embraced on the one side and railed at on the other, leant dizzily back under the force of both assaults. He felt rather weak, overpowered by the momentum of the hour. He turned shakily to Miss Avery, who, having seen off so easily the rival she didn't even know she had had, was now ardently pecking at his ear and bald head, and enquired tentatively if she was skilled at the production of lightly boiled eggs.

# Healing

## Alyson Heap

She had come to the cabin to begin the process of making herself whole again.

The jigsaw of her life, which she thought had been completed, had shattered into a thousand pieces and she had to begin again, painstakingly re-building, piece by piece, the person that she needed to be.

At first she was so cumbered by grief, so numbed with pain she thought that day was night. She was caged in this dark tunnel, fearful that she would never make her way through to tomorrow, and she would be trapped in the limbo of her grief for all eternity.

At first, the silent landscape she found herself in only served to reinforce her loneliness, but gradually to her surprise, it became a friend. This new friend invited her to scream and rail against the world, and when she was parched with crying, her new friend held her, and she wore silence like a comfortable old coat.

She thought she had found another friend in drink, but this was a false friend, the numbness a temporary respite. The feelings of hopelessness and despair bobbed like corks to the surface of the shipwreck of her life. Frustrated and betrayed, she emptied out the bottles and watched as the red liquid spiralled out of control, like her own life, and disappeared without trace, leaving just the pungent smell of loss.

## Dangerous Cocktail

And so she passed her days, her only visitors the animals that inhabited the world outside her door. Inquisitive deer would sometimes venture close to the cabin, ears cocked, their hooves raised, ready to take flight.

Instinctively she would slow her breathing and watch them, their doe-eyed beauty underlining the fleeting fragility of life.

Winter came and she left the cloying confines of the cabin, preferring to walk in the clear virginal days, where snow-laden trees formed avenues of white parasols to shield her from the glare of the winter sun. Her footprints followed on behind her as she walked, a solitary figure in a world white and unsullied.

Evenings she spent hunched in front of the fire, hypnotised by the orange flames that licked the logs like serpents' tongues, the heat reddening the pale skin on her legs and cheeks.

Sometimes she ate, acknowledging the need to eat, but not the desire. She could choose to starve, she could simply slip away, but she knew how hard he had fought to live, and she felt ashamed.

As the winter snow began to shrink away, she began to feel a lessening of her grief, and the pain began to ease. She still woke each morning remembering to remember, but now there was a gap between the waking and the realisation. The gap was filled with the hope that with spring might just come; the shoots of a new beginning.

But soon she was visited by another more destructive force, doubt.

As she listened to the rushing of the river in the valley below, gorged by melting snow, doubt flooded through her. She began to go over their life together, when each parting was like a small death, and each

## Healing

reunion, a re-birth. Nothing could have prepared her for the final parting, and because she was unprepared, there was much that was unresolved. And there it was inside her, floating like the solitary worm in a tequila bottle, an ugly interloper, doubt.

She asked the question out loud, over and over *did he love me, did he?*

But there was no answer, and even the silence deserted her, embarrassed that this was a question to no-one but her. The silence was replaced by the whimpers and keening of a child.

She turned her anguish on her father, long dead. She was desperate to feel the touch of his hand stroking her hair, desperate to hear his voice, soothing, placating.

*Papa, what will I do, how will I live......*

And she wept, for her father, for herself, and for the husband who was her world and had left her. She wept for the child she had been, full of joy and hope, and the child she would never have. She wept at the loss of a life cut short, and for all the other lives in the world that end scarcely before they begin. And when she couldn't weep any more because of the enormity of the suffering in the world, she slept.

And because she had emptied herself of grief, when she woke the next day, she felt stronger. Her memories came crowding in, but with them came an acceptance that these were a part of her, extra pieces in the jigsaw of her life that she would have to find a place for.

The air outside was fresh and she drank it until she was sated, and for the first time in many months she thought of him without pain, without anguish.

## Dangerous Cocktail

The deer came again and she watched them as they grazed. She was suddenly filled with a longing to be amongst her own, to walk amongst people and feel a human touch. She packed her few belongings and sat for a while inside the small cabin that had been her refuge for four months.

She had been engulfed in grief and she had known, briefly, what it feels like to not want to live.

There will always be a space where you walked, where you lay beside me, where you inhabited my heart. I will always wonder if you loved me as much as I loved you and there will always be 'what-ifs'. But I will survive, the final pieces of the jigsaw will slot together and I will be whole again. I can go home.

# Greed

## Peter Goodsall

I look closer. The work is genuinely remarkable! What a talent has created this! The marble, arctic to the touch, exudes warmth to the eye. I want to smooth her ruffled hair, to pull the creases flat in her heavy cloak where it has been taken by a fierce gale. I can discern no imperfection. I minutely examine every last pore. The marble is flawless; the surface almost as if it has never been worked. This divine conception sings quality against a choir of now irrelevant compositions.

Not since Rodin, perhaps, even, dare I? Michaelangelo, has God graced humanity with a touch so pure, with an eye so discriminating. All of this! I close my eyes and allow the greed to control momentarily, but just for the briefest interlude, lest Pullman spot my agitation and delight. I have been waiting all of my life for this. The elation of the true find.

There are those who create, sometimes for no other reason than they must. Then there are those who can only appreciate. Perhaps I savour the superb even more since, as I discovered early in my artistic education, the truly marvellous is beyond my mediocre grasp as an artist or sculptor.

I called Pullman over to my side so that she might share her thoughts. Yes, it was untitled. Yes, it was definitely a local commission: the sculptor lived only a few miles away from the gallery. Yes, I was welcome to contact her directly: Pullman would furnish me with her details. No, I could not even think about an offer for this one. It was

## Dangerous Cocktail

most definitely spoken for and it was more than her reputation was worth to let it go, even at the very considerable premium that I was offering. This latter suggestion seemed to irk her somewhat. Far more than was warranted to my mind. Still, you can never truly tell how such an offer will be received unless you know the vendor better than I know Pullman, so I thought little of it.

Pullman was called to the front of the gallery by her assistant. I ignored her and continued to gaze in fascination and awe upon 'my' discovery. As I wheeled around the statue I spotted a sinew of bright pink thread on the back. I would have sworn on the Bible itself that it was absent only moments before. I tried to wipe it away and succeeded in detaching it from the statue only for it to stick, unyielding, to my fingers. There was much impatient cussing and indecorous manoeuvring of my digits, as if I were trapped within my own private and hellish comedy routine. I eventually elected to snare the thread under my shoe in order to pull it from my fingers.

As I straightened up again I felt momentarily giddy. I instinctively placed one hand, still sticky, onto the statue to steady myself. I squeezed my eyes together to try and focus. The gallery wall seemed to approach me. I tried to shake my head clear, frowning to try and focus once more. Now the wooden floor, a beautifully burnished maple, seemed to rapidly advance and retreat. I sat down heavily on my coccyx. Normally I would have attended to the shard of pain that pierced my back, but my distress and disorientation were now so great that I simply gazed down at the floor as it spun. I closed my eyes in an attempt to regain control of my own body but found the room still whirling about me. As a result I opened them and found Pullman and her assistant standing over me.

"Up you get now!" Pullman was almost cheery. "We can't leave you like that now can we?"

## Greed

I tried to mumble a reply but found that I couldn't control my mouth.

The assistant, a burly man of sad, world-weary eyes and dark, unshaven, chin pulled me to my feet. A different pain, almost a sudden ache that died away again as immediately as it came, now punctured the backs of my knees. As the assistant, who I now learned was named Marchant, held me about the waist, Pullman proceeded to tug and wrench at my knees. I tried to simply stand but found that my legs remained inoperative.

"There! What do you think?"

Marchant looked down under my trunk and nodded his approval. Pullman moved to my rear. She placed her knee into the small of my back and continued to pull me upright. The same sudden dull ache punctuated my thinking. Left to my own devices I would have thought that I was going to simply slump forward again. I now found that I could not. I stayed in whatever position Pullman chose to place me. My eyes widened. I tried to swallow but found that this too was impossible!

I couldn't move! The realisation of my predicament began to trickle into my mind: comrade emotions cramping my stomach. Pullman continued to push and pull, tug at joints and haul on limbs. I just stayed in whichever pose she placed me. She would occasionally stand back, one leg extravagantly leading the other, and tilt her head slightly to one side, her eyes narrowed and her curvaceous top lip momentarily absorbed into her lower jaw. She would suddenly dart forward: the signal for a sharp crack of pain to overlay the aching.

I had no idea of what to do. The disorientation had cleared a little: I thought hard to find something, any locus, on which to concentrate. Devoid of any more useful plan, I tried to will all of my strength into the little finger of my right hand. Nothing. I strained against my own

## Dangerous Cocktail

mass and struggled with hope. Pullman was apparently satisfied with the rest of my body; Marchant being ordered to disengage his support as my tormentor reached my neck. Each time she rotated or angled my head the ache would slice across my oesophagus and clear all thought. She eventually moved onto my face. She ensured that my mouth was closed, poking and pinching with little pin-pricks of ache as if she were moulding putty.

"You'll have to hurry, he's beginning to set!" said Marchant. He began to very lightly knock a knuckle against my chest, moving with a gentleness and grace that belied his bulk, shifting with a very slight pressure of the thumbs over my fore arm and up to my biceps.

My blood chilled. This could not be! My breathing laboured. I fainted.

My eyes opened of their own accord. I found that I could still move them, albeit slowly and with great pain. I was in a room of whitewashed walls that I hadn't seen before.

Pullman busied herself in front of me with a large tray of delicate instruments before donning a bright green plastic apron that I saw mirrored my presence but obfuscated my features. She looked up at me and smiled with her head characteristically tilted, apparently concentrating on her muse.

"You're wondering what I'm doing and why I'm doing it. 'The what' is only natural and will soon become apparent. As to 'the why', well, you already know the answer to that one!"

"I don't! Please! Please, I don't! I don't! Please!"

## Greed

"No? Take that look off your face! Oh I forgot! You can't", she grinned. "Well at least take that look out of your eyes: you'll spoil the finish!"

Pullman reached under a bench and fixed a long flexible drill bit of particularly unpleasant aspect onto a meaty electric drill. She tried the drill before placing it on the tray alongside what I suddenly realised was an endoscope.

"You'll find this fascinating!" she continued. "I know I do! You see, we have a problem! The pink silk paralyses you and will preserve your skin beautifully once we've wrapped you, but of course it does nothing to help your organs. You're going to die, so your organs will putrefy. We've found that if we wait before we extract them and replace them with the correct weight in concrete, then we tend to damage the 'marble'. But, and this is the clever bit, if we extract all of your organs now then your skin is still malleable enough to resist the introduction of imperfections."

Pullman paused in her digression as she poured a bright, almost fluorescent, pink fluid into a large flat porcelain dish with a lip. She reached into it with her gloved hands, pulling a strand seemingly straight from the liquid and hanging it through the lip. The long, curling strand continued to grow, falling to the floor of its own volition in an ever greater length.

"Please don't! Please! Please don't! Please don't hurt me! Please!"

"You see, I'm like you. An also ran. Our ambitions literally exceed our talents. But not now; not any more: I can plagiarise God now!"

"You can sell the silk! Dear God please! You can sell the silk! Sell the silk you silly witch! Please! Don't you realise what you have here? This

## Dangerous Cocktail

is a breakthrough! Sell the silk!" but in my bitter desperation I already know that money is playing no part in this. This is the wealth of kudos and she is monumentally greedy.

I see her eyes glitter as she bends to her task. Dark, focussed, eyes. Pretty eyes. Concentrating but greedy. Greedy for a conclusion.

# The Rock of Death

## Elspeth Green

I have been here, companionless, soaking up the atmosphere, three endless nights. On each visit I have carefully hidden myself in the undergrowth, squelched through the boggy mass leading to the water's edge and hunkered down with an air of readiness. At the conclusion of each session my pristine white trainers have been ingrained with sludge and silt, desperately compelling me to offer an assiduous cleansing in preparation for their next day's labours. Only my body has changed; different hair, different clothes, different life within. Today I am perfect; I am as they have made me.

I will generate death.

My chosen rock has been weighed; balanced; held above my head, in one hand or both; over my right shoulder; my left. Nothing has been left to chance. Could a woman do this? Would a woman have the strength? Oh yes, I believe I could. I need to believe. I need to justify. What is my motivation? Why am I doing this?

Did he have an affair? Has he been seeing someone else? Would I care enough if I were proved right about this? Oh yes, I believe I would.

So what? How am I going to complete this deed? How would anyone in my position choose to do it? I must focus my mind; my thoughts, my ideas and allow nothing to detract from the end result. I practice at home, spinning weights above my head; press-ups in the kitchen where no one will observe me. I have crushed melons; coconuts; . . . dolls. Tonight will be the grand finale. Tonight my timing must not go awry.

I arrive exactly at the perfect moment. Tonight there are already two cars in the car park; yesterday there were three; tomorrow there will be none. The filthy green Land Rover is here, exactly where it should be. Without it, all plans would be pointless. Once again I scrabble down to the water's edge and ensconce myself within the weeds and brambles. I

## Dangerous Cocktail

carry with me a cheap, gouged vacuum flask filled with deep, rich, black coffee. I must not sleep; I must not relax. This may take time.

It is cold and my nose starts to leak. I dare not move to retrieve a tissue from the pocket of my decrepit anorak. As covertly as possible I run my sleeve across my face and trust that the slime will not show; there must be no signs of distress. Have I become too involved; do I care too much?

The deep black velvety water of the lake gives nothing away. Will it when the plans are complete? I plunge my hands into its depths and the icy droplets cling to my palms for some length before rolling back to the mire. Where is the stone? There must be no panic.

As with every other day, it is awaiting my touch, ready for the important assignment. I fondle its smooth circumference then entwine it within my arms. I lift it close to my heart.

My eyes have accustomed themselves to the dark. Because the full moon has now been joined by a myriad of golden lights, I can see fireworks in the chasmic lake. It is no longer velvety black but has taken on the appearance of streaming, rich blue chiffon. The reeds are wavering, not far from where I crouch. There is a noise, a whisper, a lovers' tryst. This is it. This is the start. My time is now.

I see two people, hand in hand. So intent upon each other they are oblivious to the world. They do not hear the screech of the owl or see the blank stare of the heron. A couple as one, only aware of the breath, the aroma, the heartbeat of each other. Slowly, stiffly, I begin to rise from my hidden perch. She screams, aware, yet unaware of my design. He faces me, discerning all.

"Go, Stella, Go!"

Without a backward glance she sprints away.

"What are you doing here? Why?"

He is ignorant of my knowledge. I will not enlighten him. They say it is blissful to have his level of ignorance. I raise the rock above my head, lever it backwards and then with even greater momentum push it towards his face.

# The Rock of Death

The weight is eased from my hands and I find myself clutching the top of a larger, softer bundle.

"Go on. Push it towards the water's edge; hide it, lose it. Make yourself safe."

I inch the toe of my now filthy trainer under a nearby boulder. With this added leverage I am able to alter the centre of balance from my burden. It topples forward. The reeds open out to welcome it; they encircle the clothing and grip it tightly. He is at peace. I am at peace.

"Well done everyone. That's a wrap. Let's hope Crimewatch get this bastard. It's much too close to home for my liking."

Charles, the Director busies himself with folding down the tripod and packing away the boom. Is he hiding a tear for the loss of a close, dear friend?

My hands will not stop shaking. Someone has placed a silver sheet around my shoulders.

That same someone calls out to the team, "Hot coffee or something stronger at the van everyone. We don't want to be the cause of pneumonia for our 'star' here."

I move as though in a dream. I banish my wig and become a mouse again. The ripples of life will soon settle and return to normal.

The car park is silent. Any self-congratulation for this performance is forgotten; tonight there is no joy. One of our film crew has been murdered in cold blood; someone has thrown a rock within our midst. Nobody feels safe. This could have been any one of us.

The feeling is coming back into my legs. I stamp my feet on the large gravel lumps abandoned throughout the car park, attempting to remove the cloying clumps of mud. The small, expensive but warming, brandy is working its magic.

"Cora," Charles shouted from behind the boot of his car "you were brilliant darling. So perfect for the part, just like Stella visualised. You are wasted behind a typewriter. I've got your number. . . . Thanks for volunteering. . . . Don't have nightmares!"

## Dangerous Cocktail

I force a laugh. Oh! Charlie boy, if only you could guess how perfect I am for the part. We'd talked, we'd written, we'd thought so much together. I loved him. He didn't even know my name.
"That's ok Charles. Like all of you, I'll miss my rock."

- Clever to hide what's really happening at the beg.
- It's a bit ambiguous at the end. So did she actually kill another member of the team? Or is she talking about long Charles + simply re-enacting what happened?

# One For The Kiddies: Another Grand Adventure

Peter Owen

"I say Paddle old fellow, this looks a jolly good place to explore, pull over here if you please, there's a good chap." Fourteen year old Jeremy Largesse-Hampton looked around for approval from his brother, Roger, sister Jane and cousin Tammy - the "Magical Mystery Solvers" as they were known - he needn't have worried, for they were all nodding their heads in agreement with his grand suggestion.

Paddle eased the sleek black motor car to a halt and the children leapt out to begin off-loading their rucksacks, frame-tent and the huge hamper of food that Tammy's mum, Aunty Bisto, had prepared for them.

"Gosh, there's enough food here to last us two whole weeks I shouldn't wonder," laughed Roger.

"Yes and we're only here for two nights, so three cheers for Aunty Bisto for being such a good sort," exclaimed Jane, grinning broadly.

"Oh yes, rather," agreed Jeremy, fiddling anxiously with the loose braces holding up his baggy grey trousers. "By the way you lot, I think Aunty Bisto may have packed some of Uncle Beamer's very special home-made cider dishes as well," he continued with great excitement.

"Whatever makes you think that Jeremy?" chorused the others, their eyes wide with wonder.

"Well," continued Jeremy in a very secretive sort of way, "It's just that when they were going up to bed last night I overheard Aunty Bisto whispering to Uncle Beamer that she would really, really like it if he could put something inside her."

"And what did Uncle Beamer say to that?" urged the others, eager to know the answer.

## Dangerous Cocktail

"Well," responded Jeremy, "He said he would pop it in just as soon as he'd finished his cocoa."

Tousle-haired tomboy Tammy smiled and patted her large black and white dog Jimmy. "It's ok," she said fondly, "I'm quite sure you haven't been forgotten - here, catch this," she called, tossing a healthy doggy dental chew into the bushes for him to hunt.

Jeremy, Roger and Jane had arrived at cousin Tammy's the previous day and, following Uncle Beamer's suggestion, had set off in the family chauffer-driven Bentley to spend a couple of days camping on their own, leaving Uncle Beamer – who was a very clever world famous scientist – to finish writing a paper on his latest project: 'Cheese and Onion Baguettes - Why not?'.

Paddle helped the children unpack, explaining when they'd finished that he would be back in two days to pick them up. He then pursed his lips in a very provocative manner, making a most peculiar 'phut', 'phut', 'phut', 'phut', phutting noise followed by some rather odd hand signals before he phutted off down the road, soon to disappear over the brow of a hill, only to reappear much later puffing, panting, red-faced and dishevelled, having realised that he'd forgotten to take the motor-car with him - how very odd.

"Right-ho everybody," began Jeremy, taking the lead as usual and sounding frightfully grown up. "I vote that Tammy and Jane carry the hamper, our rucksacks and the frame-tent between them while Roger and I scout on ahead to find a suitable camping site - it's the sort of job that only boys can do, for who knows what dangers may lie in wait for us. I myself have heard tales that some jolly fearsome rabbits hang out around these parts and I'm quite sure I shouldn't like to be charged by a marauding gang of rabbits thank you very much! And it's no good you girls grumbling like that! Why don't you just strap the frame-tent on top of the hamper and carry my rucksack and Roger's on your backs together with your own? Now, come on girls, pull yourselves together," he snapped, folding his arms and gazing sternly towards the distant hills, looking and sounding very wise indeed.

One For The Kiddies: Another Grand Adventure

"Shall I cut off a couple of sticks from that bush over there?" interrupted Roger enthusiastically, "We can use them as walking sticks just like the real explorers do," he added brightly.

"What an absolutely spiffing idea that is Rog." exclaimed Jeremy, "Well done - I was about to suggest that myself and now you've saved me the trouble!"

Jeremy flexed his arm and pointed proudly at his bicep muscle, which appeared to move a little.

"Here, look at this everybody, this is the sort of thing that can happen to you when you reach the age of puberty," he beamed, "This and a lot of other exciting things too, according to Uncle Beamer," he continued, "He says my voice should be breaking soon and that when it does it would be a jolly good sign that my balls had dropped - though quite what he means by that I'm not at all sure - here use my knife old chum, but be careful, it's very sharp," he called casually, tossing the knife towards Roger, who let it slip though his fingers, watching in horror as it fell onto his trainers, piercing the canvas and thereby leaving him with a nasty cut on his toe. Jeremy looked down at Roger's toe, turned very pale indeed and crumpled to the floor in one of his famous fainting attacks. The girls soon had Roger's foot bandaged and were leaning over Jeremy, who was still lying flat out on the grass.

"What a fine start to our adventure this is," said Tammy, slapping Jeremy's face. "Oh come on Jeremy, do come round," she pleaded, slapping him again very sharply on the end of his nose. "There, that's got you back for last year," she grinned wickedly, remembering when Jeremy had tried to wrestle with her to prove to everyone that he was the toughest, only for Tammy to somehow wrap both his legs behind his neck. How the children at the summer camp had roared with laughter as Tammy had then spun him around and around just like a spinning top.

Soon the boys were patched up and heading off to seek out a place for the girls to set up camp. Roger, leaning heavily on his stick, limped along awkwardly, while Jeremy trudged after him holding a tissue to

## Dangerous Cocktail

his nose. Good old Jeremy, he always knew just what to do; he had been a little unlucky that's all. After about an hour's slow walking the boys came upon the perfect area in which the girls could set up camp for them. They stretched out in the small grassy opening which was surrounded by gorse bushes, well concealed from any passers by, and waited patiently for the girls to arrive. It seemed an absolute age until they eventually came into view struggling gamely with their heavy load. Jeremy and Roger watched with great interest wondering just why it had taken them so long.

"Come on you girls buck up," called Jeremy as Tammy and Jane eventually plonked the picnic hamper down and threw the rucksacks onto the ground. "Roger and I are starving - think you could pitch the tent and get some food going for us while we rest a while longer under that tree over there - out of your way," he added nonchalantly gesturing towards a broken old oak tree.

"Listen everybody," interrupted Roger suddenly, "Can anyone else hear what I can?"

The children listened intently and very soon they could all hear the sound of a motor-bike coming closer. They peered through the gorse bushes as the motor-bike, ridden by two rough looking burly men, pulled up beside the tree the boys were going to lie under. One of the burly men carried a large bag over his shoulder.

"This tree looks a good place to stash it; it's got a hollow trunk - see," said one of the men gruffly.

"We can stuff the loot down the trunk and pick it up later Slasher," replied the other burly man.

"Just wot I was finking Gorilla," said the first man.

Both men began to climb the tree and when they had reached the top Jeremy dashed into the clearing and stood beneath the tree, his hands placed firmly on his hips.

"I say you two rotters," he called out loudly, "I can see you're up to no good. I suggest you stay there whilst my chums and I fetch a

## One For The Kiddies: Another Grand Adventure

policeman; we've got a large dog with us who could easily eat you up if you try anything funny!"

"Piss off you little twit," cried one of the burly men, angrily throwing a stick onto Jeremy's head.

The other children rushed out of hiding to pick Jeremy up.

"You leave him alone you big bullies, he's just reached the age of puberty and you might upset his hormonal balance," cried Jane angrily.

Jimmy began to bark, instantly silencing the burly men who weren't looking quite as threatening now. Jeremy, still feeling dizzy from the blow on his head, turned bravely to face the burly men.

"Now look here you beastly fellows, I'm beginning to get my dander up and I've a jolly good mind to beat the shit out of you both," he stormed defiantly, drawing himself up to his full height and thrusting out his chest in a most agreeable manner.

"Oh bravo Jeremy, go on punch them both very hard indeed," chorused the children jumping up and down excitedly as he turned and winked at them with growing confidence. The burly men looked down angrily from the tree at Jeremy who simply flexed his arm in a fashion that he'd seen body builders performing on television and pointed at his brand new bicep muscle.

"Come on, if you think you're hard enough," he called mockingly to the burly men.

This seemed to do the trick and the burly men, looking most anxious, began muttering something that the children couldn't understand.

"Why don't you speak up you horrid cads?" called Roger, moving bravely alongside of Jeremy, who was hoisting up his baggy grey trousers in a very menacing fashion hoping that the burly men would clearly be able to see his recent pubertal developments and become even more frightened - which of course is just what happened - good old Jeremy had pulled it off again: he could always be relied upon in times of crisis.

## Dangerous Cocktail

There was a sudden crashing in the bushy undergrowth and Sergeant Duff, followed closely by Constable Dimwick, burst into view on their large black bicycles.

"Well bless me if t'aint the 'Magical Mystery Solvers'," cried Sergeant Duff wobbling to a halt and falling exhausted off his bicycle as he called across to the children.

"Are we glad to see you kids," added Constable Dimwick, looking very relieved, "We might 'ave known you'd trap these ne'er do wells up a tree," he added, looking up at the burly men and adjusting his helmet which was perching precariously on the side of his head, "We've been chasing these villains all the way from Piddledown Fondly On-The-Water. They've stolen twenty pounds of pork and stilton sausages from Mr. Rumpsides butchers shop - and called his wife some rude names."

The children looked at each other, unable to believe the enormity of the crime the burly men had committed.

"I shouldn't like to be a policeman, having to deal with such dreadful villains," said Tammy, sounding very serious indeed.

"No, neither should I," agreed Jane. "I shouldn't be at all surprised if they're just poor people from a deprived background who never wash their hands after using the toilet or clean their teeth, and weren't clever or rich enough to go to a proper grammar school," she added most intelligently.

"Spot on old girl," retorted Roger, "If you ask me they're just grubby blighters who go around stealing sausages - and root vegetables too I shouldn't wonder - I for one vote they should go to prison."

The burly men realised the game was up and began clambering back down the tree, the man called 'Gorilla' carrying the bag of sausages.

"Thanks for doing our jobs for us you kids," said Constable Dimwick, giving a sharp blast on his whistle, "We've got some pals in a police car patrolling this area; we'll soon 'ave these villains locked up."

"That's right," agreed Sergeant Duff, grinning from ear-to-ear, "And as a special reward for your bravery I'm going to let you keep some of these lovely sausages, not only that," he added with a wink, "I know

## One For The Kiddies: Another Grand Adventure

just where you can find some hallucinatory mushrooms that you can fry up to 'ave with them - magic mushrooms for the 'Magical Mystery Solvers'.

Everyone burst out laughing - even the burly men chuckled. Everyone was very happy indeed.

"The last time we ate magic mushrooms I was able to fly - remember?" said Jeremy, laughing the loudest of them all.

What a happy ending, and after they had tucked into the sausages and mushrooms they were all trying to fly just like Jeremy, even Sergeant Duff and Constable Dimwick, who had called by to sample the mushrooms on their way to investigate another burglary.

"The burglary can wait!" shouted Sergeant Duff.

"Yes, this is much more fun," cried Constable Dimwick, as they leaped into the air from the top of a very high tree.

*This is a clever idea but the serial effects are too crude to fit.*

# Dangerous Cocktail

# MARY

### Alyson Heap

*Mary Queen of Scots was executed at Fotheringay Castle on the 5th February 1587, she was 44 years old and had spent the last 19 years in captivity. A thorn in Elizabeth's side, the cousins never met. Mary's son, James VI of Scotland became James 1 of England on the death of Elizabeth in 1603.*

### 6a.m on the morning of 5th February 1587

I do not fear death, it holds fewer terrors for me than life, but I have been haunted of late by ghosts from the past, phantoms, reminders of things long gone that cannot be undone.

Would that I could change some things. My life would have taken a different path to this rocky, treacherous way I have trodden. These last 19 years held prisoner, banished from my home, my son, my beloved Scotland, a hostage to the procrastinations of my cousin, these have been hard, wasted years.

My father's words, when he received the news of my birth, were harsh, but prophetic. He said, 'It came from a woman, and it will end in a woman'. He died soon after, from mortal wounds inflicted by the English. Ah, sweet irony, my wounds too are mortal. How came I here then, to this doleful place in time?

I was but five years old when I sailed for France, a mere bairn at the mercy of strangers. But I came to love my adopted home, and when I was betrothed at fifteen years, I was content. My beloved Francis, you

## Dangerous Cocktail

were brother, husband, friend to me. Our lives were blessed, our days halcyon, filled with promise and hope.

But my darling Francis was fragile, like a spring blossom, its petals doomed to wither and die. I nursed him when he sickened, but my dear sweet Francis died, and, at the tender age of eighteen, I donned the white mourning robes of a French Queen.

It soon it became clear that it was dangerous to stay in France, I was no longer welcome, and so I resolved to return to Scotland.

How drab it seemed when I first set eyes upon the shores of Leith. There were no crowds to greet me, I was the pretender, cast ashore like jetsam, unbidden and unwelcome.

When I came to court at Holyrood, the ladies were dull and stiff, and the lords pompous and dour.

But soon we had merriment and the trappings and finery befitting a monarch. But alas, there followed the intrigue, the plotting, the falsity and malicious inventions. My brother, Moray, who should have been my chiefest comfort, sowed discord. His peculiar art was to appear to do nothing, when in truth, he did all.

I remember he made me bear witness to an execution. I was young, so too was the poor wretch condemned that day. The executioner bungled his work, and when I saw the clumsy blows, the blood and gore, I screamed and fainted.

Dear God in heaven, steady the hand of my executioner!

Some would say my executioner is Queen Elizabeth herself.

## Mary

My cousin, the Queen of all England, has by her own hand, sealed my fate. She who all those years ago would have me marry Robert Dudley; a passed on favourite! I wept when I received the envoy, and heard what she bid me do. I, a Queen in my own right from one week old, ordered to marry Elizabeth's popinjay! I wept tears of anger and like a disobedient child, wed the man I was besotted with - Lord Darnley.

Mine eyes were blinded by his comely looks and arrogant strut. I was tricked by honeyed words and silken promises. But he was a wilful, haughty, vicious bully.

He lacked all that is good in a man. He was not my equal. He furnished feather bonnets for his fools whilst plotting against me, his only desire to seize the Crown Matrimonial, and when I would not yield, he humiliated me with vile deeds and false rumour. The protestant lords would have me cast him off, but I was with child and I would not gainsay my unborn child's birthright!

They murdered him, that handsome, lusty youth, they murdered their King!

Elizabeth knew, oh yes, my cousin knew! It was she sent Darnley to me; she knew that Darnley might well be the ruin of me and so she dangled him in front of me like a peach before a pauper. Darnley. His phantom haunts me, I see a broken body, crippled by the explosion that killed him at Kirk O'Field. I heard tell that for three nights before his murder, ghostly warriors had been seen, fighting in the lanes of Edinburgh.

And so his death was foretold.

## Dangerous Cocktail

They killed Rizzio, these same Protestant Lords, murdered him in front of mine own eyes. Dear gentle sweet, Rizzio, he whose only crime was to serve his mistress well.

They say his blood stains the floor where he fell at Holyrood. Well his death stains my heart and God's will was done when Darnley was slain, for it was his jealousy that stoked the fires of hatred that burned in the hearts of the vile men at my court!

Bothwell visits me, comes to me in dreams. Not the mad-man I hear tell of, dead these nine years passed, but the man I married.

Oh, he was handsome; he had a strength of body that well matched his strength of mind. He was rash and hazardous, high in his own conceit.

How could I love a man who had rough used me?

Do you know how it is to be in thrall to a man? To be both repulsed and yet so enamoured, you are blind to all warning? I hated him, and yet I loved him.

He was man to me, when all I had known were boys. I blush at the memory!

I lost our babies: I miscarried of twins. My mind and body were sick, I had been ill-used by my enemies. They took my reason along with the bairns, and that part of me that was Bothwell slid away with the lives we had part-formed. I mourned for those wee souls, and again I needed the protection of a strong man, I needed my Bothwell.

But he left me, fleeing when it looked as if all was lost. I had no choice but to place myself under Elizabeth's protection. I like to think

## Mary

he plotted to rescue me, that before madness overtook him he was planning the glorious insurgence that would re-instate me as the rightful Queen, and he, my husband, at my side.

I never betrayed you, my dear. When my advisors bade me divorce you and used evil speech against you, I never wanted you away. I have kept you in my heart, and what secrets we shared between us, no man shall be privy to.

So, those long years past, perhaps I should have married Dudley.

Good men would still be alive, I would look forward to ending my days in Linlithgow, the pretty palace where I was born, my life destined to end in peace, in a bed, not on a block, my head severed by an axe....

I shiver, it is cold here, awaiting the dawn.

All is ready. My correspondence was completed last evening, I have written to Elizabeth. I told her I am not and never have been 'an imaginer and compasser of her Majesty's destruction', a charge made at my 'trial'. Neither papist plotter, nor Catholic Martyr. I am an anointed Queen, her own kinswoman and the nearest heir to the throne of England and Scotland. I am to be executed for the sins and machinations of others. Had we met, she would have welcomed me as her peer and equal, but that was not to be. I wonder how she signed the warrant. Did her hand tremble, or did she with one flourish sign her name, the ink coursing through the pen like the blue blood in her veins. Ah, to have been at her shoulder, whispering in her ear:

'Elizabeth, murderer, on your conscience be it!'

Now I must be content that I go to meet my God pure in spirit. My last breath shall be that of a Queen.

## Dangerous Cocktail

What was it my old enemy Knox said - 'It is against natural and divine law for a woman to hold dominion over men'. Perhaps the old fool was right, I have been easy prey for the predatory men who surrounded me, men without honour, capable of deception and duplicity.

In my captivity they vied for my favour, promising me the throne of England, promising to restore the Catholic faith to the realm if I gave credence to their plots.

Was this my only crime? Poor judgement that repeatedly served me ill?

The English crown was mine by right! And my faith? Catholicism is my faith,

I will die in it!

Beneath this black robe I wear a red petticoat, the seamstress on my instruction has fashioned sleeves of red also. Red has always been my favourite colour, it is also the colour of Martyrdom. People shall make of it whatsoever they wish.

I shall wear an auburn wig, to cover this, mine own hair turned grey with age and sorrow. To think, I was once deemed 'the most beautiful in Europe' and now I go to my maker devoid of jewels and fripperies.

We are all paupers in death.

My ladies weep, let them mourn. They have served me well.

## Mary

Soon I will make my final journey to meet my God. I await you in paradise Elizabeth, safe in the knowledge that my flesh and blood, my son James will be King of England.

In my end is my beginning.

- Really well written. I don't like historical much but this cleverly conveys info / facts without losing Mary's 'voice' + whilst maintaining flow.
- Good balance of short + long sentences
- Good description.
- Clever use of just a word here + there in the speaking voice to place it in the past.

# Killing Nigel

## Sarah Maguire

She had pleaded guilty of course. The mellifluous voice of the prosecution continued to float over the court.
"I think my learned friend will agree that this was a malicious crime; the cold-blooded murder of a gifted young man cut down in his prime."

She suppressed a snort, scanning the court room curiously. The judge perched on his throne, regal in black and purple, visage marred only by a frown. And there in the public gallery, her husband, shrunken and aghast - poor dear man. He was mouthing at her, "Are you alright? Are you alright?"

In an unfortunately reedy tone, her defence was outlining the mitigating circumstances as to why she had taken the kitchen knife and skewered Nigel through the heart with it.

"Why? You might ask. Why indeed. In the words of my client, 'He was doing my head in'."

Precisely.

Jolted out of her reverie, she realised with a start that her husband had indeed been calling her.

"Abigail, you had me worried."

"Perfectly alright sweetheart, just indulging in a bit of day dreaming."

"I thought it might be worse."

"No, it's fine with the tele on. I'll make us a cup of tea shall I?"

She ran a finger down the craggy face of her lovely man. 'It' of course was the cacophony of noise which had taken up residence inside her, recently diagnosed by the doctor as tinnitus. She was only fifty-five for goodness sake! He'd recommended no excessive noise, no stress, no

## Dangerous Cocktail

caffeine...no jolly life in fact, she reflected, flinging the despised herbal teabag (peppermint today) into a mug.

\* \* \*

Derek was her age, perhaps a little younger; his groomed hair greying at the temples. A black suit, neatly pressed white shirt, and small perfectly formed bow tie completed the look. The notes coming from his clarinet were mellow and rounded, hardly obtrusive. In fact, had he been permitted to perform Mozart's clarinet concerto, he would have been an almost welcome companion. Sadly his repertoire was limited to just three notes, which he played with an apologetic glance in her direction. Nearby stood Pete, round cheeked, his good natured smile a reflection of the cheerful checked jacket. His many ringed fingers flexed in readiness, the burnished cornet contrasting against ebony skin as he fitted the mute. At least he and Derek had the decency to harmonise; his instrument a tinny echo of the clarinet, set a third higher.

Zack had burst onto the scene a couple of months ago. His mop of hair disconcertingly bleached down the middle. All youthful energy - he was what? Twenty-two maybe? Dashing to his seat, in skin-tight tee shirt and ripped jeans, he had attacked the drums in frenzied muppet style, ignorant of the others, absorbed in his task. Finally spent he looked up, his face flushed and exhilarated. She had been relieved to discover that he was only required for guest performances and not a permanent feature.

Abigail wondered if giving the random notes and sounds that comprised her tinnitus names and identities had helped her come to terms with it or simply allowed it to dominate her. She had once tried to explain this personification to Don but his uncomprehending gaze had quickly persuaded her not to speak of it again.

## Killing Nigel

In truth these members of the eclectic orchestra, she could live with. Tedious and frustrating yes, but manageable nevertheless. It was Nigel who tipped the balance, made her life unbearable. Nigel, who looked so innocuous. His unremarkable shirt and trousers, straining to contain his bulk, offset by the purple velvet jacket and matching bow tie, drooping beneath its own weight. Thick blond hair curled onto his collar and flopped into those blue eyes. On first sight she'd thought him winsome but now the words smug and self-satisfied sprang to mind. He played a violin or was it a viola? Something small anyway from which he produced a surprisingly strident sound as if the very cat itself was still splayed across the instrument. The notes pierced something within her, ripping and tearing at the fibre of her being, devouring by degrees.

Ironically in the severe noise against which the doctor had warned, television blaring, children playing, all was well. It was in solitude, the quiet moments and night time in particular that the motley band commenced their strange overture. And now they were tuning up again - it had been like this off and on for the last two hours. The clock glowing one fifty-six redly nearby; familiar objects creating well known outlines in their bedroom; Don's reassuring, rhythmic breathing beside her should all have been a comfort but only served to remind her how utterly alone she was in this. Sighing as the orchestra rose to a crescendo once more she reached for her glasses, slipping out of bed and to the window. Everything was in its right place: cars basking in orange lamplight; the man in the moon smiling from his fat coin-face; pin pricks of myriad stars stretching out across the night sky. She spotted Orion - always Orion - and, opening the window a crack, drank in deep gulps of cold air. Her throat constricted further, taut, heavy with stifled sobs. It was the hopelessness of it all; having something reside within her over which she had no control. The scene blurred momentarily. 'Pull yourself together woman,' she remonstrated, tasting salt. Below her, Nigel, bow scraping furiously, looked up and winked.

## Dangerous Cocktail

How she loathed him. What power had her over vivid imagination given him? What monster had she created? Letting the curtain fall she drew a deep breath, willing her body to still. Two-o-five..........time to keep Twinings in business.

\*\*\*

Child-like in spite of herself, Abigail tore at the parcel with trembling fingers. Hope apparently came in four by six inch packages these days. She set the box of magic tricks carefully on the dressing table. It had arrived courtesy of her eldest.

On Linda's last visit home, she had come upon them in collusion, daughter and husband, guilty faces raised, blinking under the flashlight of her entrance. She had caught the words, "...losing her - ," before Linda, with an over-bright smile, had leapt up to take the tea tray.

She consulted the mirror: tired eyes gazed reproachfully back. It seemed that the consultant had agreed with them. The result had been this gleaming contraption - a sound generator. According to the instructions it would, "produce low levels of repetitive sound, contrasting against quiet and helping the brain to relax." Prepare yourself for a rollercoaster ride dear - keen anticipation followed by crushing disappointment. Mind you a relaxed brain had to be a plus. The buttons glinted at her expectantly. She knew exactly what sound she would choose.

\*\*\*

They had walked past painted houses in pastel hues; past the blaring amusement arcade and shrieking of little children. They had sat one bench along from the elderly trio contemplating life - wise blind mice - each with their cap, sunglasses and stick. A little dog had dashed by, braking momentarily for a curious sniff, a blurred torpedo of

## Killing Nigel

excitement. They had strolled along the promenade, drooping flags springing suddenly to life, rippling proudly in the breeze. They had sauntered past trees, moulded through the years, sculpted by the wind's hands until horizontal and over the shingle beach which crunched satisfyingly at each step. Until finally they had arrived at the end of the jetty where, idle chatter having given way to companionable silence, they now sat peacefully.

Abigail watched the tiny dive bombers, swooping, soaring, weaving. Such precision timing – nature's Red Arrows. A lone gull sang its insistent song. She breathed in the sea's pungent aroma and lifted her face to the sun, basking in its warmth, eyes scrunched against the glare. Above her, white on blue, the clouds really were cotton wool, feathery light.
"Happy?" Don squeezed her hand. He had rolled up his trousers, bless him; his feet hovering, she noticed, just above the water.
"So happy." She squeezed back, dipping her toe into the delicious icy cold.
Over the shingle, the sea breathed. Exhalation and it spilled onto the beach, surging greedily at first before tentatively licking and exploring. Inhalation and it sucked back, rewinding with froth, swirl and a whoosh. Towards the horizon small fishing boats bobbed and toppers, simple triangles of colour, glided effortlessly by. She surveyed the vast shimmering expanse, bejewelled with a thousand speckles of light. It was perfect.

Except for something............
"Don, can you hear that?"
"Hear what love?"
The annoying whine of a power boat. Oh no. Hurtling towards them one minute, engine cut the next. That unmistakeable toss of the hair. It was him, of course it was him. The jangling, jarring note swelled. "Alright darling?" Nigel mouthed as he played.

## Dangerous Cocktail

She tweaked the volume upward.

The clouds, gathered by a dirty hand, hung heavy and lowering. Abigail stood on the beach alone, blinded momentarily by her own hair whipping her eyes, her face. She backed away as the wave crashed, drenching her with its spray. The sea, dark and angry, heaved and rolled. The small boat was faring badly - apparently submerged only to be vomited to the surface once more. And still Nigel played. The sea was stirred by an invisible spoon and the boat began to spin, a lump of sugar dissolving in some massive coffee cup. He was pleading with her now.
"Not me Abby, not me."

Disregarding the manufacturer's warning, Abigail wrenched the dial to its maximum setting.

She could hear nothing but the dual roar of sea and wind. The gale streamed gleefully around her, winding her skirt about her tightly . From the ocean, wild and giddy like herself, it crafted walls of murky water. Then, as if a plug had been pulled, the boat upended and the waters began hungrily to consume it. Nigel was drawn inexorably into the vortex, welcomed into the ocean's murky embrace. Fascinated, she watched every moment; the violin, driftwood now, floated by. She had to be quite, quite sure. She glimpsed purple for a moment; then his upturned face pale and surprised, mouth closing and opening like some fish, before the waters closed over him forever. Goodbye Nigel.

Hallo life. She pressed the re-set button. This time Abigail Summers walked free.

# Power of Persuasion

### Patricia Golledge

M r. Patel was looking very fed up as she stood trying to make her mind up.
"Close at 6.30 you know," he barked.

She gave a small smile. There were some interesting women's mags with great articles on quilting or upholstery. Susie wondered if you could make any money at it. That would be easy enough to do surely. Then of course there were Homes and Gardens, her personal favourite. Full of bespoke kitchens and designer wallpapers.

Mr. Patel rattled his huge bunch of keys.

"Oh, sorry I'll take these three; oh, right £9.50 was that?"

She searched into the corners of her purse to find the last pennies. She felt a momentary shiver of guilt picturing the empty fridge back at the flat. The excitement of the glossy pages was too much though and she lightly stroked the magazines as she tramped through the darkening streets.

Her enthusiasm evaporated as she rounded the corner. The hall light was on. Toby was in already. She felt there was a huge brick in the pit of her stomach.

"Hello Darling", she called with forced cheeriness as she entered the hall.

She was too scared even to try and conceal her bag this time. Toby sat on the couch between the Cath Kidston cushions eating Jaffa cakes out of the box with his coat still on.

"How was your day? Toby please put those biscuits on a plate!"

"Why the bloody hell should I?"

She shrugged off her wax jacket and unconsciously tidied her immaculate bobbed hair.

# Dangerous Cocktail

"Darling what's the matter?"

"What's in the bag Susie? Is it steak, or fish fingers? A loaf or ciabatta? I'd even settle for value burger rolls. Lets look shall we?"

He grabbed the bag from her fingers, took each magazine out, examined the price and threw them coldly on the floor.

"Ten quid for magazines – yet no grub in the house, no washing done. What have you been doing all day? No don't tell me – you've been flicking through glossy mags and planning on what to buy next, eh?"

Susie started to cry. She had no answer. Why was it so wrong to plan ahead for the time they would have their country house? What was wrong with getting in a few things now to make it stylish? Why could he not see that this was for his benefit too? All this was planning, research, investment in their future. There would come a point when promotion would not just be on his figures it would be on them as a whole package. He would need to entertain clients not at sterile, expensive city restaurants but in the chic elegance of their own home. The time would come when the hungry deal-closer would need to mature and change; to develop nonchalance and a sheen of sophistication. Why would Toby not see that?

He went berserk; flinging designer cushions into a pile along with the faux fur throws. The Laura Ashley bowl with the Molton Brown pot-pourri he held up in front of her nose.

"How much Susie? How much for the smelly wood shavings?"

She tried to diffuse the situation. "Darling they're not just wood shavings they are cedar shavings hand infused with wild ..."

"I don't give a fuck! How much Susie? Sorry, say that again, was that really twenty-five pound? You are obsessed with it all. All this designer posh crap. It s just useless tat and we can't afford it."

Her throat ached with trying to hold back the tears. All Susie could focus on was that he was still wearing his coat. Here he was ripping her to shreds and he didn't even have the good manners to take his coat off.

## Power of Persuasion

Toby sat down abruptly on the sofa and absentmindedly fingered the Jaffa cake packet. He looked so tired and unhappy.

"Toby?" she breathed.

"I'm sorry, Susie but you are wearing me down. We can't go on like this. I cannot understand why you can't grasp the fact that my future is immaterial right now. If you don't stop spending money on non-essentials we'll be bankrupt before I ever get the chance of a promotion."

He rubbed his hand tiredly across his face.

"You need to sort this out Susie by the time I come back from Switzerland or I'll file for divorce. I love you but I will not go on like this."

Susie sat on the floor among the glossy pages of her discarded magazines and listened to the slammed door reverberate around the flat. She picked up the Jaffa cake box and wandered round the flat. The bedroom was cold and dreary. She flung herself on the bed and lay curled up, eating the last of the Jaffa cakes. She woke up two hours later stiff and cold. Amidst more tears she huddled under the covers, fully dressed and cried herself to sleep.

Two days she lay there. She could not move, she didn't want to because after all what was there to get up for. Apart from the fear that Toby may leave her was the lingering feeling of shame. It was all her fault.

Hunger drove her out from under the duvet. The living room was as they had left it but she could only bring herself to step over the debris. She wandered into the kitchen and habit made her look into the fridge. The door closed with a pathetic thud on its emptiness.

There were no texts from Toby. The laptop he had also taken, presumably to stop her shopping on-line. She had never felt so scared or so alone, crying she returned under the duvet. The letter box clattering woke her an hour or so later. She crept into the hall, frightened of what she might find. And she was right to be scared for along with her list of instructions and a hundred pounds from Toby

# Dangerous Cocktail

there were various catalogues and junk mail offering her loans. The latter she chucked straight in to the bin and settled down in front of the telly with a cup of tea, the last of the teabags, to digest her instructions. It was quite simple. Toby had made arrangements to pay all the bills; he had given Susie a weekly budget of a hundred pounds. He would not contact her at all until he returned from his training course in Zurich. Susie did not even get dressed she headed straight back to the dark safety of her duvet.

The next few days passed in a blur, eventually she had to venture out. Pulling on her joggers and tying her hair back in an elastic band she ran quickly to the corner shop, not Mr. Patel's, though. She could not face that. Susie was soon back in her sanctuary in front of the telly, oddly fascinated with daytime television. However today it made for uncomfortable viewing.

An older well-dressed lady was looking intently into the camera. Her comforting North Eastern accent implored, "Don't worry, pet. It's nothing we can't solve. Don't be rash. You can get a way oot o' debt and you can get help with your addiction – because that is what spending is. If anyone else is dealing with debt, give us a phone."

Susie had to get out; the very items she had thought would furnish their rise in the world were now accusing her. Everywhere she looked there was evidence of her weakness. She grabbed a cardigan and ran from the flat, the TV still offering platitudes.

"Are you alright, dearie?"

Susie jumped; an old lady had appeared from behind her on the bench where she had sat crying for the last hour. She wiped away her tears and shook her head. But the old lady sat down anyway.

"Christ, dear, what the bloody hell is up? You can tell me, cos we're strangers and I don't really give a shit what you've been up to."

Such abruptness from such a stereo-typically little old lady shocked Susie. But her loneliness made her yearn for even the most superficial of human contact.

"It's money."

## Power of Persuasion

The whole sorry tale came out. But instead of sympathy the old lady roared with laughter.

"God, you youngsters are clueless. Look when I was young I had to cope with four kids, one who had TB, rationing and I still managed to skim enough money of the housekeeping my miserable hubby deigned to give me to buy gin and fags. You just need to know how to economise."

She gave Susie a calculating glance, taking her in her casual but obviously expensive clothes.

"Darling, you buy me lunch, and I'll teach you all you need to know about stretching your pennies. Deal?"

And so her education began. At the sticky table of the local Turkish café Meggy taught her how to manage her money. How to cook cheap cuts, bulking up stews and curries with vegetables. Susie learned that expensive cleaning products were not necessary, bleach, vinegar, baking soda were all you would need to get the flat immaculate. They sat there for hours. Susie taking notes on a pad borrowed from Mehmet the Turk. Meggy took her back to a time and place she had no idea had existed in the twentieth century. In her tweeds and pearls Meggy pointed out the excesses. She interrogated Susie more efficiently than any bank manager on her income and outgoings. Meggy was rude, hurtful and scornful about Susie's despair.

"You've got to look at things differently. What do you need not what you want. If you can survive without it – sell it. You don't need to eat posh on your own, you don't have to buy sixty quid boots you can get them for twenty on the market. What is it you youngsters call it – retro chic. Second bloody hand, dearie. Start a new trend with your yuppie pals."

Meggy wiped the last of the gravy off her plate with Susie's left over roll. "Christ, your sobbing 'cos he's giving you hundred quid, girly, you should be able to manage on twenty. And if you sell some stuff you could give the bastard every penny back and bugger him, 'cos, dearie he should have been helping you, not leaving you to get on with it."

# Dangerous Cocktail

Susie sat with another cup of tea gone cold; a complete stranger had just opened her eyes to her relationship and her life. For the price of a meal and twenty quid she had been shown an open door.

It had taken Susie only a week. The wardrobes were raided and instead of taking the old evening clothes to the charity shop she sold them to a chubby little West Indian lady who had a market stall. The homemade cleaning stuff was surprisingly efficient and she found a satisfaction in cooking from scratch, turning a bag of reduced out-of-date vegetables into delicious soup, or curry.

Toby was due back any day now and Susie was a different person. She looked around the flat. Proud of her hard work, she smoothed the faux fur on the back of the chair, the last symbolic item. She checked in the freezer and smiled at the little bags clearly labelled with their cooking instructions. The last three magazines were artfully arranged on the side table. In the envelope along with three hundred pounds she put a letter explaining how disappointed she was that Toby had not supported her more and that it was over.

She locked the front door, putting the key through the letterbox. Susie's head was held high. The five hundred pounds in her purse would be a good start. She had tried to find Meggy again, to thank her, to let her know about the consultancy she was going to set up but Meggy had disappeared.

Susie popped into Mr. Patel's shop, on the way past she looked at the magazines, she trailed her fingers over the glossy pages, but she turned from them, and walked out empty-handed. There was nothing in them she needed – not now.

# Amnesia

## Stephen Rigby

" Mr. Fitzgerald? Mr. Fitzgerald?
Can you hear me?
Do you know where you are?
Mr. Fitzgerald, do you know where you are?"

I heard the voice.
It was urgent, worried, almost pleading.
   I responded as anyone might to such a demand and opened my eyes.
A mistake.
   I felt a searing pain on my now open iris followed by a wave of nausea. Any scene which I had expected to see was masked by a halo of light.
   As this light dissipated I tried to move. The effort was unbearable and I stopped, my body felt tired and my muscles burnt. I closed my eyes, dizzy from the exertion and tried to gather my resolve and make another attempt at the simple task of sitting. This time I managed to place myself into a semi upright position supported mainly on my left elbow and now breathing hard.
   Without warning I felt another arm on mine and opened my eyes once more. The image was still hazy, a little like staring straight into the sun, and I couldn't make out the face which was now so close to mine. Slowly it came into focus and I defined it was female; not only female but blonde and attractive. While I contemplated her features my attention was drawn down to her mouth; she was speaking again.

"Mr. Fitzgerald let me help you.
I've called Dr McDonald and he'll be here in a minute.
I never thought I'd see it, never."

## Dangerous Cocktail

I was struggling to make sense of her statement when I realised that her use of the name, Mr. Fitzgerald, was in addressing me.
Mr. Fitzgerald.
She was talking to me.
Panic set in as I tried to associate the name with myself and couldn't.
I wasn't able to.
What the hell.
I grabbed her arm and tried to pull my own face closer to hers but as I did so darkness descended and I lost consciousness.

I next awoke to find my recent acquaintance enveloping me in her arms and hoisting me upwards into a similarly reclined posture as in our previous encounter. My vision was less blurred than before but still cloudy, and through the mist I now saw that we were not alone. Two figures stood just out of range of my still poor eyesight and they conversed. I would have liked to have listened but I was distracted by another instruction.

"Mr. Fitzgerald, look at me. Look at me."

I did so. More through the compliance which her voice demanded than choice; as for my own intention, I was still trying to focus on the visitors.

"Dr McDonald is here to see you now."

"Thank you, Mia."

This second voice betrayed no emotion, not like the first. It was deep, it was tonal and it was final. The pleasantry of the dismissal did not disguise its intent and Mia, my only contact, left me. As she did I saw her look first at me and then at the figures I had yet to meet. She

## Amnesia

moved away as one moved in. The gradual appearance was heightened by the slowness of movement. Yet as he approached, for now I could decipher the sex, so too did his companion. A woman this time, and they both came toward me.

The mystery of the situation was only diminished by a sudden spasm of pain that shot through my back. A cry tore from my throat and my guests halted for a moment. Then the male made haste, he was at my side and he was concerned. I could see in his eyes and in his mouth and the way he furrowed his brow that he was concerned.

"Mr. Fitzgerald, are you all right. What caused the scream?"

And there it was again, the name. Obviously these people believed it to be my name, and I had no other to offer them so I took it.

"My back"

I whimpered. I don't think I had ever whimpered before and it shamed me that in front of strangers I could offer such a reply. So I steadied myself and restated my assertion.

"My back, Jesus, it was my back"

The female, there was only one since Mia had departed, sobbed. I watched bemused as she stood and wept in front of me and saw the man reach over and comfort her with an arm about her shoulders. He looked back at me and whilst consoling the now distraught woman he addressed me.

"Mr. Fitzgerald, do you know where you are?"

The second time I had been asked the question, only this time I actually thought about it.

## Dangerous Cocktail

"No, no idea."
Instinctively I looked around.
My vision was clearing; all the time improving and I could now define the space. A large room with white walls and a sink in the corner covered in bottles and containers. There was a door ahead of where I lay; in a bed as I now saw clearly. To the right I could make out a television set mounted on the wall and a bed side table held a full glass of water and some newspapers. I then looked to my immediate left and the confinement became clear. A large white box stared back at me, digital display showing numbers, lights flashing across the surface and a trail of wires which lead to my bed. A stand with a bag of fluid attached to my hand was the final assertion as to my location.
I was in hospital.
Once more the darkness beckoned; my breathing quickened and my head felt light; I felt as though I would slip away into unconsciousness but this time I fought. I held on to the images of the room and let them strengthen my claim to remain aware.

"John. John. Thank God you're all right. Thank God. We thought you were dead, they said you would die. And then you just lay there, we thought you'd given up."

The woman was frantic; her tone was high and her speech hastened. The words were spoken as though she could hold them no longer.

"They said you would never wake up. I told them. I told them you would. Look"

She now gesticulated at the man in the room and addressed him.

"See. See. I told you he would. I told you"

## Amnesia

The tears flowed freely down both cheeks as she stood and stared at me.

"Mrs. Fitzgerald, please. Calm down, let me take a look at your husband."

He calmed her with his words and she visibly relaxed, her shoulders slumped and her chest eased its shaking. Yet the words were of no comfort to me, I was struck by the implied revelation of his last statement. He approached me once more and looked directly into my eyes. His gaze held me. I had taken in too much and felt unable to process all the information coherently, so I gazed back at the man before me with moistening eyes.

"John?"

He was kind now.

"John. I need to explain where you are. Can you understand me?"

I nodded, and a tear fell, or rolled from eye to mouth. I watched the woman, Mrs. Fitzgerald, as I was given account of my arrival at this confusion.

"Do you remember the accident?"

And so began a narration that lasted nearly an hour.

I listened intently as my near death collision with a motorcycle was reported to me and tried to recall any of the events that were described. But I failed. Failed to draw together any memory of the crash or the ambulance or the emergency ward. All were vividly portrayed by Dr McDonald, as I now asserted this man to be. He courteously omitted the

## Dangerous Cocktail

specifics of the numerous operations he had performed on me but I heard about each and how he had tried to stitch my crushed body back to a whole. I was treated to the reports of his near successes and finally to the despair of his perceived failure. The revelation that he held to the last was more than I could take.

"And unfortunately John, we were unable to repair the damage to the legs. I'm so sorry."

His voice eased off and he hung his head for the first time in my brief dealings with him. Now he failed to hold my stare, now his confidence failed him.
As I threw back the sheet covering my body he turned away.
She too physically recoiled as my impotency was revealed and as I drifted back into unconsciousness I saw the wreckage.
My left leg had been amputated below the knee; my right above.

*\*\*\**

I was woken for a third time by a commotion. Raised voices competed with each other, first one, then another and then a third. Each clamouring for supremacy, each louder than the last and each contributing to an increasingly painful headache. My eyes remained firmly closed as I attempted to lever myself up, an act I was becoming irritatingly accustomed to, but one that now reminded me of my loss. I could have wept with the fresh recognition of that loss but the noise in the room demanded my attention. The participants in this verbal battle could not have seen my rise for they continued to bait one another even as I raised my lids to peer out at them. Two were recognised, so too their voices now I had a visual aid. The third was new.
Another female, shorter than the others and younger.
Younger by a good few years than Dr McDonald who stood between her and my newly announced wife.

## Amnesia

Mrs. Fitzgerald looked worn, her eyes were red and her skin reflected the grey of weariness. She was unkempt, dishevelled.

In contrast the younger woman with whom she now quarrelled bore none of the marks of fatigue, nor presented an air of surrender which one might have associated with the former. She was modestly but neatly dressed and stood straight and true, pulling her small frame to its full height to gain an equal standing with those whom she now argued. Appearance was deceptive, for the vehemence with which she verbally attacked betrayed a stronger character than her form might suggest.

With the visual rendition of the scene completed I turned my attention to the aural. I did not need to strain to hear the words this time; they were thrown upon the air with force and reached me without my assent. Their subject was me.

"...but I told you to stay away. Get out. I don't want you here. Dr? Get her out"

Mrs. Fitzgerald addressed both the woman and Dr McDonald. The urgency and hysteria in her voice confirmed the intention was clearly to remove her female adversary and have the doctor do it.

"Calm down, please, calm down"

The doctor attempted now to calm the situation as it began to escalate.

"Why, why should I leave? I've as much right to be here as you. In fact probably more when you think about it. He doesn't want you, he wants me."

# Dangerous Cocktail

This apparently shocked Mrs. Fitzgerald. She stepped back, her head down, tears dripping freely to the floor. The assault continued.

"Do you think this changes anything? Does it? It doesn't. It doesn't change a thing. He told you it was over and it is. When he gets out of here where is he going to go? Back to you?"

She halted for a moment at the last remark as its impact shook Mrs. Fitzgerald further.

"Back to you? I don't think so. Back to me. If this hadn't happened that's where he'd be now, with me, not you. Where do you think he was going? He'd left you. He was coming to me."

This declaration turned the tide and Mrs. Fitzgerald lost the battle, she opened her mouth to retort but her voice had been quietened and she simply looked forlorn. The younger woman had won; she had beaten the fight from Mrs. Fitzgerald and her assertion that 'he' would choose 'her' seemed to snuff out any spirit for rally.

But not from me. The little I had heard was enough to disenchant this slight figure and to revive me in to making a reply. I broke in to the now silence with raised voice.
A short, sharp, single shout;

"Stop"

Their focus shifted from one another to me. For a moment I was scrutinised by all three and felt uncomfortable as each lowered their eyes on contact with mine.

"John?"

Amnesia

The first to acknowledge my awareness was the doctor. He immediately stepped out from between the women and was at my side, taking my arm and looking at the electronics beside my bed.

"John?"

The same enunciation, but now from the woman who had so recently and callously hurt Mrs. Fitzgerald with her words.

"Who are you?"

My question was genuine; yet concealed my own suppositions of who she was based on my increasingly coherent state of mind.
She laughed. This did not repair the damage she had done to any standing she may have had with me, but further served to enhance my distrust.

"Who are you?"

I repeated the question, louder.
She looked at the doctor, she looked at Mrs. Fitzgerald, and she looked at me.
She stuttered.

"It's me John, Susanne, Susanne. It's me."

She shook her head as she spoke.

"Do you really not remember? It's me."

But I did not remember. She held no place in my mind that I could recover. No time, no image, no smell, no hint of recognition. So that was my reply.

79

## Dangerous Cocktail

"No."
"I don't remember you, I don't remember her."

I waved a hand at Mrs. Fitzgerald, who had lifted her face to listen as I responded to Susanne and now stood despondent as though she might fail at any moment.

"I don't remember me!"

I indicated myself with an accusatory finger.

"And I don't remember this!"

I gripped the bed sheet and tore it across my body. My disfigurement was plain. The bandaging concealed the wounds but the extent of my injuries was apparent to all.
Susanne recoiled.
It was her turn to falter, bereft of immediate response she continued to move away. With her eyes fixed on my legs she stumbled and then stuttered.

"My God John, my God. They didn't tell me. Why didn't you tell me?"

She spun to face Mrs. Fitzgerald with this last question; the strength had not faded from her voice and its tone was ever more critical. She received no reply and slowly turned again to look back at me.

"I'm sorry John, I didn't know. Are you going to be all right?"

"No I'm not going to be all right. I've got no legs, look. Look."

Amnesia

She couldn't. Or wouldn't. Her eyes locked to my own as my anger grew.

"But. They can help can't they? They can fix you? Doctor?"

It was not the doctor that answered but Mrs. Fitzgerald.

"He'll be fine. You'll be fine, John"

"How can he be fine? He'll be in a wheelchair."

The prediction was blunt. It was obviously the truth, but such a truth to silence the room. I looked at my legs, Susanne looked at Mrs. Fitzgerald, and Mrs. Fitzgerald looked at me.

Dr McDonald rescued us all from this peculiar stand off.

"Right, out. Ladies? Out please. He needs to rest. This is too much, too upsetting for him. Please?"
Susanne turned. She glanced back at me over her shoulder and stepped through the open door, held by the doctor.
Mrs. Fitzgerald did not. She held her ground.

"Please."

The doctor's second request did get through and she too left the room. He closed the door and once more moved to stand beside me.

"Its not uncommon you know."

He spoke as he checked the machine, and the fluid, and concealed my loss with the sheet.

## Dangerous Cocktail

"The loss of memory. It's not uncommon. In cases of severe trauma the mind often closes off the door to those bits it wants to forget. In fact sometimes it just shuts the memory down completely, tries to erase the bad things, you know."

"Will it come back?"

I pleaded.

"It can depend really. On the trauma, and the type of injury. A massive smash such as yours and the head injuries….It's hard to say John. I'd like to be positive but these things are often psychological and that makes them more difficult to assess."

I accepted the answer but it did nothing to reassure or to comfort me.

"Sounds like a mess."

A lame attempt to lighten the mood.

"Not necessarily. There are treatments and specialists…"

The doctor had misunderstood.

"No. I meant those two. God, it sounds like a nightmare."

"Well, I'm a doctor John, not a counsellor. But yes, sounds like a mess".

I would have continued to lament the possibilities that the previous scene had proposed but was interrupted by the door opening.
Another visitor.
Another woman.

## Amnesia

My assessment of her appearance was cut short as she ran across the short divide and flung her arms around my neck. The doctor seemed less surprised than I and moved away.

"Oh Dad, are you all right, Dad?"

I wasn't sure I could take much more, not sure I could handle any more revelations without heading back to the safety of the dark. This new assertion was too much and I decided to act in my own protection.

I took hold of the girl's arms and slowly forced them from around my neck. I brought them to her side and eased her body away from mine. She took her head from my chest and looked up at me.

I returned the gaze.

And there it was.

A recovery, a hint. A reappearance, a promise. A threat.

As for an instant, just an instant, I thought I recognised her.

- Fantastically stronpening. This is really well-written, I was carried along. But I want to know the 'end' of the story... please write the whole book. What else he does? Does his memory return? Does it change his life?

# The First Spots of Blood

Peter Roberts

The first spots of blood had appeared as she coughed and she had covered them with a small white linen handkerchief. At about the same time, British troops were surrendering sovereignty at Yorktown, three thousand miles across the ocean. Those who seek synchronicity in such matters would have remarked upon the end of one struggle and the beginning of another. But while the Colonists had fought for independence for over eight years, Emily's struggle proved to be barely eight weeks.

Now, she lay dying in Samuel's arms, a grim imitation of the girl who had loved Sam so much it hurt.

Her illness, the true rout of England, had run its course and to the victor, the spoils. For Samuel, there was only this: a sorrow beyond his imagining, unfolding in their tiny room. Emily adored him. Samuel was a woodcutter, and a good man, strong and gentle. In his turn he thought her the most wondrous gift in his life. He lived through her and for her, providing their daily means: a simple lodging here in Old Port, and bread on the table. That she could fail and be taken at twenty years old was inconceivable.

The night had been endless. Emily's condition had worsened through the small hours as she passed beyond the help of their crude medication. She had declined the little laudanum that remained, wanting to stay lucid for him in their final moments together. They spoke few words, but he never left her side.

They had both come to understand that this time, he alone would wake to a new day. She had known when it was time.

"Hold on to me, my love Sam, hold me."

Emily's voice was less than a whisper and it broke his heart. He looked down at her, cradled in his arms as if in sleep. She looked

## Dangerous Cocktail

smaller now, less substantial. These were their last moments together; Sam knew it but he struggled to push the thought from his mind. Even in the flickering light of a lone candle she would see his fear; it would betray their promise to stay together for all eternity. The beautiful and careless promise that young lovers make. Now she inclined her head slowly, painfully, and opened her eyes to meet Samuel's gaze, sharing a thousand treasures in that moment as their souls danced with each other for the last time.

"I love you," he whispered. But she had gone.

In the agony of silence that followed, Samuel could hear the candle flame gutter and die. Gently and with reverence, he closed her eyes and imagined her spirit, now free, now soaring with the angels. Then he wept.

"Dear Lord Jesus, take her into Your care. Love her and protect her, until that day we may be together again. I ask this as Your humble servant."

He rocked her, slowly and gently, backwards, forwards, his face buried in her hair, her lifeless body safe within his strong embrace.

\*\*\*

She was still in his arms as the unwelcome first hint of morning seeped through the make-shift curtain to cast a yellowed taint across the sparse, cold room. Samuel had slept for nearly two hours. Now, with the dawn, he struggled to open his swollen eyes. Her body, which had only moments before been the delicate and frail figure of his one true love, now lay cold to his touch, heavy and unyielding. Of this he was miserably conscious. Yet he dare not waken, for how could he face what he had lost? Who was he now, without her? His life had surely ended at the moment she had given her last breath.

He was cold and felt himself shiver as his eyes slowly adjusted to the light. He had fallen asleep holding her, and now his body ached

# The First Spots of Blood

and cramped in protest. Closing his eyes he thought only of being able to reverse the march of time; to go back beyond this spoiled hovel that now stank of disease and defeat. He tried to remember the first time they'd made love, in the snowy woods of Leigh amongst the beech and ancient oaks, but he could hold the thought for only an instant before his mind and body dragged him back to the present. It had never snowed since, and never would.

As he lay in purgatory he became aware of the sounds of Old Port going about its business in the streets and on the quays below, just another December morning, like any other. A sled cracked along the cobbles outside, and Samuel knew it would be loaded with cotton, headed toward Corn Street and the merchant' nails. Emily loved the hustle and bustle of market days. Although they had barely a few shillings to their name, she would always throw a penny or two for the mud larks along the banks beneath the bridge, as he held her hand.

A dog was barking. Samuel wondered why he could hear it so clearly, and supposed he had left their tiny leaded window unlatched. Or perhaps the tavern's rear door at the foot of the stairs outside their room had opened. Yes, that was it, someone was leaving for the day. A young gentleman had recently taken lodging upstairs in one of the furnished rooms reserved for those of acceptable occupation. They had not had the opportunity yet to make his acquaintance but Emily believed him to be one of the new teaching staff at Colston's. She had remarked on the young man's kempt appearance and the bundle of books he would carry with great diligence, as she watched the ebb and flow of Bristol life from their narrow window. Samuel thought they must meet him, and Emily could take him up a piece of her pumpkin cake - there was no finer way to greet a new friend. Yes, they would do that, and soon.

There was a gentle *tap tap* at the door.

Samuel awoke from his reverie and listened.

*Tap. Tap*, it came again, and then the handle was turning. He

## Dangerous Cocktail

brushed Emily's hair gently aside and looked past her to the door.

"Sam? Em? It's me and Thomas. We wanted to see how you were. If you needed anything."

The door pushed open and a young woman in a dirt-streaked dress, in truth little more than a girl, stepped inside. An infant was snuggled into her shoulder, fast sleep. She saw her two friends together on the old mattress that served as both bed and armchair, and she smiled, rubbing sleep from her eyes as she did so. Samuel had once joked that their armchair was the grandest in the land, room enough for all of them and the Prince of Wales too.

She looked down at Sam and he looked back up at her. Then Thomas stirred as his mother's eyes filled with an ocean of sorrow.

"Oh no. Oh no." She shook her head and clutched Thomas tight to her, "Sam?. . ."

But the desolation in his eyes left no doubt. It was over.

***

Mary looked up at a Bristol sky that had marshalled unseasonal thunderheads like an army, a portent of the unexpected. When the first rip of thunder sounded its advance from somewhere to the north east, the child she held squirmed and shook, its tiny fingers playing out an agitated dance in the thickening air.

"Hush, Tom, 'tis only the silly ol' clouds an' what a fuss they're makin' for poor Em. I know my sweet, I know."

Mother and child stood alone, wrapped in one of Emily's shawls, as a draggle of mourners stepped through the narrow iron gates and gathered in a line. Two or three attendants lifted a pair of coffins from the cart outside and draped them in a black cloth. Mary looked around her. Only she and Thomas were here to help dear Samuel bid farewell to Em. A dozen others moaned and sobbed as the short procession began, their own loss a young man from Temple Gate who'd suffered a frightful fall from a kiln top where he'd been patching up the brickwork.

## The First Spots of Blood

Now, as both caskets were held aloft, Mary prayed that Samuel would bear the coffin as Emily had born her illness, with strength and grace.

A second and more violent crack of thunder directly overhead made Mary jump and Thomas wriggled against her, inside the shawl. Samuel approached with the casket on his shoulder. He wore the brown coat that Mary remembered with such fondness. Emily had crafted fruit cones from straw and sold them at market to buy that old coat for him. Together they had patched a hole or two but it was good enough, and Sam had been delighted when Em presented it to him. Mary remembered the absolute love that had sparked and swum in her eyes. *And in mine.*

Mary had known Sam since childhood. She had kicked stones along the cobbles with him when they were both small; and when she had tumbled hard into the old woodpile outside Stoke's Yard, it was Sam who had dislodged the splinter from her knee and soothed away her tears; and again, when her Ma had died. Then at fourteen, the orphan Mary found she could neither control nor understand the feelings that filled her head with nonsense. One day they'd be wed. One day they'd have children. One day *this day* he'd look at her and see Mary, the real Mary, burning up inside for him, and crying. And while the fairy tale had belonged to Emily, who was funny and beautiful, the tragedy had been Mary's.

For despite her impoverishment, Mary had entertained a brief dalliance with a boy-poet from Redcliffe.

This exuberant and handsome youth had promised a happy and secure future, a pledge she welcomed with gratitude. Alas, the streets of his art proved to be paved, not with gold, but with opium and arsenic.

He died without knowing that she carried his child.

The pall bearers were directly in front of her now, and as they shuffled slowly past, Mary felt the first drop of rain fall cold against her neck. She shivered and chewed at her fingers. She could see Sam, his face at once both ashen and dark, his eyes fixed on the ground ahead. Mary knew no words would ever be enough. She could never replace

## Dangerous Cocktail

what had been lost; but she could be his true friend forever; that would help him; that would help them both.

As the procession passed and moved on towards the burial site, a squall of humid air pushed the dead leaves at her feet into a frenzy, until their scratching was drowned by another thunderclap and the clouds split open. A few heavy drops quickly multiplied to a torrent, and she ran with Thomas to the shelter of Redcliffe's south wall as the funeral party huddled around the forbidding heap of earth and the joyless pit at its base.

\*\*\*

A man, a girl and a child sat atop Brandon Hill and looked across the gorge to Leigh, where the first snowfall for four years had begun to dress the treetops, inch by inch, in a delicate white lace. Around the three figures, elegant couples were buttoned up tightly against the cold. Most were taking their constitutional walk along the paths that meandered through this delightful open space high above the bustle of Bristol's town and harbour-side; yet they walked as if unaware of the picture crystallising on the other side of the Avon. As the brown and green there surrendered slowly and gracefully to white, the man sighed.

"How beautiful it is. Look. Emerging flake by flake, her white forest. Secret places and secret promises."

The girl put her arm through his and rested her head on the shoulder of the old brown coat he wore. "An' mayhap she's there still, you know? Waitin' for ya."

He pondered this as a seagull swooped and cawed and dipped below the hill line in search of food. *One day you'll meet with her again.*

The flakes were growing bigger now and began to weave a wintry blanket around them as they sat. The child, bundled up in a faded grey woollen wrap, had found a stick and was waving it like a baton as he wobbled purposefully to and fro across the whitening grass. He looked up into the falling grey sky, stretching his arms to embrace each

## The First Spots of Blood

soundless crystal wafer. Those he missed tickled his nose or settled on his eyelashes and he toppled backwards with a soft bump before crawling to his mother's side. The ladies and gentlemen of means had taken their leave as the snow had thickened, so only three souls now sat to witness the reappearance of the white forest on the other side of the gorge.

The man coughed and the girl gathered him to her and they huddled together once more as the magic enveloped them all in a thick and silent shroud of white. It covered the land, and it covered the first spots of blood, up on Brandon Hill.

> Not the genre I would choose to read but it's well written so that I am interested enough to read on. I felt it was a bit twee / stereotypical at the beginning but the way you write involves the reader & it develops well as it goes. There's a lovely balance to the story — really sad though! I can v. much imagine you writing a novel that many people would enjoy.

# Reunion

## David Mills

I'm Steve Osborne, Stevo to everyone but my sister, who has always called me scab; thirty-seven, unmarried, but in a relationship. This is the story of my sister Sally, well my version of it anyway.

Sally is younger than me by three years, and like all older brothers when not teasing her, I always thought of myself as her protector, me as Lancelot to her Guinevere. And that was one of the games that we played together, before I got too old to play with girls, about the time that I went to secondary school. After coming home from school we would generally flop in front of the telly and try hard to ignore each other and change the channel when the other wasn't looking. Mum would often shout from the kitchen or dining room if we got too rowdy. Sally was normally home first, but then one day she wasn't.
"Where's Sally?" I shouted to mum when I got in.
"I expect she's just dawdling," mum said poking her head round the door as I threw myself into the favourite swivel chair, it was dads' really, but when he wasn't in Sally and I both wanted it. When we were really small we used to both be able to fit in it with dad.
"Do you want some pop?" mum asked, "The man's been today."
"Yes please! Red, did you get red?" was my favourite chant when the Corona man had been.
"Yes I got red and don't go swinging that chair too much."
It was the usual admonishment that we got whenever we sat in Dad's chair. The time crawled round to five o'clock; telly wasn't as much fun when you watched it on your own, 'Blue Peter' had started and Sally still wasn't home. Mum was beginning to show signs that she was worried, she kept coming and asking me questions like, "did

## Dangerous Cocktail

she say she was going to see anyone after school? Which of her friends does she normally walk with? Do you know which way she walks?" The questions were interspersed with her going to the front gate and looking up and down the street.

Six o'clock came and went, dad got home from work and still there was no sign of Sally. Dad was cross like I hadn't seen for a while. He suggested I went one way back to school and he'd go another. Mum was to stay behind in case she turned. I wouldn't have wanted to be in her shoes when she got home I could tell you.

Dad and I walked to the school and back again by different routes, not a sign, not a trace. Those of her friends we saw and asked hadn't seen her since she left school either. Mum was frantic when we got home and both she and dad said that we'd have to go to the Police.

Sally, my Guinevere, was never seen again. No trace; nothing; it was just as if she had been vanished by some omniscient magician.

Things changed from that day forward. Dad started drinking, not coming home, and the short fuse that he had before became even shorter. Mum just stopped being mum, she withdrew into herself, stopped going out even for food; stopped doing the washing; she almost stopped being. Then one day, about two years later, when I got home from school she didn't answer my greeting. The house was empty and felt like no one had been there all day. The silence hung heavy in the hallway. The stairs loomed like an Everest stretching before me; I didn't want to climb them. My mouth became dry, my chest tight and my eyes began to water at the thought of what I might find around the bend in the stairs, on the landing, in the bathroom or in their bedroom. Each foot became heavier than the other with each additional stair that I climbed and with each advance the dread grew blacker within me. There was nothing on the stairs or landing, the bedroom and bathroom were empty, there was only one last place to look, Sally's room.

I hadn't been in there since the day that she disappeared. To me it seemed like an invasion; any remaining privacy that she had would be

# Reunion

torn from her. My hand reached for the knob and, slowly, turned it. As the catch clicked itself free of its housing I could almost feel the air rush past me in its escape. I knew then that mum wasn't in there but had to continue with my searching.

The room was just as Sally had left it the day she went to school, pyjamas pooled on the floor, paper and crayons spread in haphazard patterns on the desk, dolls left lying abandoned where they lay, clothes and hair disarrayed. I knew that mum had been in here though; the teddies were not in any order that Sally would have left them. But mum was nowhere. What would I tell dad when he came home?

It was dad that told me though. When he came home he had a policeman with him; at first I thought they had found Sally, but they told me that mum wasn't coming home. She had jumped off the bridge over the bypass in front of a lorry. Stupidly I asked them if she was dead. Dad just nodded, the policeman said 'I'm afraid so son.'

Well, it was about three years after that, when I was halfway through my apprenticeship, that I got a call to the manager's office. As soon as I saw the uniform I knew that it was bad news again. My dad had been killed this time, knocked down on his way to work. I guessed that he was still hung over from the night before and not really paying attention at the crossing, but what could I do, now I was alone in that big old house full of memories, full of ghosts. Every creak, each squeak, any knock was either mum, dad or Sally come to speak with me or to claim me, to take me to where they were.

Needless to say I sold the house and it made me a very wealthy teenager and a lavish twenty year old, but a struggling bloke in his thirties, well struggling no more than anyone else, just without the encumbrance of a mortgage. How things can change.

At the time that this took place I was living with Fox, a woman I had known for quite a while. I was serious about her, she was more serious about me, but we, well, I didn't want to make the final step. It was Saturday night and we had just settled in to go through the ritual

## Dangerous Cocktail

of checking our lottery numbers and then being surprised when we didn't win, when the doorbell rang. Fox went to answer.

"Steve, Steve, come quickly. Steve come here!" she shouted from the hallway.

I didn't rush: it isn't my nature, "Steve will you shift your arse!" Fox shouted even louder.

"Yeah, yeah, what is it?" I asked as I peered round the lounge door.

"This girl here claims that she is Sally, your sister. You told me that she was dead!"

Well to say I was gob smacked would be an understatement, you could have knocked me down with a feather, and in fact I sat back down on the sofa rather quickly. "Um, er, I guess you better ask her in," I called rather sheepishly from the front room.

The girl that walked in was pale and thin; 'heroin chic' would be the phrase that sprang to mind if you were talking about a model, but she didn't walk with the poise of a model. Her hair was the dark colour that I remembered, but where as I recalled it as always being shiny and full of bounce, it hung lank and loose. Her eyes that had always sparkled with life and vitality were now dark and hidden. Her body was thin and still retained the androgynous form of the nine-year-old that she was when she disappeared.

"Hello scab," she rasped, "Who's that?" she tilted her head towards Fox, stood in the doorway, her face full of thunder. She called me scab on account that I was constantly scraping my knees and elbows and just loved picking the scabs off.

"That Sally is Fox. She's my girlfriend."

I still wasn't sure that this person stood in my house was my sister, or just someone taking part in a sick joke that one of my so called mates had dreamt up. She sure looked a bit like she had twenty-five years ago, but I didn't know. How I could be certain?

"Sit down Sal, would you like a coffee or something?"

"I'd like some fizzy pop, please. Red if you've got any."

## Reunion

"I think we've got some lemonade in the kitchen. Fox sweetie, would you get some please and I wouldn't mind a beer."

"Beer! You shouldn't be drinking beer, mum won't like it and dad'll go mad when he gets home. Oh, oh Scabs in trouble."

Sally began to sing in that little voice of hers that could really grate. Funny how you forget about things like that over the years, yet as soon as they rear their heads it's like they have never left your mind.

What was troubling me was the fact that here was this woman, thirty-four, and she was looking it, with the body and language of an eight year old. She talked and sounded like my long missing sister and called me by the old nickname that no one else used. But things just weren't sitting easy with me.

"Excuse me a minute," I said to Sal, "I'll just see where Fox has got to with those drinks."

In the kitchen Fox was on her mobile, talking, I would guess, to Jane, her best mate. No doubt telling her I was a shit for telling her my sister was dead, but that she had just appeared on our doorstep. All that sympathy wasted is how she was feeling I figured. Fox quickly hung up.

"Where the hell did she come from?" she whispered.

I could only shrug, "I've no idea, but I'll try and find out. She doesn't seem to be the sharpest knife though. Is the spare bed made up?"

"You can't be serious," Fox replied, "I'm not sure I want her staying here the night."

"I can't see as how I've got a choice. She is claiming to be my sister and what do we do if she says she has nowhere else to go?"

"We? What's all this *we* all of a sudden? She's your sister!"

"Yes and you're my girlfriend, now please come in the other room and let's see if we can make some sense of what's been happening over the last twenty-five years."

The first thing that Sally asked when we came back with the drinks was where were mum and dad. I gently explained that they had both died quite a long time ago.

## Dangerous Cocktail

"They never really came to terms with you disappearing like you did," I told her.

"But I haven't been anywhere," she said. "I've been around the whole time. How do you think I managed to find you? Although you didn't make it that difficult; it is only two streets away."

"Well if you've been around all this time why have you been hiding?"

Sally thought for a moment before answering, "I wasn't hiding, you just couldn't find me."

"But," I countered, "If we didn't know we were playing a game how could we tell you we'd stopped playing?"

"I wasn't playing; I couldn't be found. I'm tired of these questions. Can I go to bed now?"

"Yeah of course you can, I'll just show you where everything is then you can make yourself comfy."

"Will you read me a story before I go to sleep please?"

"Sorry Sally, what did you say?"

"Please could you read me a story, I know you've still got my 'Beatrix Potter' books. 'Jeremy Fisher' please."

"Aren't you a bit old for a story?" I was beginning to think that I had suddenly got caught up in an episode of 'Strange but True' or some other such programme.

"You're never too old for a story," Sally replied, "And you know I always sleep better after a story."

I looked across to Fox who was just imperceptibly shaking her head. She also couldn't quite believe the way this evening was turning out. I mouthed that I wouldn't be long to her and took Sally upstairs to show her where the spare room, bathroom were and where Fox and I slept. She giggled when I showed her our room.

"You sleep with a girl?" was her childish query.

I found her some of Fox's pyjamas to sleep in and found Jeremy Fisher whilst she cleaned her teeth.

Reunion

I didn't feel comfortable as I read this child's story to an apparently grown woman who snuggled down in bed, pulled the duvet to her chin and sucked her thumb. But if it helped her feel safe and that she was back where she belonged I was willing to go along with it. I had only got a few pages in before Sally was asleep, making that contented innocent sound that only children seem to make when they are sleeping, not quite a snore, but more than heavy breathing.

"Well?" queried Fox when I got back down stairs. "What have you found out about where she's been?"

I paused before answering. I didn't really know how to phrase what I was about to say, or even if I had heard it quite right myself. "She says that she hasn't been anywhere, but that she hasn't been hiding either. I don't know sweetheart, I can't work it out. But what's really bothering me is why now, after twenty-five years; it's not as if I've got anything to give her."

"You're her brother, you can give her the time and love that she hasn't had for these years."

"I don't know Fox, I'm not sure. There's something that is just nagging away at the back of my mind."

"OK," said Fox cuddling into me on the sofa, "You can start telling me about your childhood together, like why she calls you 'Scab' for starters."

So we spent a quiet evening drinking with me telling her about the short time I had had with the girl that was now sleeping upstairs. The adventures we had on the climbing frame in the back garden that was transformed into spaceships, pirate vessels, fairytales castles. The competitions on who could jump the furthest of the swing. The split heads and broken arms that were the result of falls from the wall, bicycles, stilts, pogo sticks or many such other childhood pastimes.

Encouraged by my opening up Fox also recounted some of her childhood experiences. She told me about some of the games that she used to play with her brothers in the woods behind their garden. She

## Dangerous Cocktail

told me about her first stolen kiss with a boy called Andy inside a big hollow oak that was rumoured to be a witch's haunt. Then, later on, as the third bottle of wine was nearing the bottom, she tearfully told me about the time she was nearly raped taking the shortcut home through those same woods.

Later still in bed after I had kissed her tears away, held her tight and soothed away the dredged up memories, we shared each other.

"Why are you hurting Fox?" the voice came through the twilight of our room.

"What the hell is she doing?" Fox hissed in my ear.

"It's ok, I'll get her back to bed," I whispered back as I grabbed for a pillow to cover my embarrassment and Fox dragged the duvet over her head.

"Come on sis, back to bed." I tried to coax her with one hand whilst keeping the pillow in place with the other.

"Let me sleep in with you tonight. I've been on my own long enough; all I want is a little company. Come on Scab, you used to let me sleep in your bed; please."

"Sal no, not tonight; maybe another time. Look, we're both grown up now and it might not be appropriate."

"You just want to go back to hurting your girlfriend don't you?"

Sally began to get petulant; I remembered she could get like this when she was a kid. You just had to dig your heels in deeper than hers and eventually she'd give in.

I stuck firm and eventually I got Sally back to the spare room and made her a drink of warm milk that she asked for. I don't know where it came from, but I remembered that she liked it with sugar and cinnamon in it. As I stood there waiting for the microwave to beep I remembered the times I used to stand over the stove waiting for the milk to warm through. Sally had generally climbed into my bed sniffing, saying she'd had a bad dream again. I decided to ask about it when I went back up.

## Reunion

Sal was sat cross-legged on her bed when I went back up with the drink; she appeared to be picking at some threads on the duvet.

"What're you doing?"

"I'm trying to get rid of this smiley face that mum's sown on this bedspread. I hate it, I hate it in this bed. Please let me come into yours!"

Silent tears began to flow down her cheeks and I did what any brother would: I sat next to her and gave her a big hug. She was cold, like marble.

"Get back into bed Sal, you're cold. Look there's no smiley face on this duvet, but I'll get you another one if it'll help you sleep. And if it's any consolation I thought that bedspread was bloody awful as well."

"Ooh Scab, mum'll tell you off for swearing."

"Look Sal there's a few things I've got to tell you about, but they'll have to wait until the morning. I'm going back to bed now."

Sal's lip began to quiver, "Please don't go. I've been alone for so long, I could really do with some company."

"Look Sal I'll take the day off tomorrow and we can talk then. Tonight I'm tired and need some sleep; I expect you could do with some as well. Goodnight."

I felt a bit cruel as I closed her door, but as I said, with Sal you sometimes had to be even more stubborn than her. I went back to bed. Fox had her back to my side of the bed, pretending to be asleep. I could feel her tension as I got back between the sheets.

"Well what the hell was that all about?" she hissed between her teeth.

"I don't really know love, but I've told her I'll take the day off tomorrow and we can have a catch up then."

I tried to cuddle up to Fox's back, but she pushed me away, "And you can forget any of that you know. Goodnight."

In the morning, after Fox had left for work, I took Sal up a cup of tea. There was no answer when I knocked on her door, so I knocked again a

## Dangerous Cocktail

bit louder and went in. Sal was sat staring out the window, her fingers slowly tracing around her reflection in the glass.

"What's up sis?"

"I'm lonely. Nobody came to find me all this time. I had to come and find you. I thought you loved me, you, mum and especially dad. But you didn't try to find me. Where are mum and dad?"

"That's one of the things I need to talk to you about. But first, of course we loved you, we spent weeks searching everywhere for you. Your picture was in all the papers, we put notices up all over the area, the police hunted for you, we did all we could. Where have you been all these years?"

"You keep asking me where I've been all the time, but I haven't been anywhere. I've been around the whole time. I've never left."

"Sorry Sal," I replied, "but you're talking in riddles again. Twenty-five years ago you walked out the front door to go to school and never came home. Mum killed herself and dad drank so much he got killed going to work one day. So if you've been around the whole time why the hell didn't you say something, come and speak to us, just let us know you were ok? If you were frightened I don't think that would have mattered. We would have been just so pleased to see you. Yet now you show up on my doorstep, no warning, no explanation and you just expect me to accept it."

"Ok scab, calm down. I understand how you feel, but before I try and tell you anything there is something I need to show you. Put your shoes on and come with me."

We walked together along familiar streets following a path well worn by our younger more innocent feet. Queens Common had changed since I had last been there. Gone was the grey, cracked tarmac that used to skin our hands and knees. The roundabout that trapped ankles had gone, as had the twenty foot high slide and the wooden swing seats that knocked me out more than once as I passed injudiciously close to them in full swing. All replaced by softer more friendly options.

Reunion

But Sally dragged me on past these items of fun to another area. An area that was fenced off, with 'Danger Keep Out Signs' posted around it.
   "Sally, you never came to the quarry, you said it scared you. You were frightened of falling into it and not being able to get out."
   She didn't answer, just grabbed hold of my hand and dragged me onwards. Her hand felt colder and thinner than ever.
   "There's a path down here, it's a bit overgrown now. You go first," she said as she pushed me on ahead of her.
   I held my arm up as I pushed through the brambles. "Christ Sally, this isn't much of a path, are you sure you know where we're going?"
   There was no reply, so I turned to see if she was still behind me, but she'd disappeared again. It was as I turned back I saw it, faded, torn and almost disintegrated, but I knew straight away what it was, as there had only been the one that I knew of. It was Sally's pink satchel. I pushed forward to touch it and as I bent down, there, pushing out of the soil like some macabre fungus were some bones.
   I had seen enough detective programmes on the telly over the years to know that you left things as they were. I fought back through the bushes and once I was clear I pulled out my mobile and called the police and then Fox. I asked her if she could call home first to see if Sally was still there and then to meet me at the common.

Fox met me just as the police were stringing the last of their tape around the area. She reached into her bag and handed me an envelope; the word 'Scab' was all that was on it. I carefully opened it and unfolded the piece of paper.

*I know you're aiming for casual / colloquial / chatty style but I feel it's a bit clumsy in parts, just needs tightening up a little.*

## Dangerous Cocktail

"I told you that I'd been around the whole time. And I wish you didn't have to find out like this. But there is another letter in by satchel; it can still be read, just. It was Dad; he used to hurt me in the night too, just like you did with your girlfriend. She's nice. I'd asked him to stop but he didn't and I said I would tell a teacher. The note's from him. He came back after about five years and tucked it into my bag. He didn't bury that with me. I think he wanted it found. Then he went and walked in front of that bus. Now you know and you can put me somewhere you can find me."

The police brought the satchel out in a plastic bag, and the note in another one. He let me read it through the plastic. It was faded, but just as Sally had said.

And that brings us to today, as Fox and I are the only ones here with the vicar and the funeral director. Gently lowering the pink coffin into the ground, she won't be lost again. I gave the undertakers a copy of Jeremy Fisher to put in with her.

Oh and she was right Fox is nice, so now we're engaged.

# A Bit of a Do

### Peter Owen

My Dearest Constance,

To say I'm sorry to hear of your predicament with regard to Emily's rather odd behaviour at your delightfully eventful party, which you were unfortunately unable to "come down" for due to your "unusual" ailment – I do hope the lanolin rub is helping, you must give it time – would be an understatement.

In order to offer the advice you seek I should explain as clearly as I can the events leading up to Emily's peculiar behaviour. It grieves me to say, but it did seem obvious to me, and I think those present would agree, that Emily was extremely drunk or perhaps even "high" on some sort of drugodial substance. She had, I know from a conversation I had in the kitchen with a tearful Mrs. Lucklow, been seen "swigging" from several bottles of turpentine liquid – used by Daddy for making a rather low-grade French polish – shortly before the Turkey was carried aloft with great majesty into the dining room by Uncle Ronald and Aunty Doris.

Unfortunately, with Ronald standing at six foot seven and Doris a comparative dwarf at four foot nine, the platter was somewhat inclined and the huge bird slithered from the silverware, catching Vicar Brompsnort a glancing blow on the head as he began to rise in anticipation of delivering the ceremonial chant and sacred blessing of the festive offering. Horace the dog, making light of having four legs of varying lengths and a lazy left eye, seized the opportunity and the turkey, dragging the huge bird through the garden and into next door's stable block, closely followed by a giggling Emily.

## Dangerous Cocktail

Luckily, Aunty Pru had had the foresight to bring along a jumbo-sized part-used tin of Plumrose "special edition" spam – originally to be offered as the main prize during the post-lunch raffle in aid of Garsight Prison Inmates "Ballet and Light Opera Club". This years "deprived persons" guest of honour, Sidney "Nutter" McDruid, long time resident and principle "ballerina" at Garsight, managed to mould the spam with his bare hands into a meaty treat not too dissimilar in appearance to the departed turkey, much to the delight and amusements of the guests, though Vicar Brompsnort, still looking a little dazed and rather glum, refused to eat any of his dinner.

I managed to snatch a private word with dear old Dr. Faux-pas during after-lunch drinks, seeking his professional view of Emily's odd behaviour and any possible remedy. Unfortunately, the poor man was weighed down with his own depression and personal problems, though he did say, rather oddly, that he and his young friend, Auberon, often found complete fulfilment when covering their naked bodies with mulberry leaves and reciting passages from De-ville's "Nymphs at The Waterside". I realise of course that this is not an opinion you might look upon favourably in your present condition, though you might try substituting the leaves for a winceyette nightie and make the most of your lanolin rub during the recitation.

So, to sum up, I'm afraid I can be of little help, the fact that Emily is twenty-seven years of age and engaged to a seventy-three year old vegetarian Morris-dancer who is no longer able to wield his fertility stick with sufficient dexterity, is, of course, also a cause for some concern – I wish you well.

Yours as ever,

Bertrand

# Going Shopping

## Elspeth Green

"Things were so different when I was young, we didn't even have computers."

"Yes, Mums."

"You don't know you're born, what with everything being done for you."

"Mmm. That I do know Mums, really I do."

"I had three children, went to work, did all the shopping as well as keeping the house clean."

"You were amazing."

"What's amazing is that I've lasted as long as I have."

"Oh yes! Truly wonderful," I suggested half-heartedly.

"You have got everything ready for tonight."

"I'm going shopping shortly, when I've finished fumigating."

"Good. You know I've set my heart on chocolate cake."

"Yes mum, it's on my list."

Her voice continued and I tried unsuccessfully to block it from my mind.

The truth is I cannot wait to go shopping; it is the only way I can switch my mother off; it is the high spot of my week. She has been going on at me for months now with the arrangements for her party. My 'Palmter' - the brilliant, hand held, life giving machine - is jammed full of notes, thoughts and ideas; some she's sent and others she has directed to my brain, to assist my completion of the list.

Right now I am seated in the corner of the bath closet and steadily being fumigated. The steam is beating down, cleaning everything within sight. My waste products have been removed and the meter on the wall suggests I am virtually germ free. Soon it will be time for the

## Dangerous Cocktail

Youth Drenching and drying; then I can sort out the shopping. In the 'olden days' bath-time would have given me the freedom from my mother, but not any more; she has a direct line. It is never ending. Yak, yakkety yak, yak, in her ancient reedy voice, which, we have all assured her, has not changed over the years.

Cheryl will be joining us tonight along with her kids and the egg, but Annabel can only make it in hologramatic format. Mother's taken the umbrage over that.

"Wouldn't you just think she would have tried, after all it is a special age?" she had complained.

"Mums, there aren't any special ages these days."

"Things were so different when I was young."

"Yes Mums, I know," I stifle a yawn.

Things are so very different now.

Our dad refused point blank to take part in the experiment; that's why he was destroyed after his three score years and ten. Mum forced Annabel, being the youngest, into it, and right now she is busy working as the human part of a computer. Pity they never succeeded in completely humanising the things; they might not have needed us at all. Anyway, her job means she cannot make it; her brain has been 'borrowed' once again.

Cheryl was very young and pregnant with Tandy at the start, so she was definitely not suitable material. Mother was most disappointed at the time. I think she took it personally; where she failed with her husband she had dearly hoped to succeed with all of us. But then, three out of five family members is not a bad average; the government would have been proud of her loyalty.

Me, I am much older than my sisters. Rumour has it that our dad is not my dad, but this is something I have yet to confirm. As the eldest, and a boy, obviously the responsibility of our Mums landed on my shoulders. My mates were so jealous of my chance to make history.

"You'll stay as young and, er, sweet as you are, you lucky B....."

## Going Shopping

It was a fun time for us then, I never dreamt I would ever want things to change. Of course, the opportunity to link in partnership past me by. Not that I had the urge when I could. All I needed then were my buddies, bikes and booze. Pity the guys got left behind; all gone now sadly.

Oh Mums. I love her dearly, but there are times when I just wish she would shut up!

"You won't forget the chicken for the sandwiches and the butterfly cakes will you? I want everything to be perfect, just like when I was young."

She's off again; pouring thoughts into my mind.

"Yes mother, everything will be perfect, I'm going shopping any minute now," I responded in a similar manner.

"Don't leave it too late. Deliveries take time you know."

"Yes Mums; I'm clean and nearly dry then I'll be off. Are you comfortable in the canister?"

"No! I've got an itch I can't scratch and a headache. Things were so different when I was young!"

"I'll check your meter before I do the shopping; might get rid of that itch and you know you can't have a headache, it's impossible."

"Well I have and you'll do no such thing, just you leave my meter alone. I'll put up with it. Get on your way before you're too late and the shops shut."

There was never any point in arguing with my mother. However many times I told her, come to think of it however many times she told me, that things were different now to when she was young, she still could not comprehend that the shops now visit the people not the other way around; and I love it.

This is the only time I can totally switch my mother out of my mind. This is the only time I can truly be myself and yet pretend. All I have to do is enter our pristine, already fumigated, lounging room, place headphones around my brain and cover my eyes with goggles to find

## Dangerous Cocktail

myself transported to the world of my dreams. I am free. How sad is that?

"Good morning Mr. Thomas. So nice to see you again. Everything ready for the party?"

The attractive manager of CompterCo greeted me as I entered through the portals of her store.

This was the supermarket of my youth. The shelves were filled to their capacity with everything I could possibly desire, with only one major difference; I was alone. My trolley would be the only one; my shins were safe. There was no one around to hassle or bother me. Every assistant was in place for my bidding and without me they would not exist. I knew them all, had named them all. It was I who had dressed and undressed them. Who would serve me today: Tracey, Angela, Chelsea or Marianne?

"Mother has given me a list of things as long as my arm. I hope you have someone who can help me."

"Absolutely, Mr. Thomas, we are all here for you. Tracey, would you help Mr. Thomas please?"

The beautifully coiffured businesswoman drifted away and Tracey came to view. As well as her other obvious attributes, she always had a ready smile.

"Hallo Mr. Thomas, Alan, how are you? Not too stressed by the party? Perhaps we can cheer you up."

Tracey looked wonderful in her emerald green CompterCo uniform. The mini skirt matching so well with her elegant legs. Everything was perfect. She held out her arms to me and I found myself wrapped in her embrace. No, I must concentrate; I must not let my mind wander. Even here, away from my family, the other side would know all about my actions and thoughts; I could go too far.

"She's so excited Tracey. She loves her annual party; it reminds her of the childhood, which was so very different from today. Here's her list and I've added some ideas as well."

## Going Shopping

I unravelled the two A4 sheets of paper, which had been screwed into my pocket. Not the pocket of the white jumpsuit I had been wearing before this trip commenced, but the blue jeans and Adidas jumper, seemingly my choice for this outing. My 'Palmter' had been left behind and I was reading actual words not taking sounds inwardly.

"She wants chicken sandwiches, jelly and ice cream, butterfly cakes, cherryade and, of course, a huge chocolate cake. I think she would like some candles too but perhaps ten will do 'cause no ordinary cake would be big enough. We'll need a bouquet of flowers and I'm totally stuck what to get her as her main present. Do you know what my sisters have chosen?"

"Oh Alan, this is your shopping trip. But I'm sure it can be sorted. Leave it with me."

Her smile made my knees turn to jelly and I followed as she sashayed smoothly around the store, my eyes barely leaving her smooth, rounded bottom to stare at the plentiful shelves.

Without having to search Tracey had managed to obtain a brand new, well-oiled trolley, with wheels all working together and which whispered silently along the aisles. My purchases followed in logical order: the jelly and ice cream could be found together; the delicious, beautifully decorated chocolate cake was close by, surrounded by the butterfly cakes with their dainty featherlike wings. Amazingly the birthday candles could be found on the shelf directly above. With Tracey's help I chose a peach coloured silk shawl, knowing my mother would love it but never use it and a huge bouquet of flowers to match. To these delights were added toilet rolls, bath oils, washing up liquid and dishwashing liquid until my trolley was full to overflowing. I was offered wine tasting, chocolate sampling and sprays of the most erotic perfumes. This was heavenly.

Sadly the end of my freedom was closing in. Tracey wiggled away in front of me and I followed docilely. There had been delaying tactics of course:

## Dangerous Cocktail

"Can we have a cup of coffee?"; "I think I have forgotten the wrapping paper" but all too soon my trip had come to an end.

At the checkout was another delightful assistant. She was blonde where Tracey had brunette hair and, as yet, she had no name; perhaps I would call her Deidre or Rocky. Her legs were hidden from view, but then again, I was totally mesmerised by her heavily made-up eyes as she gazed into mine; my imagination ran riot. No, no. I must remember where I am, who I am.

"Your account will be debited direct, Mr. Thomas, Alan."

Her smile was mine and mine alone.

I checked the total box: it was a line of noughts. That was it; that was my shopping completed, it was time to remove the headphones and goggles and return to reality.

"You didn't forget the chocolate cake did you?" The sharp, anguished voice resounded around my mind.

"No Mums, all we can do now is wait."

Ten, nine, eight, seven, six, five, four, three, two, one –

By my side, almost touching my swinging seat, appeared a small white carton with the name CompterCo emblazoned upon its side. The lid opened gently and I placed my fingers upon the contents.

There were 'T' tablets, enough for each member of our party tonight, although Cheryl would have to bring her own repast; a tiny, circular, brown mound which required water to action it, eight flimsy plastic mugs, which would have to be opened before the red liquid became noticeable; four or five dried flower petals; a tiny pot of face cream. This was all my mother would need; would ever need. I turned my attention to the miniature white container of fumigating fluid and dropped the whole receptacle into the white boxed-in machine hidden at the side of the lounging room.

My household chores for the day completed, and my mother blissfully silent, I let my mind return to the days when things were so much better. Those days when there were no computers, when fresh air

## Going Shopping

was plentiful, when flowers were not rationed and cleaning was completed by a machine, but a machine pushed by man.

I remembered the days when my sisters played happily in the back yard: chase, hopscotch, marbles and fives; kept safe by their older brother, who sometimes even joined in. There were no 'T' tablets, there was no fumigation and parents could be heard to say 'You'll eat a peck of dirt before you die.'

In my mind I picture my sisters as they are today. There is Cheryl, ancient and haggard, her children no longer growing; time has at last stopped for them. Cheryl, who is long past her three score years and ten, but thanks to the eggs she fosters, still allowed to remain. Does she long for missed opportunities or is she relieved whenever she looks at me, anxious now to rest? I see Annabel, empty of thought for the time being, waiting for her mind to be restored. I see me, living in this futuristic world and yet returning to the past whenever I can, desperate to hold on.

I gaze into the mirror; the main focal point of the lounging room. A fifty year old man stares back at me. Silently, Cheryl, who had to walk up the stairs and enter on her own two legs, joins me. I am her older brother, yet she is my much older sister. Her children materialise whilst we are talking and sharing the news; such as it is. Annabel's hologram is beamed down from the ceiling and she begins the pre-recorded speech, which will be repeated many times throughout the gathering.

"Happy Birthday; mother darling. Thank you for bringing me into this world and for making sure I have all these wonderful opportunities." We thought long and hard about how this should be worded. Pleasing everyone but mostly our mums.

There is a drum roll inside our heads and my mother walks, unaided, before us. It is her birthday; she is allowed to walk. By now she will have visualised my gift to her; I hope it pleased her. She is two hundred years old and still looks fifty. Hard to believe some treatments did not work so well for her; she needs that canister for her life.

And I am her son, her one hundred and seventy five year old son.

## Dangerous Cocktail

"Yes, mother. Things were different when you were young, when I was a child. Are they better or worse now?"

- I like the idea v. much but I feel there are some loop-holes. Maybe it needs to be thought through / shaped by the author a bit more & within your? The poster at the end is not needed — it's been running throughout the story anyway. BUT I really do like the novel theme.

# The Rugby Pitch Bathed in Wintry Sun

## Patricia Golledge

The rugby pitch bathed in wintry sun
Someone has not got up to continue play
The young captain has gone down with the scrum

Anxious eyes beg for the ambulance to come
Face down on the grass – he had to be kept that way
On the rugby pitch bathed in wintry sun

Hospital machines let out a monotonous hum
Alive, cheery – never again would he walk they say
The young captain gone down with the scrum

The lads wonder if there was something they could have done
But his neck had snapped as the scrum gave way
On the rugby pitch bathed in wintry sun

The Rugby Union said, "Everything will be done
Convert the house, any equipment" – they would pay
For the young captain gone down with the scrum

Four hundred people for the funeral did come
Grieving was loud and open – no one would forget the day
The rugby pitch bathed in wintry sun
And the young captain gone down with the scrum

# Omar Kandala

Peter Goodsall

"Kandala."

Omar directed his gaze towards the crisp, theatrical man who'd called him. He was even taller than Herr Heckler, his class tutor. He wore a sharp black uniform with a peaked cap, piping and shining buttons that was both attractive and impressive.

"Come with me to see the doctor."

"Why am I going to see the doctor?"

"Don't answer back."

The man grabbed Omar by his upper sleeve, pinching his arm as he hauled him to his feet and propelled him with greater than necessary force towards the door of the classroom where he'd been kept waiting during play. He was marched towards the palatial double-doors where only the teachers were allowed. Omar was pulled through the doors and presented to an imposing leather topped desk, his feet barely contacting the ground throughout.

"Stand straight. Don't slouch. Look straight ahead."

The man looked upon Omar with barely disguised disdain before drawing himself to attention and leaving the room by wheeling smartly around to the right.

Omar stared rigidly ahead, too intimidated to fidget, as was his normal habit. It was several minutes before thought reawakened in his mind and he began to wonder what was happening. He wasn't ill. None of the other children had been told to see a doctor. There were a few less boys in his year now of course. The ones that had had the yellow

## Dangerous Cocktail

badges sewn onto their coats had all left, including his friend Jacob. Hans had told him a couple of weeks ago that his mum had said that he couldn't play with him anymore.

Omar's eyes began to meander with his thoughts. His gaze flittered, landing upon the map of Europe with the dark stain in the middle of it.

"You were told to face ahead. Stand straight!"

Omar physically started and immediately snapped to his best attention. The man who'd addressed him so sharply was short and portly with slicked hair and a thin mouth sandwiched between puffy jowls. Small dark eyes regarded Omar, in front of him now, so that he quickly limited his view to the intricate embroidery on the man's tie.

"Now then, I am Doctor Lütz and I have some questions. Do you understand?"

Omar nodded.

"Speak up!" Omar was surprised by the vehemence of the order.

"Yes sir."

"Age?"

"Eight." Doctor Lütz busied himself with a thick wedge of papers that he'd removed from his dark burnished bag of iron hard leather. He eventually sat down to regard Omar further.

"You're small for your age wouldn't you say?"

"I don't know sir."

"Of course you are." The doctor's voice momentarily acquired an edge once again. Omar subsided and resumed his rigid demeanour, swallowing his curiosity.

Dr. Lütz removed a tape measure and some fearsome calipers from his bag and directed Omar to stand against the wall below the map. He proceeded to systematically measure Omar's height, inside leg, hips and waist, finally placing the tape about his chest.

"Breath in."

The Doctor paused for just an instant before demanding Omar breath out.

"Hmm, not much chest expansion. You must have trouble with sport. Do you swim?"

"Yes sir."

"Not very well I suppose." It was a statement, not a question.

"I can swim two hundred and fifty metres sir."

"Don't brag to me boy." This was a blunt instrument, used almost absently.

"No sir."

He continued with the tape, holding it across Omar's ears, the one feature that Omar himself was self-conscious over, since some had used them as a basis for poor wit. However, the Doctor passed no comment but reached for the calipers, twisting the nut to open them wide. He placed the instrument over Omar's head and proceeded to screw the arms of the caliper together again until the sharp points began to press onto Omar's temples. Omar tried to brave the discomfiture but couldn't help grimacing.

"Stay still, don't be so childish." Doctor Lütz unscrewed the calipers once more and added industriously to his notes.

"Small cranium."

He wrote precisely and quickly, in keeping with the impression he gave while using the measure. The doctor began to place his fingers on top of Omar's head, pressing with his thumbs into Omar's dark curls. He rummaged through the papers that had multiplied on the desk and found a sheet displaying the stylised drawings of a generic human head. The doctor repeated his strange investigation, silently pressing and prodding all over Omar's head with occasional pauses as he wrote long words onto the diagrams before Omar.

"How fast can you run?"

"Herr Lütchens said I did sixteen point two seconds for one hundred metres."

"You're mistaken, that must be for less."

Omar had digested enough of his situation to understand that a reply was futile and potentially dangerous.

## Dangerous Cocktail

"Sit down and perform these sums."

So saying, the good doctor disappeared.

Omar looked in dismay at the sheet in front of him, attempting the first few additions. His arithmetic was not strong and the paper included long divisions, which his class had not yet covered.

He puzzled over the questions for what seemed like hours, occasionally erasing with great smudges of carbon that he made worse by licking his thumb and rubbing.

"This is a complete mess."

Doctor Lütz had returned, cat silent, accompanied by Herr Heckler.

"Do you expect Herr Heckler to mark this?"

Doctor Lütz reddened with the aggression in his voice. Omar looked up at him uncertainly.

"This is disgusting, appalling. Still, what can we expect?"

Doctor Lütz began to replace his equipment and papers in his bag.

"Go with Herr Heckler."

Herr Heckler led the way back through the imposing doors to rejoin the children's constituency. They trod the worn path to the hall, Omar continually puzzling as to where the other pupils had disappeared as the doors all opened on to the barren teak of lifeless classrooms. Omar heard a muffled adult voice as Herr Heckler paused outside of the hall: a voice of lecturing authority.

"Come on boy." Herr Heckler ordered.

They dived from the pacific corridor through the membrane of the doors into the predatory realm of the full school hall. Four hundred heads targeted Omar's journey to the front.

The tall man with the wonderful uniform that had taken Omar to Doctor Lütz interrupted his discourse to welcome Herr Heckler. On the temporary screen facing the pupils a slide comprising a number of diagrams of the human body, each labeled with bold text, was being projected. Omar recognised one of the diagrams as the same as Doctor Lütz had written on when he'd been feeling over Omar's head. Doctor

Omar Kandala

Lütz emerged from a side door and soundlessly descended onto the chair provided.
The man continued. "I am sure that you are all aware of Kandala." Omar had reached the front by now and was placed facing the assembly with the screen and adults behind him.
"Doctor Lütz here has undertaken a thorough examination of this type over the years and will now present his results together with the specific information he has gathered on Kandala."
Omar's vulnerability began to increase as he tried to digest the words shooting over his head to the naïveté arrayed ahead of him.
Doctor Lütz rose and regarded the mostly expectant faces; although some were already bored and examining various physical attributes of the hall.
"Kandala here is an example of a black and white cross and should be a warning to us all as to the deleterious effects that can occur when pure German blood is diluted by that of inferior races." He paused but failed to register that his advanced vocabulary was already losing the vast majority of his young audience. Doctor Lütz continued to efficiently explain his theories and how Omar was one more and classic example to support them. His competence as a succinct and entertaining lecturer was, however, appreciated only by some of the adults. A few of the teachers, including Herr Lütchens, rove over the audience with their eyes or stared at the floor or ceiling rather than regard the speaker.
"Note especially Kandala's cranial capacity. This is significantly smaller than any of yours and indicative of the recurrent lower intelligence quota of the inferior races." Doctor Lütz continued, testing the attention span of the most avid student and most of the teachers as well. "The science of phrenology teaches us." Here the doctor began to point to the head diagram with a baton. "That the capabilities of the different areas of the brain are reflected in the physiognomy of the skull." He then continued in crushing detail to relate precisely why

# Dangerous Cocktail

Omar was as incapable as Doctor Lütz demanded his genetic inheritance cause him to be.

All the time that Doctor Lütz pursued his thesis Omar felt that he was carrying a burden as the object of attention of over eight hundred disapproving eyes. In a room of so many he began to feel greater and greater loneliness until by the time that Doctor Lütz had finished and called upon Herr Gross, the headmaster, he stank of solitude, ready to cry but retaining his dignity within his throat.

To Omar's dismay Herr Gross began to reinforce Doctor Lütz's comments that even to his young ears had proved so relentlessly derogatory, pointing at and touching him as he did so, the penetrating, acidic, voice washing him in debilitating anecdote and hear say.

Eventually the timbre of Herr Gross's voice changed to that of authority instead of explanation.

"Thank you very much for your time Doctor Lütz," He nodded at the tall Lieutenant Hittorf. "I'm sure this talk has been most illuminating and a lesson to us all."

At this, the headmaster raised his hands palm upwards, drawing the whole assembly as if they were held on invisible string. At a direction from another teacher the pupils began to file out line by line while Omar stood and watched, unsure as to whether to follow when his class began. As Omar looked at him, Herr Heckler instructed him to stay where he was. "You're to fetch a letter from the headmaster's office directly."

At the conclusion of the manouvre to empty the hall a glance by Omar caught the gaze of Herr Lütchens whose chin moved with a sympathetic mouth before he quickly looked down and followed his pupils into the corridor.

"Come with me."

Herr Heckler lifted Omar's arm and momentarily pulled his sleeve indicating the particular exit Omar was to follow. They walked in silence, Omar concentrating on the flowing gown that glided ahead of him. Herr Heckler stopped outside of the headmaster's door and rapped sharply twice.

"Come."

Omar had never been in this office before. For a student to be brought before the headmaster he had to have performed a truly heinous act meriting the very worst of punishments.

"Kandala."

Herr Gross looked at him, his fingers together.

"You are to give this letter to your mother. I hope now that even you realise that you do not belong here. We are all engaged in a great endeavour. We are building a strong and new nation and such an enterprise requires the strength and character of the Aryan race. Herr Heckler has brought your book and coat. Keep the letter safe. Dismissed."

Omar looked in bewilderment at Herr Gross and then turned to Herr Heckler who gave him his things before pulling the door open and motioning him to walk through.

All through his walk home Omar wondered what had occurred that day. He wondered what the others would say at school tomorrow and whether he'd passed the difficult arithmetic test that Doctor Lütz had given him. The envelope that Omar carried was not sealed and his curiosity won over his conscience.

Omar gave the slither of paper to his mother apologetically, his face screwing into misery at his failure to make his mother proud of him. She absorbed the news that he was no longer attending the Leibnitz Gymnasium without shock but held Omar in a tight cuddle. "It's alright my darling, whatever they told you, it isn't true. You're a good boy, a wonderful little boy and I love you. I love you so much." At this her hold on Omar tightened still further, the safety and warmth of her proximity alleviating a little of Omar's pain. "We're going to have to go on a trip through the country now. On the train. You love trains don't you?" Omar nodded as his mother caught a tear on his cheek with her thumb and he forced a weak smile. "It will be an express, very fast.

## Dangerous Cocktail

We'll be rattling along." She attempted enthusiasm, Omar's smile strengthening at this news as he choked back more tears. "It's alright, don't fight it. It's alright to cry. Even big boys cry now and again." Frau Kandala managed to maintain her calm façade in the face of her raging anger and the aggressive pain that always ate into her when faced with such injustices.

Over his mother's shoulder, Omar spied the newly framed studio photograph, which interjected his misery with memories of his mother parcelling him into his most uncomfortably starched Sunday best. For the first time in his life, it occurred to Omar that he was black.

# Nothing But The Truth

Rosemarie Ford & Alyson Heap

## CHARACTERS

A retired Detective Inspector

Diana Harrington. A 'county set' lady in her early forties.

Mrs. Brewer. A housekeeper in her sixties.

## PROPERTIES

*Detective Inspector.* Armchair, table with table-lamp, a detective novel.

*Diana Harrington.* Table, vase of roses, elegant chair with shawl draped over the back. A pink envelope, used in the final speech.

*Mrs. Brewer.* Small kitchen table and chair. Silver (to polish), silver cleaning cloth, china cup and saucer, 50's style telephone.

# Dangerous Cocktail

**SETTING**

Present Day. An ex-Detective Inspector, sitting in an armchair, is reading a crime novel. He recalls his first case as a young Detective Constable, back in the 1950's.

Scenes take the form of flash-backs, with the lady of the house, and the housekeeper relating events. All three characters are on stage for the duration of the play, which takes the form of short monologues. Each character is in cameo spotlight when speaking, the rest of the stage being in darkness.

**OPENING SCENE**

A retired policeman is sitting in an armchair, reading a crime novel.

# Nothing But The Truth

## POLICEMAN

They always get it wrong, crime writers. They give you some twists and turns, a few red herrings and then – case solved. Bit different in my day, no DNA testing back then. You flew by the seat of your pants. Old-fashioned detective work and gut instinct.

I remember my first case as a detective constable, back in the 50's. Moral standards were higher in those days, on the surface; but scratch the veneer and there was all sorts going on.

Caused quite a scandal, the Harrington case. Rich man blasted with his own shotgun, a scorned mistress, open and shut case. I suppose by today's standards some of the evidence could be called 'circumstantial'. But back then that's all we had.

Lois, that was her name, Lois Marshall. The case sticks in my mind, bit like your first love, you never forget it. Or maybe it was because of the outcome.....

Felt sorry for the wife. I can see her now, neat she was, twin-set and pearls, not a hair out of place.

## DIANA HARRINGTON

The roses have been wonderful this year, the floribundas are glorious; it was a shame to pick them. Richmond likes flowers in the house, so I make sure we always have plenty. Mrs. Brewer complains it brings on her hay-fever, but I insist: I say to her,

'The master works very hard, the least we can do is keep his home tip top.'

She's quite precious, Mrs. Brewer, very loyal. When Richmond complains about her gossiping, I tell him we are very lucky to have her. Some of the stories I hear about the girls in the village, well, they seem to lack any sense of moral decency.

## Dangerous Cocktail

They would rather be canoodling with boys than earning an honest wage.

It's getting quite late, he should be home by now, and it's started to rain.

He works much too hard; I do wish he would relax more. He has his boat of course, and he's passionate about shooting. I can't abide it, all those people waving guns around, it's positively dangerous!

I wonder if Mrs. Brewer will think to bring the laundry in....


## MRS. BREWER

Mrs. Pritchard at the Stores 'as bin on the phone again. Wants to know what I thinks of the latest gossip.

'Gossip' I ses, 'gossip means nowt to me. Folks should mind their own' I ses.

'No need to poke your nose in where it ain't needed'.

'Oh,' she ses 'An' there's me going to tell you about the letters,'

'What letters,' I ses - not a bit interested,

'The letters what got sent' she said.

'I don't know what yer on about' I ses

'Seems to me if your business is a General Stores and Post Office, chances are one or two letters will come your way !' I laughed at that. Mrs. P didn't, 'fact she ignored it.

'They was perfumed' she ses; 'pink envelopes, very posh'.

'Lovely, I ses,' but I've got the silver to do, 'not that I likes doing the silver: the polish sets off me allergies. Then she gets all agitated.

'Don't you want to know who picks 'em up every day, regular as clock-work, for the past week or more'?

'The vicar' I ses, an I laughs fit to burst me stays.

'Your Mr. Harrington' she ses.  Well, that shut me up.

'Praps theym for the Madam', I ses.' From a lady friend, she knows some quality does the Madam'.

# Nothing But The Truth

'Oh no, definitely for 'im' she ses. 'e's got 'is own box number'.

I gets angry now. 'What you insinuatin Jesse Pritchard ', I ses, 'They'm devoted, Master Richmond and the Madam.'

Put the phone down on 'er, I was that mad. Made me feel quite poorly, nearly 'ad one of me turns......

Oh Lor, there's the rain, best get the washing in ......


## POLICEMAN

Funny things, words. They can sound the same but have quite different meanings. Take the word 'sent', add a c and you've got, scent. It's the same with things people over-hear. Look at the Bentley case. The lad shouted 'Let him have it!'

Back then everyone thought he meant.' shoot him', now they're saying he could have meant, give him the gun.

Let him have it.

Thinking about 'scent', there was a bundle of perfumed letters found in the Harrington case. She'd sent them, the mistress. They were locked in his bureau. Seem to recall there was one missing, but I read the rest. Pretty standard stuff, undying love and all that. Towards the end she was getting a bit agitated, putting the pressure on him to leave his wife. Said if he really loved her, he'd tell his wife the marriage was over. They never do though, do they, they never leave their wives.

Dangerous Cocktail

DIANA HARRINGTON

Our new tenant came for coffee today, Lois. She's taken the Gate House.
Richmond has known her for years apparently, her husband was a business associate. Deserted her, poor lamb, ran off with his secretary. Caused quite a scandal at the time according to Richmond. I don't remember him mentioning it, but then he can't abide tittle-tattle. I said of course I didn't mind her coming here, the Gate House will be perfect for her, nice and secluded, and Richmond can keep an eye on her.
It's so typical of Richmond to think of others.
She seems perfectly pleasant, a little 'giddy' perhaps, and a tad heavy with the make-up. Richmond doesn't like me to wear make-up, he always says he prefers the natural look.
She sails, like Richmond, and I believe he's taking her shooting.
I always think it's unnatural for women to shoot, how can a woman take pleasure in killing things?

MRS. BREWER

That woman was 'ere again today, for lunch would you believe. Flighty piece if you ask me, make-up plastered on like one of them Tiller girls. Giggles all the time an' all, at the master's jokes. They ain't that funny. Madam ses 'er, Lois and the Master's a-going off sailin' tomorrow. I didn't say nowt, but I over 'ears the Master on the telephone, 'e was talking to the Major. I 'ears 'im say, 'Alright old chap, you can take the old tub (that's what he calls 'is boat) over to Cally for the weekend, just bring me back a bottle of conyack.' Then, as 'e walks past me on me 'ands and knees polishing the parkee, 'e laughs and ses, 'Silly old fool don't know 'is stern from 'is arse, 'e'll end up in the briny.'
And off 'e goes 'ooting with laughter!

## Nothing But The Truth

Well, I don't know where Cally is, but I was thinking, if the boat ain't 'ere, where are them two a-going.........

### POLICEMAN

Messy business. His shot gun had been tampered with.
Clever though, the mistress had loaded 20 bore cartridges: when Harrington loaded the gun with 12 bore they jammed. Blasted his face off. Lots of witnesses, it was one of his weekend shoots for his cronies. The mistress was screaming, splattered in blood. Good actress, by all accounts. She could well have got away with it, looked like an accident, but I found the empty cartridge cases when I was roping off the body. Proud as punch I was. The Super called me in to congratulate me - said the lab boys had found another set of prints on the gun, and they were treating the death as murder. The prints were the mistresses of course. She tried to blame the wife.

Didn't wash with me. You only had to hear how distraught the wife was. She heard the explosion and the screaming and apparently came running down from the house. They say she howled like a banshee before she collapsed, had to call in a doctor.

She didn't shoot, you see, hated guns by all accounts. Had cause as it turned out.....

### MRS. BREWER

You could 'ave knocked me down with a feather when I found out it were true. It were a Tuesday; I was in the store over by the fresh veg. Master walks in, bold as brass, an' pushes a note through the winder. Mrs. Pritchard does that pursin' 'er lips thing she does when she sees 'er 'usband Bert 'eading off down the lane on 'is bicycle. Sort of a disapproving 'I know what you're up to' type of look.'

Dangerous Cocktail

Ain't got time ter tell you now, but suffice to say, I knows as well! Anyways, she goes to the pigeon-'oles and makes a song and dance of looking for summat, but even I can see there's only one thing in 'em: a pink envelope.

She 'ands it over and 'e takes it outside. I follows 'im. 'E's standing behind the bus shelter - 'e can't see me. I'm one of the invisible class, see. Anyways, 'e opens the letter, reads it, smiles, then 'e sniffs the envelope with a look on 'is face. Well, I can't describe that look. Needless to say, twern't ever a look I saw on the late Mr. Brewer's face.

## DIANA HARRINGTON

I couldn't face going back to court for the sentencing.

Of course I want her to hang. She's ruined my life - may she burn in hell!

What will I do without him? He was everything to me. My darling Richmond, I can't believe I'll never see him again. She was evil, a manipulative, vile temptress.

We gave her a home, a roof over her head, all the time………

The police have taken all of the guns away; the cabinets are empty. I am haunted by guns. All those years ago in Kenya Daddy would take me out with him; it was second nature to me, game hunting. I would carry Daddy's guns for him, even load them when I got older. But then one day one of the guns jammed, and one of the Masai was killed. I can remember the blood, the panic. The beaters ran off and Daddy had to carry the man's body back to the farm. Daddy made me walk in front of him in case the smell of the fresh blood attracted wild animals. I was so frightened, I vowed there and then never to touch a gun, ever, ever again.  For years I had nightmares. I could see that man's head exploding like a ripe pomegranate.

For Richmond to die like that is too horrible, too horrible….

## Nothing But The Truth

**MRS. BREWER**

Star witness me, the judge thanked me for bein 'eloquent and succinct'. I think it were a compliment. I told 'em about the secret letters, 'ow I knows they was lying about the sailin trip, 'ow the madam didn't 'ave a clue what was a goin' on, and 'ow Lois whatsername was no better than she ought to be. A bloke in a wig got up and said 'Objection!' I ses 'objection fiddle - it was the truth and I'd sworn on the good book to tell the whole truth an nothin' but the truth.' The jury laughed at that.

Never knew juries was allowed to laugh.

Then I tells 'em about what Mrs. Pritchard's Bert 'eard. E's station master an' there's not a lot gets passed 'im. 'E knew Fanny Downend 'ad left 'er old man afore 'e did. Saw 'er get on the 10.50 to Ilchester with a suitcase and a new 'at. Bit of a give-away, a new 'at. Anyways, Bert sees the Master on the platform with 'er - Lois.

They was 'avin a blazin row. 'E's shoutin', she's cryin', then 'e yells at 'er,

'Don't you understand? It's over, finished, I don't love......' Then a train pulled in an' 'e never 'eard the rest. She storms off; 'im followin' 'er with a face like thunder.

The man in the wig gets up again and ses , 'Objection, your honour, hearsay!'

I ses, 'Course it were hearsay- Bert heard 'er say it!'

Ah well, it's all over now. Best get the madam 'er lunch. Not that's she's eatin', poor mite; she'll waste away if she's not careful. She keeps rockin', like a child and cryin', 'Daddy, Daddy why didn't you take the gun?'

Grief's a terrible thing, terrible....

## Dangerous Cocktail

**POLICEMAN**

The housekeeper was a good witness, I recall, gossips usually are. Had a way with her; the jury liked her, you could tell. She made them laugh. The evidence was stacked up against Lois. Enough to hang her.

Another witness to the argument at the station came forward - the vicar no less.

He was shocked, seems he and Harrington were shooting buddies.

Then there were the fingerprints on the gun. Lois never denied handling the gun, but her story was that Diana Harrington asked her to put the gun back in the cabinet. Seems Richmond had left it out and Diana couldn't bear guns lying around.

But Richmond Harrington would never have left a gun out, never.

Her version of the row at the station was that Harrington was pleading with her not to leave him and that when he shouted it was to tell her his marriage was over, and it was his wife he didn't love. End of the day, the jury didn't believe her. They were on the side of the wife. Diana Harrington sat through the trial, cool as a cucumber. But her eyes - her eyes were haunted   She wasn't there for the sentencing. When the judge puts on the black cap, you know it's all over. Lois went to the gallows protesting her innocence.  She was 29 years old.

Mrs. Brewer, the house-keeper, became a minor celebrity for 5 minutes; retired to Sussex to live with her sister, I believe.

Diana Harrington, well, no-one heard of her again. Some say she never got over the death of her husband, locked herself away.

Strange how something that happened all those years ago still seems so fresh, it plays on my mind, you could even say, it haunts me.....

# Nothing But The Truth

## DIANA HARRINGTON

She's here, Lois. I see her at night, she's looking for something. I tell her to go, leave me alone, but she doesn't hear me.

Daytime is bearable. I fill the house with roses, they remind me of Richmond.

I have forgiven him you see. That harlot was to blame. She wove a spell around him. It's all in this letter; I read it again and again. I found all of them, in his bureau.

I thought my heart would break, but then I met her and saw her for what she was, a hussy, a gold-digger. She didn't love him, not like I loved him. Oh Richmond, my sweet trusting Richmond, what have I done? What have I done? It was easy, I'd done it before: guns are easy to jam, and then they explode and it's all over...

But my plan went wrong again, just like all those years ago when Daddy gave his gun to his bearer. It was Daddy who was supposed to die! Daddy, who came to my room at night and hurt me. I hated him

Lois hurt me too, so I wanted her to die. But you gave her your gun Richmond; you gave her your gun and you used the one that was meant for her!

I heard the explosion and I ran out and I saw her standing screaming and there you were my darling, your face ripped open in a hideous scream...

I'm so cold. She's here. She's looking for something - is it me Lois, are you looking for me?..........

- I love the different characters in this & the different 'voices'. It's a clever way to tell the story from. Not sure abt the end... I guessed it which is annoying! Still v. enjoyable

# Just a Normal Day!

## Elspeth Green

Today began just like any other boringly normal day; I got up. The shower was warm; this was slightly different, admittedly. Perhaps I was the first in our block of flats to welcome the day. Maybe it would prove a good omen.

I breakfasted in the standard way: muesli, yoghurt, juice and coffee. My eyes unpinned and I continued with the rest of my routine: dress in skirt, blouse, jacket, check handbag, put on coat, exit front door, carefully ensuring the lock had caught. Off to face the big wide world - big deal!

No doubt, to you, working in a radio station sounds glamorous; in reality it is anything but. I am the lowest in the human food chain, the receptionist. That's me folks, the one on the end of the telephone when you want to speak to Happy Harry Hawkins and answer his latest stupid question. Did you really think you would get to talk to him? Sorry, you got landed with me, Miserable Miranda Mowbray in all her glory.

Work continued as usual: the weather forecast disappeared; a morning guest arrived drunk and had to be sobered with coffee; I did the filing. Nothing at all out of the ordinary, that is until I went for lunch. Munching on a tuna panini and supping a latte coffee, I stared through the plate glass window of a coffee bar to the world beyond. There must be more to life than this, surely? What comes now? How do I spend my next forty minutes of freedom? Can I engender some excitement into my life?

The answer to those four questions was a resounding 'Zilch!' I picked up my saggy, black handbag and slid myself precariously from the wooden seated, high stool. My tights snagged on a miniscule

## Dangerous Cocktail

splinter and I felt the pull run right across my leg. No spares, a trip to the supermarket was obviously obligatory.

Overlooked by many, but right next to Costmark and hidden down a side street, is a tiny charity shop. The charity is unusual, but if Superannuated Sorcerers need support, who am I to complain? I have been tempted many times by the gaudy items of clothing on view through dusty windows. Today was no exception. There before my eyes I espied the most glorious, emerald green, velvet waistcoat, just calling to me.

Thoughts of tights escaped my mind as I entered through the creaky, age-blackened portal and stood before the counter. At this point it could be expected that I would describe an ancient, wizened character, but no, the charity hostess was about my age and dressed in a very ordinary manner. She soon drew the model from the window and undressed it. Before you could say 'abracadabra' the waistcoat was over my shoulders and fully buttoned; it was perfect.

As is so often the case in these places, temptation increases and I was soon rummaging through the shelves. There were trousers, jumpers, pots and pans and a very plain 'Brown Betty' teapot. Brown Betty teapots produce the most perfect cup of tea, much better than one teabag per mug. My resistance was lowered when I found that it was amazingly clean inside. I questioned the hostess.

"Is this brand new, it looks so clean?"

"Dunno. This is my first day here, but it looks ok. What can you expect for ten shillings?"

"Ten Shillings?"

"Sorry, I mean fifty pence."

"That goes back at least thirty years, before my time and yours I should think."

"I was reading a book on the sixties to pass some time."

I handed over my two pounds and fifty pence then shovelled my purchases into my black portmanteau. Time was galloping by and I still had Cheeky Charlie to organise before my day's work was complete.

## Just a Normal Day!

Ignoring the tattered tights I ran back to the radio studio and relative normality.

That is, until we stopped for a coffee break. Amazingly, the producer had offered to make it, so I had time to sit back and draw breath. The teapot was peeking out at me over the clasp of my bag; I hauled it on to the desk. Quite a find really, only a slight chip on the rim. Hang on a minute; I had not noticed that before. What a shame. I ran my thumb over the fault to see if the mark could be removed. Sadly it would not shift.

To my knowledge, no one entered the room. Margaret was still out making coffee, but someone was sitting on the desk behind me, cross-legged - actually on the desk! He was dressed to look like a Beatle, from the time of their red LP not the blue. His beige jacket collar-less and the matching trousers flared. The outfit was wrinkled and barely covered his enormous frame.

"Hiya! Look, I know this sounds stupid; I am the genie of the teapot."

"The what?"

"The teapot, y'know, that thing you've just bought at exorbitant cost from the shop."

"It was cheap, actually."

"Well, whatever," my Beatle Genie went on, "the thing is, I've come from it and you've got three wishes, I guess you know the routine."

"Yeah! But we're not in Pantomime land here, I deal with reality."

"This is reality. You've got three wishes and I want to get on with them 'cos someone's waiting for me."

"Ok, ok, I'll play your little game." Obviously I am hallucinating. " 'I long to return to my little flat to enjoy a bottle of warm, red wine and a big box of chocolates, with a red bow.' How's that for my first wish?"

Beatle Genie, hereinafter referred to as BG, looked a little surprised and he raised one eyebrow. "It's unusual, but I'll play along. Hold tight, here we go."

## Dangerous Cocktail

There was no rushing of wind, or howling, or spinning. I blinked and when my eyes fully opened I was back at my flat lying comfortably on a fireside chair. The little coffee table to my side held one bottle of Navarra and two glasses from my miscellaneous selection. Next to this was a huge box of chocolates; Superman might have delivered them but they had been a Christmas present from my doting Aunt. Sadly the only person with me was BG. The curtains were closed and I was wearing my new waistcoat; so soft and gentle to the touch. He had even remembered to bring along the teapot. Tonight was not the night for cups of tea.

"That's grand, spot on, well done. Did I drop off to sleep? It's been busy at work. Did Margaret lend you her car? Even the wine came from my own cupboard."

"Oh! Mistress, trust me. You have two wishes left. Just command."

I was quite willing to continue his game, whoever he might be, but decided to give my wishes more thought. Eventually the obvious idea came to me.

"I'd like a George Clooney look-alike to join me."

BG raised the other eyebrow and the more astute will realise I should never have mentioned 'look-alike'. I blinked again and without dramatic entrance I discovered a life-sized, cardboard cut out of George Clooney balanced against the second fireside chair.

Now, as I have never had a cardboard cut out of anyone, let alone George Clooney, it did seem matters were becoming serious. Whatever was happening? I must make a sensible decision for my third wish. I swallowed two glasses of wine and six chocolates whilst deep in thought. A slow smile spread over my lips. The answer was obvious.

"Are you ready for this BG, it wont be simple. I've given it a lot of thought."

"Good, I've got things to do tonight. What is it, riches, new home, brand new car?"

"No," I answered, the smirk remaining on my lips "I want a hundred more wishes."

## Just a Normal Day!

He leapt from his cross-legged position upon my ancient carpet and aimed his fist to the sky in a powerful salute.

"Yes, yes, yes. I'm free. I'm free. I'm free. Jean's waited long enough. Now we can catch up."

"What do you mean Genie, how come you're free?"

As I questioned, I could feel my body contracting, the oxygen was pumped from my lungs and within the blink of an eyelid I found myself in a dark brown room. Leaving no time for exploration, the roof hatch was closed; darkness descended. I ran my fingers along the cold wall but could find no comfort.

"You were too greedy. Too greedy."

My eyes became accustomed to the light and I spotted a tiny opening. The words floated down what appeared to be a tall chimney.

"You have your one hundred wishes to share with others. It's your turn to be left awaiting for someone as greedy as you."

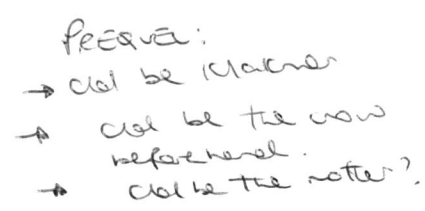

# The White Crow

## Martin Mickleburgh

Klakmer blinked, looked down, looked up, blinked again. The contours of a landscape began to emerge from the blare of blue light reflected from the snow. A plain, stretching before him, virtually devoid of features, broken only by a single distant tree, black and twisted. Far, far away to the south and west – he took his bearings from the sun – there was a rim of mountains whose height he could not begin to fathom.

They had pushed him out, slamming the great oak doors shut behind him. The sound had had no echo, as if it were a detonation inside his own head. Of course he had known there would be snow – the courtyard had been ankle-deep in grey slush for two months at least. But this light: he had not been remotely prepared for it; it was as if this very first moment of freedom needed to mark itself by distending his senses.

He turned about; the prison blocked entirely the view to the north, and yet, he realised, looked at from the outside, placed just so in the midst of the plain, it was of no great size. How could the measureless dank corridors and the countless cells be contained within it? He felt suddenly dizzy, unsure of his own scale, vast or tiny. To the east was the forest. That must be where the birds came from, the only living things that had made an outside to his inside in all the time he had been imprisoned. How long had it been? How many years? He felt the same giddiness again as time concertinaed in and out. He put his hands to his face, ran his fingers through his beard and wondered what he had become.

Freedom. Klakmer took the word in his mouth and ran tongue and lips around it. It had an alien ring, as if it were a dubious harbinger from some other continent of the soul. He had never expected his

143

## Dangerous Cocktail

liberty, never thought he would see beyond the blackened walls of the fortress, and yet, here he was, free to walk this endless snowy plain. A dim wonder bloomed and dispersed in the base of his brain.

And now he must make a choice: which way to go? They had given him no clue, merely told him he was released and pushed him out through the doors. They had given him a coat, a leather flask of water and a couple of cakes of hard biscuit. Then he noticed that, as far as he could see, his were the only footprints in the snow. Surely there should be a road?

He felt a swirl of fear unfolding in his belly. He must choose. He had never had to choose anything when he had been inside, and that, he reflected, must have been for most of his adult life. The act of choosing felt suddenly steely and murderous, like an imminent betrayal; he recoiled from it. He turned about once more, looking for some guidance, and then, finding none, he fell to his knees and buried his face in his hands.

Only when it came to him that he must choose or die right where he was, twenty yards from the doors, did he stand up once more and wipe his eyes on the sleeve of his coat. The air was still but so cold that it made his eye sockets ache and pinched the inside of his nose as he breathed in. It smelt faintly sulphurous. A thin film of cloud the colour of dirty sheets was sliding across the sky from the east. He felt naked, absurdly exposed, and then the choice made itself: he began to stumble towards the single tree.

He reckoned it to be perhaps two miles distant. The going was hard, the snow often up to his knees. Within minutes he had lost all sensation in his feet. When he judged himself to be half way to the tree he stopped, turned, and looked back at the prison. It had all but disappeared as if the land itself would expunge it. His memories felt tottery and insubstantial, suddenly reduced in scale. How long? Twenty years? Could it be so many? He took a pull of icy water from the leather bottle and set off again.

## The White Crow

The air began to move around him, little siftings and flurries at first, but growing into a steady breeze that thickened in time to a dull wind. The cold penetrated the ancient brown coat and he flapped his arms around his sides even as he walked to keep warm. The dirty clouds slid across the face of the sun and the temperature dropped still further.

Klakmer began to hum. It was a hymn he had heard when he was a child in the city. His mother had sometimes taken him to the church on a Sunday in order to be warm for an hour or two and to beg from the lace-swagged ladies at the church door at the end of the service. He could remember their perfume, those ladies, cloying and exotic, bringing notice of another world as they swept past; they were plump, rounded and pink; watching them, he had often wondered what it would be like to eat so much as to be so glossily firm, and then his mouth would water and he would cry and then, perhaps, one of these creatures would stoop and drop a coin into his mother's hand, clucking and sniffing, patting his lousy head and then wiping her hand on a kerchief in order to be rid of him. In time he had learnt the hymns in the way that a parrot or an idiot might: mouthing them with no whit of understanding of their language or purpose. Thus redemption, forgiveness and love had slid past him, leaving only the tunes which had borne them and fitted them for the human breast.

When, some time later, he looked up, the tree appeared to be no nearer, as if it receded even as he approached. He looked behind him; the fortress was no more than a blot of sullen grey in the snow, and now he could see that the mountains extended right around behind it. He could not gauge its distance. How far had he come? How long had he been walking? He looked back towards the tree and noticed what appeared to be a hang-fruit of snow in its uppermost branches. He could not remember it being there before, and how had one small clot of snow clung when the rest of the tree was bare? He bowed his head and trudged on.

As he walked, he began to wonder what process had chosen for him the tree as his destination. What would he do when he got there? Did it

## Dangerous Cocktail

have some significance imparted by its solitude in the plain? He lurched to a halt. What if there was in truth no reason to head for the tree? What if his imposed choice had been no more than the arbitrary clicking of a dumb machine? He noticed that the sun had passed its meagre zenith and was heading for the western horizon. In the tree's upper branches, the lump of snow, he was sure, had moved. He shook his head violently as if to chastise his eyes for such deceit; but there was no mistaking it, unless, of course, it was his memory that deceived him. He plodded on.

He tried to remember his mother's face but it swam like a protean swarm that would not coalesce. Blood on the snow: yes, he could remember that, and the way her fingers had been splayed as if in shock at being so suddenly overtaken by the final darkness. Blood, exquisitely red on the blue-white snow. And a voice: She was mad anyway; coming from behind him but when he had turned and looked up there were so many gathered around that he had no idea of who might have delivered the judgment.

The cold crept up his limbs so that, in time, he could no longer feel his thighs and forearms. He pulled one of the biscuits from his pocket and tried to break off a corner but his fingers were too numb to hold it sufficiently firmly. He put the whole biscuit in his mouth and tried to bite off a lump, but his jaws were too cold and refused to clamp about it. The absurdity of being in possession of food which he could not eat made him laugh: he stood still and threw his head back and vented a great guffaw. And as he did so, what had been the clot of snow in the tree grew wings and flapped lazily into the air, rising some five or ten feet above its erstwhile perch, allowing the wind to hold it there, and then it settled back down again.

Klakmer's mouth sagged open in wonder. It was a bird, a white bird. White in the midst of this white wasteland as if the snow and the wind had conspired and bethought themselves to make a little plaything for their amusement. Unthinking, he tried to pull the leather bottle from his pocket to take a swig but his hands failed him and it slipped from

## The White Crow

them and lay inert at his feet. He knelt and tried to seize it using his hands like flippers but it was too slippery and eluded his grasp. That was when he realised that he was going to die, that they had given him his freedom so that he might expire somewhere other than in the cell he had occupied since the day of his incarceration. He stood up and gazed at the white bird. It seemed to beckon to him, not by any formal gesture but by its mere existence and its high place in the blasted tree. He began to stumble forwards again, leaving the leather bottle where it had come to rest in the snow.

He felt a great press of tiredness, such tiredness as betokens a life running down and the folding in of the darkness. But he kept moving, pausing every twenty paces or so to look once more at the bird. It stayed exactly where it was and, as he drew nearer, he realised that it was looking at him as intently as he at it. When he was close enough he saw that it was a crow, a white crow with pink beak, pink legs and pink eyes. It shifted a little from side to side on its perch at the top of the tree and, when he finally arrived beneath the branches, it uttered a raucous stammering Klak-Klak-Klak, calling him by name.

He fell to his knees beneath the tree, clutching its trunk, resting his cheek against the bark, though in truth his face was so numb that he could barely feel it. Some instinct pressed him to remove himself from sight of the fortress so that they might not see his end or take any pleasure in it: he inched his way around the girth of the tree, stumbling over the planes of its roots which were of such size as to break the surface of the snow, deep as it was. When he judged himself to be on the opposite side, he gathered himself with his back to the trunk and his legs stretched out in front of him. He tipped his head back and gazed up at the bird. The cloud had cleared and against the sere blue of the sky the crow seemed hallowed, as if marking an un-guessed compassion in the universe, as if its singular being was a corridor along which mercy might pass and he might be thus shriven.

Klakmer thought of his great sin and began to hum the hymn once more. The white crow cocked its head to one side, listening intently,

147

## Dangerous Cocktail

and then it stepped into the air and dropped down on the snow close by his feet, eyeing him the while. As he hummed, it sidled this way and that, unsure, to Klakmer's clouding eye, where to take its place; or then again, perhaps it was dancing.

The sun set in sudden catastrophe and the firmament waxed indigo and violet.

Presently, above the low chant of his hymn, Klakmer heard a whistling thrum coming from the east. He turned his head to see – such unspeakable effort – and beheld a vast plume of black birds heading towards him in the failing light, arrow straight in their track as if drawn magnetically to him. He continued to murmur the tune even as they filled the sky before him. He looked back at the white crow; it had stopped its lurching dance and was staring at him, moving its head from side to side so as to engage first its left eye and then its right. It paid no heed to the black swarm approaching. He held out his hand to it but it backed away, until it was fifty feet from him, just beyond the purview of the tree. He thought to throw some crumbs from his biscuit to it, but he knew that his hands were beyond such use.

All the while the sound of the approaching birds grew louder and presently their shadow, cast before them, as if by their own black light, lapped around him and the temperature seemed to plummet. They gathered in a great boiling mass of tattered flapping wings, circling not around him but around the white bird, which continued to hold him steadily with its eye. They began to shriek, spewing accusations, louder and louder, some spark of vengefulness leaping from brain to brain, surging and heaving, reeking of death. And then, as one, they fell upon the white crow.

It was over within thirty seconds. They lifted in a single mass, wheeled and set course for the forest whence they had come. The snow was smeared bright red, and white feathers drifted in the sighing air. Klakmer began to weep.

# Doing it for Uncle Arthur

Peter Owen

FATHER: "Ah, come on in Simpkins and sit yourself down; there's a good lad."

SON: "Good morning sir, thank you sir."

FATHER: "Now tell me Simpkins, how long have I been your father; how many years have passed since 'ere we met?"

SON: "Nearly eighteen years now sir."

FATHER: "So – nearly eighteen years you say eh Simpkins? Well Mummy and I have had a little chat and we've agreed that it was high time that I had a 'little chat' with you Simpkins, man to man so to speak – not that you quite a man yet eh Simpkins?"

SON: "Not quite a man yet sir."

FATHER: "And have you any idea at all what this 'little chat' will be all about Simpkins?"

SON: "No sir I haven't a clue."

FATHER: "Well I'll tell you Simpkins shall I?"

SON: "Thank you sir."

## Dangerous Cocktail

FATHER: "Have you ever heard talk of the birds and the bees eh Simpkins?"

SON: "Well I joined the field study group at school sir, and I can remember 'donkey' Harrison and 'dopey' Jenkins saying disgusting things when Mr. Thomas showed us some blue tits and a willow warbler sir."

FATHER: "Hmm not what I had in mind Simpkins, not that at all. Let me put it this way Simpkins, do you know from whence you came my boy?"

SON: "No, not really sir. I thought it was Portsmouth, but I'm not too sure about that sir."

FATHER: "Well I'll tell you Simpkins shall I?"

SON: "Yes please sir."

FATHER: "Many years ago Colin – I feel I can call you Colin now that you're nearly eighteen Simpkins – and you must call me Father."

SON: "Nearly eighteen now sir, yes Father."

## Doing It For Uncle Arthur

**FATHER:** "Many, many years ago Mummy and I did a very wonderful exciting thing together, something that resulted in Mummy bearing forth a child, and that child, Colin was you; can you begin to imagine what that wonderful exciting thing was Colin?"

**SON:** "No, not really father."

**FATHER:** "Well, Mummy and I quite deliberately, passionately and without prejudice exchanged place, on the sofa Colin, while the cushions were still warm, and lo and behold three years later you were born, I can remember your arrival in this world very vividly Colin, it was nine months almost to the day after Uncle Arthur came to live with us – it was a truly wondrous thing Colin, truly wondrous."

**SON:** "Yes Father truly wondrous, Uncle Arthur's been with us a long time Father. Why does Mummy still go up to his room most afternoons Father?"

**FATHER:** "Well she has to go up and 'manage it' for him son, she tries to 'manage it' for Uncle Arthur most afternoons as you've rightly noticed, and when he's feeling depressed she has to 'manage it' some evenings too. It's all very tiring for Mummy but she feels that she must help Uncle Arthur 'keep his pecker up'; she's a very wonderful woman your mother, Colin, we should be very proud of her, proud of everything she has done and is still doing for Uncle Arthur."

**SON:** "I can hear her up there now father, doing it for Uncle Arthur."

## Dangerous Cocktail

FATHER: "Good old Mummy, Good old Uncle Arthur eh Colin?"

SON: "Good old Mummy, Good old Uncle Arthur eh Father?"

FATHER: "I want you to promise me Colin that you will never ever let a woman sit on a warm chair you have recently vacated, until you have married her, whereupon it would of course become a perfectly normal and exciting thing to do. There's nothing to be ashamed of, its not in any way unpleasant or dirty, married couples often change their seating arrangements after a fine meal and a glass of wine together Colin; it's then that the wonderfully evocative exchange of warm seating may bear certain fruits, and that Colin is exactly what happened between Mummy and I three years before you were born, and before Uncle Arthur came to stay – now pour me a cup of tea and one for yourself, there's a good chap."

SON: "Good old Uncle Arthur eh Father – one lump or two?"

*Not 'my cup of tea.' Are they always abt sex?*

# Memories

## Rosemarie Ford

At last the muse has visited me and I hope these jottings recalling past memories will bring a smile to your face and perhaps you, in turn, will stop awhile and think of those of your own.

I am going to keep this in some sort of chronological order and, therefore, first being first, I am ashamed to say that this memory rather shows the nastier side of my character. I was the only child at Winford Hospital who refused to eat bread covered with brown sugar and milk. I demanded tomato sandwiches and a glass of cold milk. This same menu I had every night during my two years of intermittent visits to hospital.

I recall the girl in the bed next to mine had to have blood tests. As you can imagine in those days, the needle was not the elegant small objected it is today. I was so terrified of being included in this 'operation' that I used to turn round in bed and hide under the sheets. This would have been all right but I did not allow for the fact that I was wearing a frog plaster from my toes to my chest. As I turned in my bed the weight of this plaster promptly pulled me to the floor. This, again, proved my stubbornness, as it would not have happened had I allowed the staff to put cot sides on the bed. I can only assume that they agreed to leave these off since, with the heavy plaster, they did not believe I would have the strength to pull myself around in the bed. After the incident, cot sides were promptly replaced!

I was thus indulged because of the large polio outbreak in 1947/48 (the exact date escapes me). I and a little boy were the only children in our ward to escape polio. He went into the men's ward and I went into a lady's ward where I was thoroughly spoilt because my parents could only visit me by waving through an outside window for six weeks!

## Dangerous Cocktail

The days of hospital stays have now gone and at the age of five I start at a very small, private school with a total of ninety-six pupils ranging in age from 4 to 16. This school was operated by two ladies who, in retrospect, could only have been in their forties but as a small child they seemed to me to be so ancient it was not true! It was a huge Victorian house with the kitchen in the cellar. There was, I remember, a Miss Way and a Miss Starr. Miss Way always wore black – very Edwardian. I attended the school from the age of five until the age of ten and it brings back many happy memories. I particularly remember one of the senior girls telling us all stories in the lunchtime whilst sitting under an apple tree in the playground. The sun shone through the branches, because in those days the sun always seemed to shine. Music lessons were held in the 'ladies' lounge.

We were only allowed to use the tradesman's entrance with the exception of Parent's Day when we could use the main front door. To this day the smell of cabbage always reminds me of Miss Way as she stood in front of the black-leaded stove; the Edwardian equivalent of today's Aga! This was the kitchen, which was in the cellar of the school. It was very dark and I could imagine servant girls preparing food on the huge wooden table where we gathered for lunch. The table was covered with a huge oilcloth, which could be sponged clean. The packed lunch eaters sat at one end and the cooked lunch eaters sat at the other end of the table; never the twain shall meet!

My first test at school was also my first experience of nerves when taking exams. It was all very hushed and I was aged about seven. Just as the test started I wanted to go to the toilet but was much too afraid to ask! The next thing we heard was the sound of running water from beneath my chair as the puddle formed; coloured navy blue from my new school bloomers. How ashamed I was although I was never frightened to ask to leave the room again!

## Memories

The other day a friend mowed my lawn and the smell of the grass brought back lazy days when I found myself at a senior school. In stark contrast to my little private school the senior school contained twelve hundred boys and girls. Yes! In those days we were lucky enough to have lawns, commonly known as two hockey pitches. These lawns were covered during lunch times with girls on one side and boys the other; separated by what you could term the Berlin Wall. This was, in fact, a drive the width of two cars, which you crossed at your peril as prefects diligently patrolled it so that no 'hanky-panky' could take place!

As I go on thinking of schooldays I have another memory from the coach, which took us to school. Returning home one day one of the girls had with her a glass bowl full of the gruesome results of her cookery class, pretending to be cauliflower cheese. Although it was not a pretty sight, I wonder if it really deserved to be thrown out of the window by one of the boys, whereupon it wrapped itself around the face of a cyclist as he was being overtaken by our coach. We left this poor many lying on the grass verge covered in white gunk. The school received an extremely irate letter following that event!

Another tale of the cookery class was from a parent-teacher's meeting: My mother was sat with a friend of hers and the cookery teacher, who was no friend of mine, joined them. She refused to teach me cooking in the event of it being too dangerous due to my restricted height. My mother's friend seized the opportunity to get back at this teacher on my behalf, by asking others around the table if they had managed to eat any of the recent, horrendous meals brought home under the guise of Irish stew; with fat floating in it. My mother said the teacher's face just coloured up, which I found very satisfying. The quality of the Irish stew is further underlined when it received, the similar fate as the cauliflower cheese. This time the stew was thrown out of a train window, with the resultant solids and fat dripping down the window, potatoes and meat all looking the same.

## Dangerous Cocktail

During these days, a bowl of boiling water in the sink with soap powder in it for hand washing brings back the thought of Mondays, which was washday. In our house at least it was pre washing machine.

The gas boiler was filled with water and switched on with a good measure of Lux soap flakes. I remember father's white shirts going in with blue whitening after the collars had been scrubbed well. Starch would be added to the collars and cuffs when they were retrieved. My mother used to congratulate herself that she had the whitest washing in the street, and rightly so! Father used to mangle the clothes when he came home at lunchtime before they were attached to the line. It was well into the 1970s before my mother agreed to have a washing machine. Even then she only agreed on condition that she had the least mechanical or technical requirements to operate it. The business of washing dictated our lunch, or dinner as we called it then, to be mashed potatoes and vegetables with cold cuts from the Sunday roast.

Tuesdays brought cottage pie, shepherds pie or chicken casserole if the Sunday joint was chicken. Wednesday we had lamb or pork chops; Thursday was a cheap day of sausages or pies; Friday, of course, was always fish and Saturday was cold meat and pickle in the winter or salad in the summer. Sunday, of course, was mostly roast beef as chicken was a delicacy and red meat much cheaper. Such a regimen and my father would really be furious if mother tried to ring the changes because she got so bored with the same menu week after week! There was, of course, no pasta; the only slight variation being the occasional rice.

The smell of an overheated car brings to mind a trip to the Mendips with a crowd of twenty year olds in a very ancient Rover. When I made the suggestion that we had run out of water in the radiator, the driver was not amused by this remark. He told me not to be so silly, but on inspection I was right!

## Memories

And then we come to the days of Victoria.

Victoria was a 1925 Daimler hearse. She was majestic in the extreme and cost us the princely sum of £25. Her purchase was decided by six of us sitting in a pub one night, talking about holidays and the cheapest way to do them. The smell of oil brought back the memory of Victoria and the oil she used to puff quite happily through her exhaust.

Patrick saw the vehicle advertised in the Evening Post by funeral directors. He decided that it might be a good idea for a holiday vehicle and brought the idea to the pub table, where it was all agreed by a drink. We owners used to travel in her all wearing deerstalker hats; we thought we were perfectly normal human beings! We also took paying guests. She could seat twelve comfortably and we took her on holiday with seven occupants, all sitting on a variety of seating stretching from deckchairs to the back seat of another car. Our luggage was inside but roped firmly to the roof was a canoe. This was purely for decoration as it had a hole in and stood no chance of ever floating again; we thought it looked just right. Also in the luggage was a barrel of rough cider to help us on the journey.

We were going to spend a week camped on Julian's parents' lawn in Cornwall and borrow their garden shed, which was furnished as an extra bedroom. As Victoria only did 8 miles to the gallon, we allowed plenty of time to get down to our holiday destination; which involved staying the night on Dartmoor. Warmed by the cider, I was told off for laughing, as was Julian. We were asked to leave Victoria to calm down. Together we walked along the main road, which crossed Dartmoor and as we looked back the hearse was parked with a ring of mist, pretty well half way in line with the bonnet. Nearby there was a tent and we have often wondered what those people must have thought in the morning because they had gone before we left.

Our trip to Cornwall was nothing if not eventful. The old Cornishmen thought we were attracting the devil by using a hearse. We offered rides, but nobody accepted. Perhaps they were proved right,

# Dangerous Cocktail

because one night Julian fell in St Mawes Castle and compound fractured his leg. Had we taken him to hospital, everything would have been ok, but due to the anaesthetic known as alcohol, we got him home to bed. Poor Julian! The next morning he awoke to find his leg like a zeppelin and, of course, the next we knew he was travelling to hospital at the speed of light. He had to stay in Cornwall with his parents and has suffered arthritis as a direct result of that jape, ever since.

Rather than smell, I have an evocative noise, which is when a loud engine, such as a motor mower, starts up.

It reminds me of driving the invalid carriage I had for six months before I learned to drive. I used to commute to Bristol daily in this contraption and during winter I had a blanket on my lap with a hot water bottle wrapped inside – no heater! Unfortunately it was the sport model and had a soft-top, which could be folded back. However, in windy weather or when travelling at speed, the air used to cut through the join between the body of the machine and the canvas roof like a knife. I managed to wind the vehicle up to 60 miles an hour going downhill with a good, following wind. A friend's father following one day in his Porsche verified this. You can imagine that the cold inside the cabin was probably worse than outside!

Of course, I had no steering at this speed as the front wheel lifted from the ground; it is a miracle I am still here!

In that vehicle my brakes failed one day and I ended up at Clarken Combe, buried in a bush! On another occasion I was hit in the rear when in a queue. The man behind, who said he didn't see me, pushed me across three lanes of traffic. Heaven knows how they didn't hit me! My father was getting even more neurotic about my driving to work. After one day, when it had been snowing badly, all of my wheels locked and I skidded straight across the main road and through a farm gate, which was thankfully open. I ended up in a bank of snow in a farmyard, from which I had to be dug out. My father said:

## Memories

"You're not driving that thing any more - I'll take you to and from work until you've got a car."

The following day we went in to Bristol and he kindly bought my twenty-first birthday present, two years early, in the form of a Fiat 500. That was the start of my halcyon driving days.

I was a founder member of Clevedon Motor Club, which is still in being as a skittles team! We spent about two Sundays a month rallying. Petrol was much cheaper then and the traffic much less! And - I am ashamed to say - there was no breathalyser.

When we were in operation, rallying, we had one or two things happen. There was the day I was navigating in a Ford Mexico and we headed for a herd of sheep at sixty miles per hour. We skidded our way through, missed the sheep, but broke the sump, leaving all our oil on the road. Luckily we were near the lead and on the right route, as the car behind picked us up. It is just as well because we were in the wilds of the Cotswolds, long before mobile 'phones were ever thought of.

Another rallying experience was when I had a Fiat 500 and lost all the gears apart from reverse and first. I used to break half-shafts with great regularity, but losing the gears was a new experience. I had to reverse, in the dark, up about a mile of a long hill. Luckily, the pub where we were meeting to end the rally was at the top. Another breakdown occurred during the evening rush hour in the centre of Bristol. A very kind young policeman came over and pushed me in my little Fiat 500 onto a parking meter but then asked for the sixpence – and yes, I mean sixpence! – to pay the meter charge.

The smell of beer on a hot summers' day recalls Saturday lunchtimes and my visits to the pub with my dear old dog, Sean (full name Sean Connery-Ford) yes; I followed every 007 film for many years! Now Sean was given to me as a King Charles' Spaniel, crossed with a Jack Russell terrier. He grew and grew to become an old English sheep dog cross retriever-coloured dog with wool rather than hair.

## Dangerous Cocktail

Back to Saturday mornings: Sean used to sit on the front seat of my Hillman Imp and was taller than I was. He used to hoof it into the pub for his present of a large ashtray full of Double-Diamond and a full packet of crisps, donated by the publican. This was all well and good but he used to get drunk and was rather given to farting all the way home. When I took him into the house he created his customary 'charming aroma' and my teetotal father greeted me with:
"That dog's been drinking again!"
The dog took several hours to sober up!
Another Saturday morning occurrence that I remember was when a friend was directing me into a parking space at the pub. I parked brilliantly, switched off the engine and got out of the car, only to be greeted by Rodney, the friend helping with the parking, who said:
"Well done Rose, but please will you move off my foot!"
My front near side wheel was very neatly parked thereon. It is just as well the engine was in the back!

In my days of helping with the Samaritans, I was very amused one day when I went down and opened the door to be met by a very gaudily dressed transvestite; complete with colourful makeup, blond hair, high-heels worn down at the heel and fishnet tights. I asked him in and when we had been sat down for a while and been chatting, he suddenly remarked
"I've never spoken to anybody like you!"
To which I replied, "I've never spoken to anybody like you!"
Thank goodness we both laughed because I do not feel this is really the right reaction for a Samaritan counsellor when speaking to a client. After all, why should he have any problem with someone who is only three foot ten?!

I must say I have been very lucky with the human race; they have treated me very kindly. But I have had one or two occasions when I

## Memories

have been taken where I do not want to go, or where help has been a little amiss.

There was a time when I was waiting for a friend on the corner of Baldwin Street in Bristol and, I admit, I was standing on a zebra crossing; perhaps that was my mistake. This dear old lady came along and caught hold of my elbow – truly – and then held my hand and marched me across this zebra crossing. Before I knew it I was on the other side of Baldwin Street. I had not intended to go there at all, so then I had to turn round smartly and walk back again. Her face was a picture, but she did not listen to my 'Oh no, I don't want to go', or anything, bless her; she thought she was doing me a good turn, so there we go.

On another occasion, I had parked my car outside my house and was actually listening to tennis on the radio. It was an exciting point, so I got the wheelchair out and placed it on the pavement. I then just sat in the passenger seat listening quite happily, when all of a sudden this dear man came along and said

"Oh, can I help you?"

Before I knew it, the chair had been carried up the garden path to the door. At which point, of course, I had to say to him

"Excuse me, can I have my wheelchair back, because I can't manage without it?"

He was so taken aback and in such a state, that he caught hold of it and did not put the brakes on. The chair swung round and must have delivered a huge bruise onto his leg. Never mind, people mean well!

Another experience I remember was when I was beginning to learn to drive but we had not got around to fitting the extension pedals. A friend said he would sit in the car while I sat on his lap, to get the feel of the gear stick and steering wheel. So we sat driving around and around a field. That was my first experience of driving; some say my driving never improved! I hope I have reason to doubt that! I know my parking never improved – but then, parking is never easy for a lady is it; really?

## Dangerous Cocktail

    I hope these little note-lets from me have helped you to think of your childhood and young times; but before I leave, I must tell you about my great aunt's house in the Cotswolds:
    She had a chemical toilet and this puts the cap on all smells! Whenever I go anywhere near caravans or anything similar, the smell of that toilet instantly reminds me. You had to go down to the bottom of the garden past some buildings. I was frightened to death going down there! Thinking of that house and when staying in winter days, I had to climb into bed up a little pair of steps because the feather mattresses were so high. But oh! It was so cosy once you were in! You just disappeared into all these feather mattresses. When you think about it, they must have been terribly unhealthy. Heaven knows how many dust mites and so on were in them.
    My great aunt always used to heavily salt her vegetables. She used to have to cook for two great uncles, (both well over twenty stone), herself and her sister in law. I remember once, as a small child, standing aghast as she put a full tablespoon of salt in a small saucepan of runner beans. Unbelievable how the older people used to live! Also the beans were kept salted-down in a pot, so they had salt on them in the first place! Oh well, they were happy days.

    I have had a lovely life. The more I think of the noises, sounds and smells, the more it all comes back to me. I have many more recollections, but do not wish to outstay my welcome with you. Hopefully, one day, you will do as I have done and sit down to think of things. Just jot them down and very soon many happy memories will come flooding back.

## It's Cool

### Peter Goodsall

Johnston allowed his head to flop forward, revelling in the sudden coolness of the storm. His arms were open to the rain. The all embracing humid warmth had for long hours been his great burden, confining his ambition to the discarding of his heavy overcoat.

Now low rumbles had grown to insistent threat; pyrotechnics that lit an entire sky had given way to individual fingers of light, probing, seeking out who knew what, but forever attempting to find their mark. Then something had marked him. Again.

-oOo-

He had been found face down in a field with a ragged, smouldering hole burnt right through the back of his coat to blackened skin. Puzzled paramedics had radioed for the A & E Doctor to come to their location, fearful of causing more harm to a seemingly *compus mentis* man with no apparent pulse.

Dr. Mitchell smiled warmly at Johnston as the Paramedics scooped him into the back of the ambulance.

"This time you seem to have been affected a little more severely Mr. Johnston," he said.

"How's that then?" replied Johnston groggily, feeling himself drift further away from the voices and clamour about him.

The Doctor pushed his glasses back to the bridge of his nose, that place where they should be, that was precise and under his control. He swallowed.

"I suspect some permanent damage to your spine."

He allowed a pause for the news to sink home.

## Dangerous Cocktail

"I can't say for definite without extensive further testing."

"Testing?" managed Johnston. "You mean scans?"

"Yes quite, we'll start with some x-rays."

But Johnston could manage no more, slipping into ignorant unconsciousness.

He was lucky to have awoken only minutes after the ambulance had arrived back at A & E, having been able to resist all further enquiries as a consequence. Dr. Mitchell sighed as he looked in exasperation upon his patient.

"Even given your, if you'll forgive me, frankly irrational fear of x-rays, or, indeed, MRI scans or even an ultra-sound, what has occurred is readily apparent. Some of your vertebrae have been fused by the lightning. To be honest, I'm amazed that you seem to have suffered no permanent neurological damage."

Johnston feigned a tick but soon stopped when he was ignored by the other.

"I'm rather afraid that you'll never be able to bend your spine at this point again.", continued Mitchell, pressing his hand hard into Johnston's back.

"Oh well, it's cool, reckon I got off light."

"Yes; I'm curious Mr. Johnston, your records indicate that this is the twenty-third time that you have been struck by lightning. Is that true?"

"Oh aye. Twenty-three would be right."

"Do you work out of doors?"

"Aye."

Seeing that this was all the information that was to be volunteered, Mitchell opted for a slightly different tack.

"Well, I'm astonished that you're still here. Do you have any idea why it is that you seem to have been quite literally struck so many times?"

Johnston shifted his gaze down to the copious notes strewn across the bed, risking a quick glance in the direction of the Doctor.

"No, no. None at all."

## It's Cool

Mitchell's eyes narrowed.

"You know not to stand under a tree in a storm, hold an umbrella, or indeed any metal object?"

"Oh aye; of course."

"I'd have thought that you would have taken cover indoors at the first hint of rain, let alone storms that have been forecast for days."

"Oh well, still here aren't I? It's cool."

The Doctor cocked his head to one side.

"Well, I don't think there's anything else to be discussed Mr. Johnston, please come back to me should you experience any additional ill-effects."

Johnston concluded that the consultation was over and rather stiffly, with a curious half-rolling, half-standing motion, slid off the bed and stood upright.

"What was that?"

"What?"

"That kind of ... crackling sound."

"I didn't hear anything."

"You do realise how important you could be to medical science, don't you?"

"If you think I'm spending what little time I've got between the four bland walls of this even blander building speaking to bland men you've got another think coming."

Johnston started at his own vehemence.

"What little time I have to myself, I mean," he finished lamely.

The Doctor nodded slightly whilst stroking his moustache, staring intently at Johnston, and then in one sudden, swift movement took Johnston's feet from under him, so that he collapsed with a great rustle into a heap on the floor.

"*That* kind of crackling sound," replied Mitchell, continuing to keep his eye on the ball: watching Johnston intently for signs of retaliation. But Johnston did not even remonstrate, simply lying on the floor as if the very life had been drained from his limbs until eventually, with

## Dangerous Cocktail

deliberate slowness, he turned his head so that he could observe his antagonist.

"Jujitsu, third dan", smiled Mitchell by way of explanation.

"Can you do this?" exclaimed Johnston. His speech was slow, slightly slurred, as if he'd had one too many but was not yet working towards complete paralysis.

"No," replied Mitchell, still smiling.

"I don't know what you are, how you came to be, where you're from, but you're not in any text I've ever read."

Johnston eye-balled his new-found antagonist and wondered whether he dare gamble on the truth. It had been so easy thus far. Until now he'd never been knocked unconscious, until now, he'd never been discovered: until now, he'd never been examined.

"The paramedics said that you were only a few feet from a metal pole stuck into the ground. Are you sure you know never to touch a potential lightning conductor in a storm?"

Johnston was getting progressively groggier.

"Whether I touch metal in a storm has nothing to do with you," he ventured. But there was no force behind it: all his energy was spent.

"Given you current location, it has everything to do with me," snapped back the Doctor.

Johnston's eyes pleaded with Mitchell for him to stop stabbing at the truth. The Doctor had ceased to be a mere obstacle: he was graduating to nemesis.

"If you don't let me go, take me back, I'll never come back again. I'll never *know* again. I'll never *be* again. The strike can't have transferred its energy with the same force. Please!"

"I'll make you a deal. We do an M.R.I., *then* I'll take you back to your field, Mr. Crow."

"Mr. Crow?" queried Johnston.

"Of course! Mr. S. Crow! Why Johnston?"

Johnston saw that he was beaten; worse: that he could not afford the time to argue.

## It's Cool

"It was the first name I came across when I learnt to read. 'Johnston's Baby Powder': an old tub was lying on the ground in the woods." He paused. "Please. Now!" His voice was little more than a whisper.

Mitchell rubbed his hands together in delight. Finally, to go with fortune, the esteem of his peers, fame.

Johnston despaired. This time was different: this time he'd been discovered. Now he would be a curiosity, a thing, not Mr. Johnston, but property.

# Rimes Last Case

## Cynthia Grimm

*Lovely opening!*

Rimes was poised, arms outstretched towards the clear waters of the sparkling ocean below him, when the telephone rang. He sprang upright in his bed, momentarily disorientated. Had he drowned? It took him a few moments to realise that the ringing was his telephone beside his bed. He looked at the red eye of his digital clock, 3 a.m., and with a muttered curse he snatched up the receiver and growled,
'This had better be good!'
The voice on the other end was that of D.S. Reason.
'I'm sorry to bother you sir, but I thought you'd want to know. We've got a report coming in of another missing child…'
D.I. Rimes sank back against his pillow - why him? Why now? A madman on the loose on his patch and only four days to go to retirement.
'I'll be right there', and the cool blue waters of the Med began to recede.

The incident room was buzzing, no shortage of volunteers in these circumstances; it could be any one of their children missing. The map on the wall was scattered with drawing pins, the multicoloured heads dotted around like Smarties. Each one meant a child gone missing, a sighting, a possible suspect, but thank God, thought Rimes, so far none of them indicated a body.
He rubbed his chin wearily. 'Any leads?' he asked, to no-one in particular.
A young sergeant turned from her computer screen, 'No sir, no leads. A few crank calls; we'll follow them all up, but we've drawn a blank'.
Rimes shivered, someone had walked over his grave.

## Dangerous Cocktail

Where were they, these children, were they alive or dead? He needed help.

'Come with me, Reason, I've got an idea'.

His deputy snatched up the car keys from his desk, and followed his chief out into the car park.

'Where to, Sir?' he asked as he jumped into the driving seat.

'We're going to see my grand-daughter,' Rimes answered.

An hour later they pulled up outside a chocolate box cottage in a hamlet that Reason was pretty certain wasn't even on the map.

He raised his eyebrows as he nodded towards the cottage, 'Nice,' hoping that he would pick up some clue as to why they were here.

'She loves gardening' was the only reply he got, as the older man eased himself out of the car, knees cracking. He sighed as they walked up the small pathway, and muttered under his breath, 'I'm getting too old for this'.

Reason followed behind, side-stepping the shells that had been sunk into the concrete path. The name-plate next to the polished brass door-knocker pronounced proudly that this was 'Cockleshell Cottage', although they were a good forty miles from the sea. D.I. Rimes knocked hard on the door-knocker, the vibration setting off wind-chimes that tinkled like fairy bells.

A young woman opened the door, her face lighting up when she saw who her visitor was.

'Pop-pop!' she cried, flinging her arms around Rimes, 'how lovely to see you'.

Rimes turned his head slightly in the direction of the detective sergeant, his eyes screwed up as if taking aim. D.S. Reason raised his hands in submission. It really wasn't his place to comment on the nick-name, but he filed it anyway; it might be one to tell the lads later. Once they were in the lounge and seated, D.I Rimes introduced Reason to his grand-daughter.

## Rimes Last Case

'This is Mary. She's a criminal profiler, one of the best'.

The young woman smiled. 'All down to you Pop-pop; all down to you.'

She offered them tea and scones, with cream the colour of butter and squashy strawberry jam and they sat companionably, the last of the day's sunshine languishing on the hearth and a pinky glow suffusing the cottage.

D.I. Rimes wiped the crumbs from his mouth and, leaning forward towards his grand-daughter, related to her from the beginning the events of the last few days.

Mary listened in silence, and, when he had finished, got up and walked over to the French doors and looked out onto her garden. Her planting was orderly, in rows, interspersed with tiny cloche hats on sticks, like little people marching through the flower beds. This was her own invention, to prevent birds pecking at seedlings and cats scratching up her beloved plants. She loved this garden, it was the perfect antidote to her work, here it was all about beginnings, not ends.

She turned back to the two men, who were looking up at her expectantly.

'He's a loner, an itinerant worker perhaps, but familiar with the area. He could be holding a grudge against somebody, an employer, a figure of authority. He hits back where it will hurt the most, the most vulnerable. He very likely has a rapport with children, prefers them to adults, they trust him, he could even be a youth worker, these children seem to go willingly, some in broad daylight.' she paused,

'You haven't given me a lot to go on Pop-pop, that's it I'm afraid.'

Rimes stood and walked the few steps over to his grand-daughter He kissed her cheek and held her close to him. She was very precious to him, she was all he had, but was she any more precious than any one of those missing children?

## Dangerous Cocktail

'Take care, Mary, and thank you, we best be going.' As he turned, Reason was surprised to see a tear in the older man's eye. He wouldn't share that one with the lads.

Mary watched from the doorway as the two men got into their car, and thought how old her grand-father looked, and how glad she was that at last he was retiring.

'Pop-pop,' she shouted and he wound down the window,

'I don't know why, but I just have a feeling that these children aren't dead'

D.I. Rimes smiled, 'Thank you Mary, please God you're right,' and with a wave they were gone.

'She's very smart sir, you must be very proud of her', D.S. Reason didn't want to give too much away, but he'd been very taken with her.

'Oh yes, I am. She was a little devil when she was young, never did as she was told, in fact usually did the opposite'

'You mean she was quite contrary, sir'

If Reason was expecting a reaction from Rimes, he was sadly disappointed.

The next morning D.I. Rimes was at his desk early; the situation unchanged overnight.

The phone lines were busy with the press, anxious parents, even the Home Office, all being dealt with calmly and politely by a team of his best officers. But Rimes didn't feel calm, he had been asked to extend his leaving date. For how long? What if this case went on for months, years even? His reverie was broken by D.S. Reason sitting opposite, his outstretched hand holding a telephone,

'Sir, you may want to take this call, it's a tip-off'.

Rimes groaned, he disliked tip-offs, nine times out of ten they were time-wasters.

As he took the proffered receiver he mouthed to the man opposite,

'Name?'. The D.S. shook his head. That was fairly typical, people rarely left names unless there was a big reward.

## Rimes Last Case

The voice was male, local accent and nervous, very nervous.

'It may be nothing' he stammered, 'I work for the council, Cleansing department, bin working with a bloke for a few weeks, and, well, he's a bit odd.'

'How do you mean, Sir, odd?' Rimes put his hand up to his head in a gesture of despair.

'Well he's foreign- not that I hold that against him', *Oh I bet you do,* Rimes thought, *I bet you do.*

'He don't mix with us, see, just listens to his walkman and jigs about a bit'.

'Jigs about a bit?' Rimes thought he might explode.

'To the music like. Anyway, we all think he's odd.'

'And what makes you think he's got anything to do with this case?'

'Well he's been working down the docks: the council's got a contract down there, pest control. He's been sleepin' in one of the warehouses. Thing is I went down there the other night on me way home, just to check if he needed anymore stuff, you know, bait like. He wouldn't let me in, just pulled the sliding doors enough to speak to me, like. Thing is, as I was walking away, I heard something. '

D.I Rimes leant forward in his chair, the hairs at the nape of his neck bristling.

'What, what did you hear?'

'Children, I heard children laughing, inside the warehouse'.

Rimes felt his heart begin to race.

'Where is this warehouse exactly?'

The water was cold as ex D.I Rimes waded in, the expanse of blue sparkling like cut glass ahead of him. He swam with powerful strokes, out, out into the vast ocean, sloughing off the dust and grime of the city, and the passed few weeks disappeared with each stroke. Back on the beach he lay looking up at the sky above, as clear and cloudless as he felt. He'd done it; he'd cracked the most important case of his career

173

## Dangerous Cocktail

and re-united all of the children with their families. The loner had gone, leaving the children behind in the warehouse. He smiled as he remembered the scene when they pulled open the doors- kids everywhere, listening to walkmans, playing pool and table- tennis. There were tables groaning under the weight of food, party food, junk mostly, every child's dream. He hadn't hurt a hair of their heads, in fact the kids loved him, he was their friend. At first it was an enigma, why had he done it- who was he trying to get back at? Then they had found the letter. It was addressed to his boss at the Council. Seems he'd done a good job down at the docks- eradicated the rat infestation, but wasn't happy with his pay. No overtime! All that work, all that heartache because of a loner, a rat-catcher. The police in his native Germany had drawn a blank, he hadn't returned to his home town, in fact he'd disappeared off the face of the earth. Ah well, It wasn't his problem now. Rimes stretched his arms lazily over his head and began to give some thought as to where he would eat dinner that night. He like it here, he liked the Mediterranean lifestyle, and he liked the way the locals shrugged and said 'manana '. He might even stay....

The mayor of the sleepy Spanish town slapped the strange young man on the back, and in broken English managed to communicate his grateful thanks. At last someone who could rid them of the plague of rats that was terrorising the populace and bringing disease and death in their wake. He didn't know how they would pay him, but he seemed a decent enough chap, hadn't he already charmed the children- they wouldn't leave him alone.

# The Other World

## Martin Mickleburgh

It is our memories that bind our lives together, fastening the fragments of collected experience into what we think of as a whole, an I. Our present is anchored by memory into our furthest childhood, a place as alien as the ocean floor. What was it really like to fly free of words, to be unfettered by hope or belief? What was it like when almost everything was novel, everything unexpected because we had no expectations; when we were governed by rage and ecstasy and life was experienced whole and raw, not fragmented, packaged and finally obscured by the alchemy of language. Imagination struggles to find purchase on so strange a world, and most of our early memories are gradually civilised and tamed as we recall and retell them. Most, but not all. A few still have that pungent immediacy that marks them as authentic. They are like snapshots from that other world. They will spring to mind complete and unbidden, triggered perhaps by the smell of crushed pineapple weed or of bonfires in November; or, as in the case of my earliest memory, by something as simple as silence.

My early childhood – until I was five and a half – was bathed in noise. Not, you should understand, the drone of traffic or aircraft: our little hump-backed street was visited once a week by the coal lorry, but was otherwise empty; and the nearest airfield – airport would be far too grand a name – was at Elmdon, thirty miles away on the other side of Birmingham. No, my sonic cradle was the sound of industry – the steady heartbeat thump of the steam hammer in the foundry at the end of our street; the clattering of castings and girders being moved around in the steel yard across the road at the end of our garden; the muffled

## Dangerous Cocktail

peal of loose-coupled freight being shunted in the marshalling yard a mile and a half away. And when we went to Bilston to visit my aunts, the blast furnace at Stewart and Lloyds being fed: when the little truck full of coke reached the top of the slope up to its mouth, the doors would open and a great plume of white-hot cinders would hiss into the sky; and as the coke was dumped in, the furnace would roar and the ground would tremble.

The noise of industry wrapped itself around me, a presence as familiar, as unquestioned and consoling as my mother's arms. It seeped into me, long before words could disarm it, and as a pioneer in my wordless wilderness, it laid a claim on my heart that endures still. My very first memory, short-circuiting all the intervening years, is of silence, of a morning of perfect silence.

I must have drifted up slowly from sleep because the silence did not come as a shock. Perhaps if I had been younger still, the sudden departure from normality would have been alarming; or if I had been older, I would have been overflowing with questions as to how such a thing could happen. But I was at that age when the new is hailed with pure delight. So I lay in bed, the eiderdown pulled up to my nose, full of wonder.

There was nothing. No steam hammer. No freight train. It was as if sound itself had been subtracted from the world.

Time passed. Then, as if banished sound was making the most tentative, the most guarded re-entrance, I heard "floooopf", so delicate that it was hardly a sound at all and so quiet that a clock-tick would have buried it. I had never heard anything like it.

My wonder redoubled, I waited. It must come again. Two minutes. Three. Four. And then once more "floooopf". This time I could tell that

# The Other World

it was coming from outside the window. I jumped out of bed, dragging the eiderdown around me. I had to rub away the frost from inside the window with the sleeve of my pyjamas – our house had only one coal fire and was bitterly cold in the winter. What I saw in the last light of the moon was beyond all delight, surpassed all wonder: the world was covered with snow. Gone were the blue cobbles of our yard, the two scruffy flowerbeds and the handful of withered bushes; gone were the soot and smoke, the dirty red bricks and grimy roofs, gone was every hard edge, to be replaced by smooth, shimmering blue-white. It was as if I had fallen asleep in Bradley and woken up in another universe.

Out of the corner of my eye, I caught the first tiny movement as a block of snow, perhaps two feet square, detached itself and slid down the slate roof of our kitchen and landed in the yard with a gentle "floooopf". A camera lens clicked. The anchor bit into the ocean floor.

Much later, I managed to work out when it was the world had turned white and sound vanished: it was Christmas day 1953. I was just three years old.

# Consequences

## Deborah Grice

Pain raining down like a million tiny bolts of lightning, a storm of remorse and god's displeasure dripping down from heaven leaden as sleet in these northern hills.

I stand on the rain-sodden heath, stricken, as the heavy sky sinks towards earth with its burden of water. Sheep, innocent as children, turn their expressionless eyes towards me, indifferent or resigned.

Only in the violence of the storm is this pain bearable, the riven sky a mirror to my heart. Lash down, rains! Bare-headed as Lear I will rail against the ordinations of the gods. Pain as a consequence of love! Who ordered these myriad crucifixions? Seeing the pattern of these things I can almost believe in the Grand Design, God's masochistic sacrifice the required price.

In the white waste-lands you lie wired into alien systems that keep your heart ticking like a German clock, as far from this peat-black moor as you will ever be. How I wish for you this rain and this dirt, this goodly soil smeared on face and hands, these heavy boots mired with the claggy earth. You float on a cloud of morphine, half-way between heaven and hell, waking with the white-hot pain of angels falling and calling my name when you surface.

How could I have failed to protect you? I, who cupped your face in the gentlest of embraces; I, who once drew a bright circle around you that seemed to raise you from the earth so you floated free of her snares; I, who stroked your wrist-bone as the needle bit deep into your flesh and the white-coats took you away. They chopped out the bad bits

## Dangerous Cocktail

and saved the rest, but it wasn't enough and now, although your blood flows orderly as a canal and everything that can be regulated has been regulated, you are sinking down towards chaos and the formless void as steadily as this rain falls on my head and soaks into my clothes, skin and bones. Thin and papery: your body in that heartlessly bright ward with its heartlessly bright nurses and its cruelly white surfaces. I hate each gleaming scalpel and each sterilised syringe, each white polystyrene cup and each pastel print chosen to match the pastel walls.

When you were young and full and bright you dazzled me in summer valleys, golden flesh gleaming and overflowing from a red bathing costume, throwing yourself into the churning river, the splash and laughter ringing loud and echoing. Hale and hearty your sturdy girlhood before I knew you, a Betjeman girl with hockey sticks and sturdy thighs, growing into radiance, holding court at tennis club dances. Wide-hipped you bore my set of sons easily, splendid in your no-nonsense way. Boys suited you, a good-egg sort on sports days you did them credit in your long-legged-bright-head-scarf-and-scarlet-lipstick kind of way. We loved in a lazy taken-for-granted ease with boys and dogs and horses and boats and picnics in abundance.

Who created the Serpent, God or Man? Did Adam, bored one flawless day, conjure his sibilant coils out of his own wayward mind? Whispering rebellion, whispering other truths, whispering other ways of viewing God's orderly paradise. Do we seek out the sin that starts the story? The tableau unfreezes, the plot begins, the endlessly splitting and multiplying plot. Now there is knowledge, now there is uncertainty, now there is the Herculean labour of deciphering the truth. Now there is begetting, there is pain, and jealousy, desire and temptation. Now there is the questioning in the brain, and the corruptible flesh.

When did the voices begin? Poison enters by the ear, as Hamlet knew. Who whispered 'bovine beauty' as I saw, suddenly, the appalling limits of your flat brown eyes; wanted, suddenly, things you could never even imagine.

Did she find me, or did I seek her out, my Puck, my darling, my demon, my elusive, serpentine, indefinable chameleon? Shattered in childhood, her mind a kaleidoscope of broken mirrors in which I found all my other selves, dancing and twisting, never touching, terrifyingly and exhilaratingly multiple. Fingers touching on the tightrope. No certainties, no rules. No limits, then, to the subtle variations of her sensual imagination, Eve's more exotic and intoxicating fruits, all to be tried. Biting and bitten, I am delirious, hallucinatory, transcendent and utterly, utterly lost. No limits, then, to pain and confusion, no net under the wire. No limits to her flights and her falls.

As abandoned, as bright and as brief as the butterfly: fragile wings against the storm.

They found her hanging, twisted in a thread of her own making, turning slowly, reflecting in the many-mirrored chamber.

I hung there too, for a long time, a time out of time. Paralysed, web-bound and beckoned by ghosts.

The hands of the clock tick on in the empty room. Time leeches away.

---

Eventually, I dropped back into your lap, tightly curled, afraid.

As the cow licks the new-born calf, instinctively, you reach out and claim me, heal my hurt, feeling its depth, unknowing of its origin, outside its reach.

181

## Dangerous Cocktail

The undeserving Prodigal feasts: showered on him is all the love garnered up in each of his absent years. There is no justice: thank god. Some larger mercy surrounds us, as the dough rolls around the bowl absorbing all we are caught up in the whole.

And so we rolled down the years, fattening like a plump snowball, unstoppable.

Until now. Until you slammed into that wall that never gives an inch, that is immoveable and impersonal. There is no justice. This should be my pain, my death. And though I pour every vestige of love from my veins into yours, your blood is growing thinner and weaker and I am losing you to the whiteness.

There is no understanding of this.

Though I stand here on the moor until the rain washes me away; though I lay down in the desert until the sun bleached my bones white as the sand, there is no understanding of this.

Only dissolution.

# Rest

## Patricia Golledge

It was cold, so cold. The mist hung round his shoulders like a leaden shroud. The air was bitter, even in the lee of the asylum walls. His lungs ached on every inhalation. The sun had begun to rise, slowly. Its pink fingers did nothing to warm the cold early spring morning. Red sky in the morning shepherds warning. Was he to have no luck on this, his final expedition? Tired beyond tired he stopped and held on to the icy brick. How could he go on? But tramp on he would, as he had always done. It hadn't even been ten miles but this last was draining his very soul. Ten miles, God he had walked thousands of miles in his life. This was how it had begun with the escape over these walls and then the roads, north to south, east and west. Sometimes they were encrusted with the salt of the sea, other times knee deep in the vilest effluent the golden paved city excreted. Always at his shoulder was the fear. The winds of the mighty Atlantic had not blown it away as he had prayed to the Lord, holding tight to the ship as each mile took him farther away from this land. The spectre was still there through the heat of the Pennsylvania summer and the scorching dryness of the New Mexico deserts, even the freezing gales off the Canadian coast did not free him totally. True sometimes it faded, but not for long. He had thought to banish it with his repentance and atonement. He had tried to return, twice, but they did not want him, and he had fled each time, again to the roads, to live hand to mouth – always hungry, always searching for the nights rest.

Rest, that was what he now craved. He could see it before him now, the lights in a few of the windows. The cool pale halls would give him the rest his mind and body craved. The track along the side of the kitchen garden wall was rutted. The frozen ruts felt like blades through the soles of his once sturdy boots. Blades, blades glinting. He stopped,

## Dangerous Cocktail

looking around him, his now silent world seemed soaked in blood, puddles of it along the lane to the gate. He shook his head and wiped the greasy grey hair from his forehead. It was only the weak sun on the ice. He shook his head as he marched on – what a silly old man. After all there had been much more blood, rivers of it flowing into the gutters. Cool, quiet blood which took longer to clean from the marked cobbles than to spill it. The flow of blood was meant to cleanse but it only besmirched all those touched by it. The whores, their pimps even the famous police inspector had been contaminated.

He could not let those thoughts overwhelm him now. Block Four was in sight, he must keep on, step by step. He would be able to rest. No need for the pretence, no need to play a part. He could be himself – flawed, devout, wanting only the security and rest. The main door would have been deterrent enough to those sane enough to notice it on their admission. He had no fear of it, he knew what it contained. It had not changed these past decades. He leant his lined forehead against the wood. It was pitted and scarred and held no warmth. Unchanging. Unlike this world, this world he could no longer hear. And glad he was. The noise of traffic, of telephones, picture houses; of cannons, screaming men and animals; all these he didn't want to hear again. This noisy new century. The smell of leather, horsehair, the quiet methodical noises of chisel, hammers, these he missed. His arthritic hands could no longer tack the cloth to a chair; his mind could no longer keep its path. The feel of his tools, of knives, of the yielding flesh, sliced open to reveal the innards of the corrupted vessels. These things he had not felt for a lifetime. His mask was slipping more often and the fear increased with each stranger's suspicious look.

He mustered enough strength to pull at the bell. The sound insignificant and hollow in the cold air. He stood, face pressed to the wood feeling for the sound of footsteps when the door was flung open. Dazed, he merely stared at the youth. Somewhere in the depths of the tiredness he wanted to laugh at the irony of such fresh faced innocence in a place full of madness.

## Rest

His voice was rough; loud.

"I'm turning meself in, lad. I'm an escapee. Eighteen-eighty-eight I left, I'm turning meself in"

Hesitant hands brought him in to the hall. He sat alone on a hard chair, conscious only of the need for sleep. Footsteps jerked him out of the fog and he stood up, every muscle aching. Yet the face, the dark hair and round face sparked something...

"Mr. Rich? Is that you, can you tell them I've come to turn meself in"

The middle aged man took his arm, to lead him on to rest? To sanctuary?

"After forty years, I didn't think to ever see you again. Come on lets get you settled. Young Brightly, here will take you to get fed."

He shuffled off behind the young figure, warmth slowly creeping into him again.

"Oh, and Jack, welcome back to Broadmoor."

# Tone

Peter Goodsall

Click.

The sound is constant. The sound is forever. Before me there was no sound.

I am pure. The tone is frequent, immaculate, as sanitary as the scene that I regard. No change. Change is bad. Change will bring panic. Change will mean that events have strangled all of the moments that preceded them and ripped apart the calm. Change will mean crisis.

Screws are turned, gases and fluids that snake their way through brightly coloured pipes, or tubes of no colour at all, are forced into the resisting container of chemicals in solution that has something wrong with it. The thing to which I am linked, physically and with all of my energy, so that it may awaken from it's sleep mode, becoming fully operational once more, like the other containers of all different sizes that flit and spin about it, but with jerky movements. All of these receptacles, that change one with the other but are strangely constant, applying energy to the maintenance of another receptacle. These objects must take much energy to create: too much must be invested in them for them to be simply abandoned. It seems to me that it would be most efficient to simply switch them off and scrap them when they malfunction.

This container never responds to the others. This container must hold something special, something that must be preserved at all costs, but its controls are faulty. Why do they not simply take the insides out of it and place them in one of the others? My pure tone is the only

## Dangerous Cocktail

indication that the container merely requires servicing, that it is not empty of energy and should be removed to wherever obsolete containers are kept.

The container and I maintain one another. Both of us demand constancy, sustaining our perfect equilibrium with the music of pure sound, pure tone, perfection.

Tone is more frequent now. No! Irregularity! No! This cannot be! Tone misses emission. Tone misses again. Chaotic tone is more then less. Extended tone breaking into vibration and disorder. This cannot be allowed to happen. I scream! I scream again! My screaming imposes order, frequency, drowning the jumble of confusion in which I am embroiled.

Many containers, moving so fast that they are almost graceful, dash and, given their limited speed, almost bustle. Screws are turned. I am under constant observation. It is as unsettling and frightening as my new mental indigestion. The slow rumble of receptacle-sound is swamped by my screaming. A container looms over me and I am screaming no longer. The chaos courses through me once more. I can feel spikes (that should be but smooth bumps) stabbing at me, strange spaces where there should be marks. The rumble of the containers is more frequent, more compelling. Lights suddenly flash their urgency. A tempest stirs in the tentacles with which I reach to the receptacle. Another tube. Small cylinders: simple, insignificant, machines are applied to the broken container. Still the chaos! Still, I am in turmoil! Please make it stop! What can I do to make it stop?

The machine that the receptacles move has appeared. I have sometimes thought that it must be wonderful to be able to move, but this machine only seems to appear during moments of chaos. And I cannot abide chaos. A container presses upon the damaged receptacle. A loud rumble. A huge blow thrusts into me. The chaos has vanished! Oh thank you! How wonderful! No! Now there is only space. Emptiness. I demand a perpetual, incessant, repetition. They have taken it away from me. They must return my order, my reason. Another massive belt

## Tone

surges into me. Again, blissful order. But so fleeting! In my distress I failed to observe the container that is prone when the first spike surged through me. Now I find that it is suffering as well. It distorts and moves so fast for one of the receptacles that I see it fly. Still more space. Vacuum where there must be matter, energy, life. The impact of another strike, yet more powerful and another. Momentary hope for me in a terror of hollowness.

Another! Another!

All of the containers have stopped moving. All of the rumbling has gone. The tempest has moved out of my vista and I am empty, starved. The containers yank and lurch inelegantly once more: slower if anything. Until there are only two left. Two containers and me and my hollow belly demanding that my tentacles receive their frequent pulse.

No! Don't touch that!

The room has blurred. The bed, the curtains, the containers (funny walking bags that are almost full of water); the blue or brown balls with which they are forever confronting me: they're all leaving me. Everything's becoming indistinct. Everything has formed one cloud. One cloud that is floating away to join the pulsing, radiating light in the corner…

Click.

The sound is constant. The sound is forever. Before me there was no sound…

# Mrs. Throttleback

## Peter Owen

All who regularly survive Mrs. Throttleback's Sunday morning underwater line dancing classes (meet ten a.m. at beach kiosk – Stetsons absolutely imperative during high-tides) may like to know that Nigel and I have just returned from Tadcaster, where we were drawn to say farewell to Mummy, who passed away on the fourteenth of last month.

Shortly after our arrival in Tadcaster a large contingent of Mummy's friends from the W.I. turned up and, taking their lead form a Mrs. Tartlove, began to file with heads bowed into the room where Mummy lay in her fur-lined casket, the eerie silence punctuated only by their restrained singing of the hymn "Lo She Hath Gone" (no. 321 – Anciently Unusual – 1603 limited edition). Each of them bore certain gifts, of which there appeared to be an abundance of plum jam and beetroot chutney, which they placed beside Mummy as sustenance for her journey into the afterlife. Their eldest member, one hundred and nine year old "Queenie" Arkwright, held upright by fellow members; one each side of her, with a third positioned at the rear in case of a backward fall, scattered pink rose petals over Mummy while a certain Mrs. Golightly, accompanied by "Sidney Trump and his Tea-time Five" tried her absolute best to overcome a rather unfortunate speech impediment and severe nervous twitch as she attempted a song and dance routine that was, I'm afraid, totally incomprehensible.

Mrs. Tartlove afterwards very kindly tried to console the prostrate, tearful, figure of Mrs. Golightly – who had "toppled over" after a particularly aggressive twitch had rendered her immobile – by enthusing that she had definitely recognised the words "Jesus" and "supermarket trolley" during the second verse to which "Sidney Trump and his Tea-time Five" added that, if that was the case, they'd been

## Dangerous Cocktail

playing the wrong tune and promptly stormed off – it was all rather moving.

Nigel, of course, volunteered to serve as a pall-bearer, an opportunity, as he amusingly put it, to try out his new toupee that had arrived on the morning of our departure. The toupee came complete with a battery-operated head-warmer, which was to be worn discretely under the hairpiece, its temperature controlled by certain head movements that Nigel was sure he would soon master. Poor Nigel, it was well past the freezing point as he and his fellow pall-bearers hoisted the coffin onto their shoulders. It soon became apparent to me, as I watched Nigel's increasingly bizarre head movements, that he was experiencing great difficulty controlling the temperature of his head-warmer.

As the cortège proceeded with slow dignity along the aisle towards a solemn Reverend Slammingham I could detect thin wisps of smoke emerging from beneath Nigel's stove-pipe hat. My darlings, I knew what was happening, but what was I to do? Should I breach the silence – 'Nigel dear, I think wiggy's on fire', or remain silent and pray – I chose the latter.

It was at this moment that a group of partially-sighted cyclists from the Tadcaster Wheelers Disabled Persons Cycling Club pedalled their way through the chapel en-route to their winter camp at Barnsleydale Tump, making their exit after a series of mishaps with various members of the congregation, including lone piper Mr. Thumble, who was forced to make hasty adjustments to his distorted chanter before he was able to blow off with any resonance. Then, with a strangled cry of anguish, Nigel, with flames beginning to leap around his head-ware, had to relinquish his hold on the corner of Mummy's coffin and make a dash for the "gentleman's room", where he was able to plunge his head down a vacant toilet pan. The driver of the hearse very kindly offered to take Nigel off to Tadcaster Royal, which he did at great speed. Poor Nigel, his head swathed in the Tadcaster W.I. hand-knitted flag of

## Mrs. Throttleback

remembrance, stretched out in the rear where a short while ago Mummy's coffin had lain.

Meanwhile the remaining pall-bearers wilted under the uneven weight distribution and Mummy's coffin slid to the floor with a resounding crash, its lid sent spinning towards Reverend Slammingham, who, belying his seventy-three years and early stage dementia, leapt out of its path shouting obscenities that saw choir-mistress Cynthia Temperate and her ladies of the 'All-Hallows Choir of the Desperate Virgin' (senior section) running from the building, vowing never to return.

The rest of the service proceeded relatively smoothly after Mr. Jenkinson, at twenty-eight stone the heaviest person present, had replaced the lid of the coffin and reluctantly agreed to Uncle Bertie's suggestion to 'jump up and down on it' until all were satisfied that the lid was secure.

There was a further peculiar moment when Reverend Slammingham caused a murmur of unpleasantness by requesting "The happy couple to come forward on this joyous occasion and receive the good Lord's blessings", smiling seraphically upon the weeping congregation and imploring of them "Who amongst you carries the ring?", there then following several disturbing bodily "thrusts" and worryingly enthusiastic laying-on of hands by the Reverend on a very confused Aunty Norah. Daddy's friend, Mr. Pontefract, felt obliged to leap to his feet and point out to Reverend Slammingham in no uncertain terms to press the fucking button and send Mummy through the velvet curtain.

Poor Nigel; he does look odd, though I daren't tell him so: his toupee is charred beyond recognition, yet in his dazed state of mind, he still insists on placing the remnants over a small unblistered section. The rest of his head resembles a peeled beetroot (Tesco, sixty-nine pence, vacuum packed). He hasn't eaten for three days, though he did try a little goose and a spoonful of broth this morning. I have saved the goose-fat to spread over Nigel's head. Nurse Sidebottom thinks it might

## Dangerous Cocktail

lessen the swelling and help ease the inflammation a little, and being waterproof, it does enable him to walk out in a light shower.

Yours as ever,

Prunella.

# Passing Trade

## Martin Mickleburgh

I am old. I am too old for the sea. By the salt in my bones and the rime in my beard I am too old for the sea.

Seventy-six years I have crossed and recrossed the trackless wastes where there is no mark of man, no beacon, no middle part of any journey, only the leaving and the arriving and in between the endless, timeless sea. Seventy-six years I have schooled myself in wind and wave, the pelagic moods of my solitary love.

Such things I have seen in the furthest ocean that would shake the Almighty in His high heaven and stand to nothing his gifted order. Such things I have witnessed as would tax Lucifer's heart. Such beauty. Such merciless, pitiless beauty, where sky and sea stare at each other in abject confusion, where the worth of a man is less than the spindrift that fills the air, where his voice at full stretch is a whisper to the wave's cry and the ceaseless roaring of the wind. I have seen the bergs, as big as cities and of such blue as would break your eye; waves like mountains marching, ship-swallowers, sightless furies, turning about the whole southern ocean, endlessly hurling themselves at unseen enemies. I have seen the Horn in her finery of terror, and the doldrums where you might sit in the centre of a world gone to glass.

All these things I hold in my heart, memories, the sea suffered and endured; by these things am I measured as a man; in them my soul is shriven.

But there is one sight for which I would trade all these others to witness again.

It was the fifth of September, eighteen hundred and sixty-six. I was sixteen years old and four before the mast. We were south-bound out of

## Dangerous Cocktail

London for Durban, beating against a steady westerly south of the Lizard. The sky was lightening behind us, painting the high clouds driven like smoke before the wind. The second mate spotted them, down by the horizon and headed towards us: tea clippers. He called out their bearing and every hand crowded to the rail for a glimpse.

We knew of their race, could recount their passings from Anjer to Cape Verde; and their names – such names! – Taeping, Ariel, Taitsing, Serica and Fiery Cross. They were the fastest, most hard-driven ships on the face of the ocean. For ninety-eight days and fourteen thousand miles they had pursued each other, from Foochow bound for London, each bearing a million pounds or more of the first of the season's tea and a bonus of ten shillings a ton to the first to arrive. Fiery Cross had dropped her pilot first and stood away for Turnabout Island and the South China Sea; she had made all the early running, first past Anjer, first past Mauritius and making three hundred and twenty-eight miles in a single day. By the Cape, after the long charge across the Indian Ocean, Ariel was snapping at her heels, but fell back in the South Atlantic to give the lead to Taeping by St Helena. By the line, the three ships were beam to beam. Then Fiery Cross sailed into a calm and had to watch Taeping inch away from her: after four hours she was hull down; another two and she had gone. Ariel, out to the west and unseen by both of them, caught a slant and by Cape Verde was ahead by twenty-two hours while Taitsing and Serica, trailing all the way from Foochow, closed to within a day of them. That was the last we had heard. And now the leading pair were bearing down on us in the dawn light.

The skipper put us about so that we might parallel their course as they passed, the better to see, the better to remember.

On they came, taking form from the blooming light. I thought that they had the look of angels, creatures of the narrow place where beauty begets terror. How can a soul be so magnified in the simple sight of man's work? I cannot say, and yet, as they came on, I swear they trailed glory in their wake.

## Passing Trade

It was the boy, sent to the masthead with the skipper's telescope, who first called their names. "Ariel! 'Tis Ariel to windward and Taeping by her lee and a mile astern." To hear their names, to be alone on the sea to witness them, was to be so graced as to be, for the brief time of their passing, unbound by death or mortality.

We looked on in wonder, no further word spoken between us, bound together into this oldest of rituals: the passing of ships in great waters.

And then she was upon us, a bare fifty yards to leeward and making fourteen knots: Ariel the bride of the ocean, decked in her wedding weeds, wimple white over bible black, sporting ringtail and watersail, Jemmy Green, moonrakers, skysails and stuns'ls and every fancy racing sail that could be bent to spar or stay. She lay low to the water as if caught in its embrace, long, sharp and impossibly narrow, all her brass finery rigged for home and polished to a fiery sheen. She dipped and lifted in the quartering swell, breathing spray which hung about her like a garland, glittering in the rising sun. The sea rumbled beneath her forefoot, speaking to us in a voice barely below the threshold of comprehension; the wind wailed in her rigging.

For a few moments the world was perfect with us; we imperfect beings were redeemed by beauty as impenetrable as adamant. Man's work outshone God's.

As she passed, her master, Captain Keay, standing aft by the mizzen stays, lifted a hand in a simple act of greeting; but we took it as a blessing, a gesture of infinite compassion, one poor soul for another, a mark of the bright world already retreating.

She fell astern of us, while Taeping passed away down to leeward. In twenty minutes she was hull down. Then she was gone.

They are all gone now: Ariel lost running her Eastings down, engulfed from astern by one of those southern wave-mountains; Taeping wrecked on Ladd's Reef in the South China Sea; Serica, Kaisow, Taitsing, Fiery Cross, Sir Lancelot, Titania, Lahloo, Spindrift, all lost: dismasted and hulked, driven ashore or swallowed by the sea. Their light has gone out of the world, and none to replace it.

## Dangerous Cocktail

I am too old for the sea. Too old to leave her take my body and breath as hostage against her whim: she has taken my days and left me my memories in trade, each one a trial in mortality for each is an I-was-that-and-am-no-more.

But I say this: I am more than my memory for I carry to this waking hour the mark of that day, steady as a riding light on a starless roadstead, the day of the world made anew in man's image, of the passing of Ariel, beauty incarnate, across the face of the deep.

# The Life Model

## Alyson Heap

She rested her cheek on the kitchen table, and, like a blind man reading Braille, she traced her fingers across the pitted surface. Each dent, each scratch and groove, held a memory, every inch of the scrubbed pine was a testament to the last twenty five years.

It was here, at the kitchen table, that her children had eaten marmite fingers with grubby hands and snotty noses, here they had fashioned works of art with her home-made play dough, licked spoons and bowls of cake mix clean with their puppy soft tongues, and here they had each shaped their destinies. One minute they were lovingly drawing stick figures labelled 'mummy and daddy', and then in the blink of an eye, they were scribbling hormonal love-notes in sprawling writing, to nubile young girls with fresh faces and bright, white smiles.

Now, she had it back, all to herself, this precious table with its vacant chairs.

She didn't really want it, the echoing space, the yawning linen baskets and the empty cupboards. Where were the tins of baked beans, the pots of instant noodles and the plastic squeezy sauce bottles, their lids crusted hard because no-one ever thought to wipe them? That was her job, along with the cooking and cleaning, the ironing and all of the other unpaid jobs she did because that was who she was, the nurturer.

She pressed her ear hard against the surface, and listened. Here were the sounds of her life. The pit-pat of small hands tapping out tunes, the clatter of impatient knives and forks, and the laughter, the light high-pitched giggling that suddenly turned to deep melodious

## Dangerous Cocktail

man-laughter. She missed that. Tears trickled down the side of her nose and onto the table-top, melting through the surface and disappearing. She raised her head and impatiently wiped her face with a sleeve, so redolent of so many occasions when her sons had done the same, sitting at this very table. No they couldn't ride their bikes to school unless they wore helmets, no they couldn't always have their own way, and yes, sometimes girls were spiteful and duplicitous, and no, they wouldn't always feel this unhappy. But she might.

She was well aware that time snatches things away unless you fight to keep them; she was losing the battle. The memories were fading, and taking with them the last few years of her life, leaving a void like a yawning chasm deep inside.

And that is why she had decided she would look for a job.

Her husband had snorted, an unspoken 'Who would employ you?' sound.

It would be easy to acquiesce, to believe herself unemployable, past the sell-by date of usefulness, but she was going to prove him wrong. Her credentials were impressive, her C.V a triumph over adversity- yes, she who had scaled mountains of ironing, performed life-saving techniques with elasto-plast, open-heart surgery with just a hug and a cup of cocoa, she could do anything. Hadn't she grown from seed four strong, healthy and heart-stoppingly beautiful human beings, mediated wars and prevented fratricide by negotiation on countless occasions? She was a contender!

Taking a deep breath, she placed the three neatly clipped job advertisements in front of her on the table.

## The Life Model

The first read:

*PART TIME POSITIONS*

*GREETINGS CARDS*

*Exciting opportunities to join a small friendly team of merchandisers. The role involves calling upon local supermarkets to assist with re-orders, tidy displays, and the display of new and seasonal ranges. Experience not essential.*

For this job she would wear a dark pin-stripe suit and a crisp white blouse. Her make-up would be light, her lipstick red. Her shoes would be black leather with low heels, showing a hint of sheer black tights as she walked purposefully and confidently amongst the supermarket aisles. She would have a flair for choosing the best selling ranges, and her sales figures would soar. Her superiors would beg her to take on a bigger area and soon the job would be full-time, with training meetings in the evening and nights out with her fellow employees. Her husband would begin to complain, 'I never see you', and she would think, how strange, coming from a man who had never really looked at her. But there would be younger, more dynamic women snapping at her heels. They would be more in tune with the upwardly-mobile buying public, and eschew her choices of animals in soft focus, and heartfelt verses in country gardens. Instead they would fill the shelves with cartoon faces and cards with micro-chips that spewed out obscenities in loud nearly-voices. She would be passed over and ignored, her opinions worthless and targets unattainable.

She sighed. Screwing the square of newspaper into a tight ball, she discarded it and reached for the second clipping.

# Dangerous Cocktail

*DEVELOPMENT WORKER- SUPPORTED VOLUNTEERING*
*We are seeking a skilled and sympathetic person to develop and run an exciting project to support people from disadvantaged backgrounds into volunteering. Experience an advantage, but training will be given.*

    For this job she would wear linen, comfortably creased. Her sensible shoes would be hand made in Scandinavia and her chunky jewellery bought from a women's co-operative in Bangladesh. She would speak in a borrowed voice, enunciating clearly and compassionately. Her clients would soon come to view her as a surrogate mother, and they would sit together drinking fair trade coffee, whilst she gently eased them into the world of volunteering, offering them the chance to make a difference.

    She would grow to love each one; she would fret over them, shoulder their worries and fight their demons. And as she watched them, battling against prejudice and handicap, she would see in their eyes the people they could have been. At night she would lie in bed and grieve for them, her surrogate family, and by day she would ache with tiredness and a longing to make the world a better place. A place where the weak were strong, the disabled able, and all of these, her children, accepted into the society in which they were side-lined. Her health would suffer, and her family would watch her bloat with the canker of disappointment, see her legs swollen with the weight of it all, and they would beg her to leave the job that had stolen their mother from them.

    She realised with great sadness and a heavy heart, that she couldn't do this job.

    That left just one:

# The Life Model

*LIFE MODELS*

*Clothed and unclothed life models required to sit for A-Level and BTEC Art and Design drawing classes. All classes are supervised by a college lecturer. Experience is not essential, but a mature and professional attitude is essential.*

For this she would wear a smudge of blusher and a slick of lip gloss. She would lounge, head tilted slightly toward the ceiling, on a velvet couch, her hands resting comfortably on her naked thighs. Each bloom and fold of her body would be captured in charcoal, pastels and watercolours. Each dip and curve would be minutely observed, cherished and replicated, and she would share her glorious self with the best and the talented. She would raise a paean cry for women everywhere, the nurturers who have given all to arrive at this point in time when they can say:

'This is me, this is who I am'.

And when she gathered her family around her, at the kitchen table which was the beating heart of her home, they would all acknowledge this strong, brave woman. Her husband, fiercely proud of her, would fend off any suggestion that this was not a seemly occupation And above the fireplace, she would hang his favourite portrait of her, the one that showed her complete and fulfilled, in all her magnificent, iridescent, naked glory.

This was it, this was the one.

# I Have Trapped An Angel

Peter Goodsall

I have trapped an angel.
It is fluttering within my glass.
I have trapped an angel;
It watches all the world without
Pass.
I have trapped an angel,
Crying
In the debris of its freedom.
I have trapped an angel,
Beautiful, haunting,
(A golden one).

I have caught a demon,
It is conniving within my glass.
I have caught a demon;
It watches all the world without
Pass.
I have caught a demon,
Revelling
In it's coming freedom.
I have caught a demon;
It was an angel
Beautiful, haunting,
(A golden one).

# The Artist

## Elspeth Green

Are you comfortable sat in that chair, with your feet curled under you and your head placed gently against the cushion? I was sat in that very same position not so long ago; it is probably still warm from the heat of my blood. Do the soft arms welcome you into its depths? Do you belong?

I see you have a mug of hot chocolate beside you, dripping with luscious cream. He served that concoction for me, as well. We laughed at how different we were from those who drank beer or wine. As the perfect couple we planned to be different, something special. We had no need to reach for alcoholic stimuli.

How did you two, the next 'perfect couple', meet? Was it by accident at the gallery? Were you both gazing in excited anticipation towards a painting yet to be unveiled? Is this his usual lair? Did you both walk backwards towards the tiny Edwardian loveseat swathed as it was in deep luxuriant velvet? Was the collision something to bring a smile to your eyes and lips? I remember his hypnotic gaze; how safe it made me feel. Oh for that confidence now.

Safe. Safe? When I look at you and see life repeating its pattern, I am aware of what will happen next. I stretch out my hand to you. Despite the energy of my efforts it is impossible to reach you, to warn you. You must fear relaxing in this man's company. There is nothing I can do to save you from your fate. Do you wish to be saved?

On that loveseat we shared so much; he offered powerful thoughts. 'This moment is filled with joy and challenge.'

His eyes held my gaze and he stared deep, deep into my soul. I could not answer, I could barely breathe; pain filled my chest. Unformed words crowded my brain. It was not possible to share those words; somehow he understood my every meaning; there was a bond. Without

## Dangerous Cocktail

a question or further thought he ran his lips along the nape of my neck. I rocked my head back against his face and should have left. I could not move; his power was too strong for me to leave. Was that how it was for you?

Your eyes have raised; you are looking towards me. Ignore the rich, dark tones of his voice; listen only to me. I have the knowledge; I can save you from repeating my mistakes. Compel yourself to wish to be saved.

No, he has won; he has filled you with himself. I know for I have been where you are now. You believe that you, alone, hold this man; he is your disciple. You are wrong. He is holding you, bending you to his every whim. You are no longer free. You move when he asks; you breathe when he tells; you smile when he allows. Bless you; you cannot be saved. Time has wandered too far.

He has left you alone, why? To prepare the room for you: is that what he said? I know. That was the same explanation he offered me. Look up, look into my eyes, see that I am calling to you; pleading with you. Escape now whilst you can.

You lift yourself gracefully from the all encompassing chair and walk towards me. My heart is filled with hope. You gaze directly into my eyes. Can you not take your mind further within the picture before you? Contemplate the artistry? I am here; I can help. This need not be you. Smile at me; let me know that you have seen.

I place the palm of my hand flat against the window. Although the opening appears wide towards the sun my fingers are still restricted by glass. Can you not see the movement within the cottage, the movement that is I; listen to me, listen to me. Inside my head I am screaming at you.

"Get out; get out now whilst you can move, whilst you still have power within your skeleton. Before the beverage takes its toll."

You return to your chair, relaxed and at peace with the world. I recognise the feeling; I know that it is too late. You too will find yourself in this cottage, held captive by the pressure of glass. You

# The Artist

cannot move, your breathing shallows, only when he speaks will you respond. He will speak; believe me. He will make demands upon you and you will follow like a small child or a puppy, pitifully aware of his master's voice.

I try once more to beat against the glass; my fist burns with the pain.

"Get out, get out: run, run, run!"

Your eyelids gently close. It is too late; there is no rescue.

I drop within my prison. There is nowhere for me to relax. I am locked inside a pictorial facade. He showed me the way. He took my hand and raised me from the chair. He gently guided me towards the room I believed he was preparing and introduced me to his art.

The walls were filled with paintings: some large, some small, some welcoming and some repulsive. There were nudes, landscapes, bowls of fruit, portraits; one I recognised as a facsimile of myself. A huge easel dwarfed the rest of the room and left no space for furniture. On it there was a massive painting draped with a red silken curtain.

"You are here as I present this artwork to the world."

He whispered the honour into my yearning ear. Taking my hand he guided me to a silken tassel. It needed no pressure but dropped to my touch and the curtains drifted apart.

I realise now that the painting was nothing. It was of little value, of little worth. With my gaze I truly believed that all the colours in the world had joined together in a celebration of his art. I gasped in breathless wonder at the vision before me, yet this cottage with roses around the door was not exceptional. Why did it have such a powerful hold over me?

My hand was now clutched tightly within his own. With a certain level of haste he pulled me towards the doorway once again. I was not allowed the opportunity to study for myself the other works and judge upon his level of ability.

"First we will set my masterpiece where I have planned; I will share its beginning, its middle, its end with you. Help me to lift it through. Be careful."

## Dangerous Cocktail

Together we found the space above the chair. There was a greasy black rim around the velvet wallpaper. This artwork was not a new addition. Where we were placing it, the frame had always lived. There had been many similar unveilings. To my willing eyes it brought completion to the room; its absence had been stark, its return a joy. I spread my arms with pleasure and longed for the room to enfold me once again.

"Come with me, you can't rest yet."

He took my hand and drew it close to his chest, the roughness of his jacket catching on the softness of my skin. I gasped.

"Don't be afraid," he whispered, "You have nothing to fear from me."

Lamb-like I followed my mentor. I would shadow his lead wherever. He pulled me towards a small oak door and guided me through its portals along a narrow gravel pathway. I could smell the spring-like air long before the realisation dawned upon me that we were outside in the country. This home, his home, had moved from city to green-belt without stirring an inch. Hysterical laughter filling my lungs. I ran towards a nearby apple tree distanced from the ancient orchard. I flung myself upon the antiquated wooden seat surrounding its trunk. From where I rested the origin of his watercolour could be viewed: the cottage, the roses around the door, the chintzy curtains; it was faultless. I screamed with demonical laughter again; the same frenzied clamour.

As my gaze rested upon his, I realised I had travelled too far. Was it my laughter, or my attempt at escape? I was unsure. He grabbed both of my wrists, his grasp too strong for me to react against, and shook me violently. I felt the burning sting as his hand then swept against my cheek: backwards, forwards and then again; twice, three times, maybe more. He flung me hard on the sun-dried grass and rolled upon me. I could feel his tears touch my cheek; stinging as they soaked into the grazes his strength had left.

Then calm. Without a word, without a murmur he lifted himself from my body and held his hand out gracefully towards me. My fingers

## The Artist

were placed in his. I was temporarily oblivious to the change which had gone before. Silently he drew me, once again, along the gravel pathway, steeper this time. We made the return journey, towards the tiny doorway. I crouched down low and believed we both made our entrance. There was a heavy weight upon my shoulder as I was forced ferociously towards the blank, white wall.

"You'll have a long time to regret laughing at me."

I dropped upon my haunches and gazed at my surroundings. This was no comfortable lounge, nor was it a room filled with artwork. This was blank, this was cold; this was nothing. In front of me was a white wall with four windows, two high up, two low down. Each window had four squares of glass and four small handles. Chintzy curtains surrounded each casement. There was a white door in the centre to complete the balance and a pristine doorknob had been finely painted.

My breathing slowed and I began to use my fingers as well as my open palms to discover my surroundings. There were no ridges; there was no depth. What I had thought were windows were clear spaces. I pushed my hands through and found them met by a plain sheet of glass.

"I am part of the masterpiece above your head. I cannot be seen. I cannot be heard. But I am here. Save yourself, do not let this happen to you."

I stand by the window to watch; it is all that I can do. Suddenly my world turns a deep shade of red. Each window is covered by red silken material, though the light continues to shimmer through. I hold my breath as the covering glides to the floor and I can see once more.

I can see you, your unfocussed eyes gazing directly at me. Do you appreciate only the colours, not the style of this work? Are you aware that you have studied it before or is your drugged, befuddled, brain oblivious to the beginning and the end? Again I scream,

"Get out; get away. Leave him for God's sake!"

You do not hear me. You cannot hear anything. All you can see are his eyes, his lips and his body. Do you not know his plans?

## Dangerous Cocktail

I feel movement as the painting is raised again to the wall. I know as he takes you gently into his arms. I hear him utter the words:
"Don't be afraid. You have nothing to fear from me."
Yes you do; yes you do!
I watch, helpless as you laugh, at first with joy at your surroundings and then hysterically. I see his face change at his erroneous belief that you see him as the jester. I feel the strength pouring into his body as he shakes you and slaps you hard around the face. I feel as your jaw snaps and gently rub my own as I gaze down. He throws you upon the emerald coloured and flower-splattered carpet and I watch with impotent horror as he begins to tear at your clothes. Your bruises are my bruises; your blood is my blood; our agony is shared.
I hammer at the glass imprisoning me, using my hands, my feet - my whole body. Eventually, with one final pound, it smashes into a million pieces. Without thought for my own pain or maybe because of it, I fling one huge crystal as far as it will travel. He has rolled away from you and the glass reaches its destination. It is he who will have a long time to regret the laughter. I sense the blood dripping from my body; my eyes screw tightly closed. I know that you are safe. You are free. It will take time but we are free.
"Stay with me love. Stay with me. You're ok. Everything's fine. I heard your screams. I've called for help. Just you hang in there."
I floated back, but stayed no time. My saviour had covered my nakedness.

It is another white room which this time has depth. There is no sky; no flowers; no chintz curtains. It is calm, warm and peaceful. Someone, a blue angel, is holding my hand.
"Welcome back; you'll be fine now. You lost a lot of blood; it was a nasty gash. You'll soon feel better."
I journeyed through a deep, dark, tunnel towards the sunshine. The glare pained me; my eyes remained closed. Deep in my soul I knew he had survived; he would be able to laugh again.

## The Artist

I am not safe; we are not free. I cannot bear to be in this world with him. My decision is made. My eyes flutter. I close them gratefully for the last time.

# Resurrection

### Deborah Grice

I wait under the earth.

My fingers are long and plentiful, grappled into the ground around roots and rocks. In the darkness I stretch out my elongated limbs and yawn. Yet I am content. My hour will come.

Down here, in the soft, moist darkness, there is plenitude and life, alacrity in all its creeping, scuttling forms. Here the rich earthworm drills his way downwards; the bright waist-coated beetle scurries home. Here the secret mole moves in his mysterious ways, both velvet and claw.

Down here we know things hidden to those who live in the daylight. We know what moves in the darkness; we know what crouches, waiting. We can see with our ears and our noses. And we have a seventh sense that recognises the smell of death. The silence just before the stony drop of the kestrel; the soft padding around the farmyard fence: deafening sounds to those who live in the darkness and have a hundred ears.

I know the sweet voice of the nightingale, and I know the soft thump of a body when it falls onto the leaf-mould. We are no strangers to bodies, here in the forest. This is the hunting ground of the weasel and the stoat; small creatures freeze under the shadow of the owl's flight. We feed on death and decay here; we flourish.

## Dangerous Cocktail

But humans fall heavily, and do not lie easily in death. *She* lies above me, stretched out in the loamy soil, an unnatural bedfellow. I know her too, from a time when both of us were more upright.

I heard the tyres first, sibilant on the wet road leading into King's Wood. The engine, purring slowly in a low gear, pausing, then coming on. Headlights swinging round with the bend that leads into the mossy lay-by at Hook's Hollow, picking out the silhouettes of amputated trees and the ghostly skeletons of dead foxgloves. The engine subsides; there is a quiet click, then I feel soft-soles creeping above me. The leaf-mould stirs and mutters: I listen, and hear the first strike of a spade clunking against small stones. Harder, the next time, shaking my roof, then again and again, a steady rhythm. Only two pauses, with laboured breathing. It does not take long.

Steps again, retreating then returning. She must be wrapped in a rug or blanket, for she slides easily across the forest floor towards the shallow grave. Now the soft fall of soil onto her body, and the scattering of bracken, moss and stones to cover the fresh scar of red soil.

A pause, and an absence of sound. Then rapid steps and the forgetful slam of a car door. A curse, the roar of the engine, then he is gone, leaving her to the close embrace of the earth and the slow investigations of the worms.

Foxes glide by in the darkness, on missions known only to them. The deer sleep, curled in secret coverts in the tall bracken. Badgers scent the air warily, and retreat into their caverns of earth. There is a foreign scent in the air tonight and it does not smell sweet. The forest is become a human graveyard.

Usually humans lie together in death, weighted down by stones and heavy crosses of marble, seeking safety in numbers and in prayers and

Resurrection

remembrances. The loneliness of *this* death is undisguised; her only mourning the shriek of the owl.

There is a Spirit that moves in the woods, an indefinable presence. Even those of us who dwell here do not entirely understand the how and why of it, only that it moves and lives and breathes and sighs and that sometimes even men can sense it. The ancient trees know it best, the old oaks in the heart of the forest, gnarled and twisted with the blasts and droughts of countless years, their hearts dried with age, their leaves green and moist. *She* knew the spirit of the place: I have seen her press her ear to the trunks of the tallest beeches on a windy day to hear the groan and creak of their sinews, like the timbers of a tall ship at sea. She could sense and feel the life that pulses through all things, her body pressed closely against the smooth trunks. It could not save her: it does not save. It simply Exists.

There is a darkness in the soul of man that we know nothing of. I feed on death, yet kill nothing. Man kills without eating, against the laws of nature. This corpse, I remember when she played here as a child, running wild in the forest as if she belonged here, making dens, collecting acorns and sweet chestnuts that the trees let fall. She learnt the tracks of the deer and the foxes; knew where the badgers built their setts and how to freeze, upwind, to watch their cubs frolic and cuff each other.

There are spirits that oppress; and those that listen. She would lie down on the peaty soil to see what it smelt like, how it felt under the body. She lay on the mossy turf in summer, her nose close to the scents of the forest, watching the logical trails of the ants. I sensed her spirit rise in the autumn when she leapt to catch the falling leaves or run rustling through great heaps of them. She hunted for me and my kind, not wrenching us up from the ground, just observing our delicate forms and subtle colours. Humans warned her to beware of us, how we could

## Dangerous Cocktail

disguise ourselves to dupe her, how dangerous we could be. Did they warn her about her own kind, who do the same, but with intent?

I think men have become sick since they left the forest. Or rather, since they cleared the great trees with axe and bow-saw, turning life into timber. The forest is not what it was: only patches remain, and mankind, rootless and disconnected, is lonely in spirit.

But we know nothing of loneliness. We are all one in the forest; rock and root and branch and soil. The sky seeps into the ground, the trunks push up into the air. Flesh and wood alike rot into life; the plump grubs grow into young birds that falter on the edge of the nest and fall to feed the foxes. All things dissolve one into another. Without the whole, there is no life.

Man inhabits the dead world, where things live separate lives. Isolated, their souls rot inside this prison of their own making and fear pervades the earth. Some know this. They come here for comfort, like the girl. Cold comfort now.

Now she lies close to me, her flesh and mine almost touching.

Waiting for the only certain resurrection we know.

# The Cave

### Deborah Grice

Hang high in the heart's altar
that candle-flame for love that once
transcended the grey cave we have not outgrown.
Bellying dinosaurs that thrash our tails
and roar, outwitted.

I will lay down in the snow to die,
turn my ancient bones to ice.

Over-evolved, our tiny hands
make the machine spin
that threshes the whole world,
yet cannot hold down
one ounce of joy
beyond a single second,
fistful of ice dissolving.

The moon lights the mountainside;
you paint the blue enchantment,
the revolving clouds.
Yet within the caverned rock,
the unceasing drip
ends in stalactite
not fountain.

## Dangerous Cocktail

So let your brushes dry,
let mountain peaks be only themselves,
give willow bridges no story.
Let the heart weld to
unthinking granite,
kind in not being so, or otherwise.

The darkness holds no terror,
the cave no light.

Cover my body with broad brush strokes,
dissolve my bones in great washes of white.

# The Dauber

## Martin Mickleburgh

Audrey lost no time in branding me a cynic, and she should know, hailing from such a sneering tribe of misanthropes. I think she regarded me as a romantic for all of two weeks – though perhaps less: she has an easy way with concealment – and then the truth dawned: I was in it for the money. All around me my fellow students were ardent to the point of boredom, pledging eternal troth to the muse or the Great God Art (gold letters, outlined in red). All I wanted was to sharpen up my skills as a painter to the point where I could make a decent living from turning out portraits and landscapes to order. Lazy, you see. Physically, intellectually, morally and emotionally.

I had known from an early age that I had some small talent; I don't believe I was ever deceived – I always knew it was meagre fare, enough to get by on, enough to be amused with. And so, armed with such intellectual provincialism, I never thought to try my hand at anything else. I flunked everything at school with the exception of art, and it took all the string-pulling the dear mater could manage to find an art college willing to take on such a dead loss. Well, in the end it was Loughborough, hell-hole of the East Midlands. So far, so very far from Surrey.

It could have been worse: three years living off the state, and of course I met the beloved, Audrey Ellington, known to friend and foe alike as the Duke. She was studying physical education at the TT college, and she was most decidedly physical. Did I mention that there is one respect in which I am rather less than entirely lazy? No? Well, perhaps best left unsaid. Naturally a trainee teacher was not considered quite the done thing amongst us arty types, a bit shabby, if you like, a bit down-market. But, do you know, I found the old trout really rather endearing: she actually liked my daubing. I painted her portrait, a

## Dangerous Cocktail

month after we met, a violent purplish sort of rendering which she said reminded her of Francis Bacon. She was so sweet. Still is for that matter. Seventeen years have rather knocked the edges off the enthusiasm, but I still regard her with more than a modicum of fondness.

Which is more than I can say for her appalling kin. The very worst kind of new Northern money, hideously vain, slurping Moet like dandelion and burdock pop, reckoning their worth in BMWs and Rolex Oysters and those dreadful Jimmy what's-his-name shoes. I thought I'd descended into the bowels of some ghastly BBC2 comedy. Her mother – Iris – took an unwelcome shine to me: a bit like being thought well of by a hyena. She declared that I was just what the family needed, a bit of class. I shudder at the memory. She sequestered Aud's portrait and hung it in state over the living room fireplace – a nasty mock-Georgian affair that was straight from an MFI catalogue. I wore my embarrassment stoically and consoled myself with double helpings of Duke pie; I think Aud understood completely my need for condolence, and in time she grew to rather enjoy it. It gave her a sense of power.

In those early days, I often wondered quite why Aud had elected for teachering. With the amount of loot sloshing around the Ellington nest, she could just have stayed put and lived the good life without lifting so much as a finger. Two things decided otherwise.

The first was obvious enough: she had far too much physical energy for her own good. She was never happier than when she was charging up the side of some Lake District fell – with me hollering encouragement from a comfortable perch at lake-level – or running a half-marathon for some or other benighted charity. It was as if the fates had decided that she was to play the part of a furnace. Lucky old me to be on hand to toast my appendages as occasion demanded. The one thing she couldn't do was sit still.

The other reason didn't really surface for a few years. Aud was not given to gushing, down right taciturn if truth be told, so it took that long to wring it out of her. Thing is the old gannet had a conscience:

# The Dauber

couldn't bear to have the tribe roll in dosh without, as she saw it, returning something to the impoverished. So, with no great intellect to speak of but with a body determined on conflagration, physical education was the natural choice. No, I didn't see it either. At first. But she had a point: children liked her because she bounded about like Tigger on methedrin and because, having so few words, she never told them off. And she, in turn, doted on their approval. As neat a bargain as you could wish.

We got married two years after she finished at Loughborough. Deciding where to live caused our first major fight. I was all for a swift return to the bosom of the Home Counties: kick off the dust of the Midlands and never darken its portals again. But Surrey was just too far from Manchester for the Duke. Unlike me, she set some store by being a good and dutiful child. So we rowed about it for a month or more and then decided to compromise on staying right where we were, about half way between our respective home ranges. In one way at least, it was a most favourable choice: whenever we found each other unbearable, we never had to invent something to argue about.

We plumped for a riverside cottage in Zouch (anyone who thinks multi-culturalism is a modern phenomenon has only to consider our absurd place-names), with a garden and a golden retriever. Aud cycled into Nottingham each day to teach and I plunged into my career as painter by appointment to the muddle-classes and commenced growing fat. And happy. The one great benefit of belonging – at least by marriage – to the Ellington horde was that they had lots of friends who had more money than befitted them and who thought a portrait infinitely more upmarket than a photograph. I was delighted to indulge their opinions and relieve them of aforesaid spondulix. Needless to say, once my mother's set found out, they couldn't bear the thought of some upstart Northerners stealing a march on them in the small matter of furthering the career of one of their own. Commissions poured in.

I bought a little car and trudged up and down the M1 and the M62. I quite liked being on the open road, master of my own destiny, so to

## Dangerous Cocktail

speak. The only disagreeable thing was that, being cheek by jowl with one or other family, there was no opportunity for playing away from home. Not that that was a great inconvenience: once she'd got the hang of it, Aud never lost any of her energy or her sheer carnal delight in sex and was always happy to entertain my appetites. She did get lonely, poor thing, when I was away for more than a couple of nights. But I rather think that kept her, shall we say, hungry.

We settled into a feather-lined rut, Aud and me. She turned down promotions – 'have to keep things simple', she'd say – and I painted and inflated. I'd never been what you would call thin, but my weight stayed under control as long as I couldn't afford much food. All might have been well if our only income had been Aud's teaching and my daubing. But the blasted Ellingtons would insist on 'presents', dispensed without any particular occasion, a couple of thousand here, a couple of dozen there, 'just so as you can afford a few little luxuries'. I can hear you drooling from here: who wouldn't kill for such bountiful in-laws? The problem is, it's corrupting. Now don't run away with the idea that I'm some sort of anchorite at heart, or, worse, an acolyte of the protestant work ethic. But the thing is, if you don't earn it, you don't value it. So we frittered away our windfalls. The very first one was spent on a hilariously appalling cruise to Norway on a boat built to Noah's own blueprints, peopled by soaks and sharks and women with necks like turkeys, entertained by the sort that the Skegness Palace had expelled as being beneath its dignity. It rained continuously. Half the crew went down with some vile stomach infestation. The other half were permanently sea-sick. We drank and ate our way into oblivion.

Truth to tell, that's probably where the rot first manifested itself. I'd always been one for a good blow-out, never one to turn down a hillock of food. But that was always in the singular, occasioned by a wedding or a wake. On that wretched boat we ate continuously for seven days and seven long, intemperate nights. I took to waddling about with my trousers undone, clutching my belly. Aud grinned and grunted and shovelled away just as much as me and then burnt it all off by running

## The Dauber

round and round the deck in the pouring rain; and then came back for more. The old bump and grind was quite a strain, when we could manage it.

Bodies are so unfair.

That set the pattern for the next thirteen years: we ate like hogs when we could, Aud ran it off and I held on to it. Being fat was a disquieting experience: it seemed that everything slowed down, as if I was permanently wading through treacle. No more running up stairs in pursuit of an amorous Aud, no more sexual athletics or silly games of tag along the weir. Even walking the hound came to require a certain resoluteness of purpose. Worse was the way that I sometimes caught Aud looking at me as I got dressed, as if I were faintly malodorous, a thinly masked pig. Those looks had a dizzying effect, as if I was looking over the edge of a cliff whose base I couldn't make out. I consoled myself with more food.

And this is not to say that being fat was bereft of benefits. The thing is that fat people are curiously anonymous. We have a way of gliding through the world while the thin majority looks the other way: their only response to us is either barely veiled disgust or relentless indulgence of our humour. Fat people are supposed to be jolly. All our anguished utterances are mistaken for the sort of musings that pass for wit on the stand-up comedy circuit. I have to say that rather suited me: I could be as violently rude as I liked and people took it for farce.

Thirteen years. Ah me.

I often wonder if, had I not seen Emma Rush-Butter's exhibition, my body would have found some other means of sabotaging me. The truth is, you see, advantages or no, in the end I had come to think of it as the enemy. Stated baldly, is that not absurd? And yet I felt such a detachment from that fat carapace that I could think of it as not me; instead it was somehow other, inhabited but separate. The exhibition gave the lie to such nonsense.

I had known the Rush-Butter quite well at college, had even made a half-hearted attempt at waving the old willy at her, but she was far too

## Dangerous Cocktail

committed to The Great God (gold letters outlined in red) to be susceptible to something as earth-bound as sex. I never thought much of her art; no, let me be more honest: I always thought she was from the crap end of mediocre, going through the motions of art because some fool teacher had told her she had some talent. Her work was dreary, repetitive, utterly uninspired and uninspiring. And yet she was so lamentably earnest, determined that she would make a name for herself, convinced that she had the makings of a second Vincent. I found it all very entertaining while we shared the hell-hole, and then I forgot about her. Until the exhibition.

Aud and I had decided to take a day trip to the Smoke, so that she could have a shot at disposing of the latest act of largesse from the tribe and I could wander around and look at paintings. The thing is, you see, I actually *like* painting, and I like looking at what other people have made of it. It gives me a certain, almost carnal, glow to look at a Vermeer or a Turner and think of myself being, in no matter how small a way, part of the same rush to self-expression: a sort of hunger, if you will, to make marks on canvas that represent your own good self and nobody else. Oh I know I was low-grade stuff, a mere artisan, but I knew my own worth, knew what I could and couldn't do.

So, while Aud shopped I was wandering about one of those poky little galleries in Camden when I happened to notice a flyer announcing an exhibition by none other than the Rush-Butter, at the Tate Modern to boot. At first I thought I must be mistaken but I rapidly realised there could only be one Emma R-B, and a quick glance at her biog confirmed the worst. Dip.A.D. from Loughborough – she actually seemed to be proud of the fact. For reasons that I could not fathom at the time, my interest was immediately aroused to fever pitch: could she have actually come good despite all my worst imaginings? Could I have been so bone-headedly wrong about her? A taxi got me there in twenty-five minutes, and I fairly pounded up to the gallery; perhaps it was the pounding, combined with my rotundity, which set the whole ghastly business in train.

## The Dauber

I stood before her...no, I can't force myself to call them paintings; before her pictures, the old ticker going nineteen to the dozen and the old lungs heaving like a pair of ancient bellows. It was awful, truly, unremittingly awful. There was not a jot of fire or insight, not a single stroke of the brush that was in any way remotely original, no shred of humble craftsmanship, no passion, no hunger, no anguish, no joy, nothing nothing nothing. I began to laugh. I tittered. I sniggered. I smirked. I chortled. I hooted. I howled. I uttered great yelping guffaws. I clutched my sides in merriment. I laughed so much that I had to sit on the floor. Tears rolled down my cheeks and I laughed until no sound would come out. That was when my heart decided to have its own little joke.

It was like having a sack of cement dropped on my chest. I knew straight away – do we understand these things instinctively? – what was up, and half of me dropped, as if through a trap door, into that skull-bound terror which is the first, face-to-face confrontation with one's mortality. But the other half could not stop laughing; in fact the very notion of dying of laughing at Emma Rush-Butter's ghastly musings was just about the funniest thing that I had ever conceived. Apparently I giggled all the way to hospital in the ambulance.

In the hospital is where things finally began to get serious. It was after the initial chaos of yelling doctors and po-faced nurses and scans and injections and monitors and all the paraphernalia of pseudo-scientific nonsense that masquerades as modern health-care. However they had summoned her, Aud appeared at my bedside, very suitably concerned for my well-being in her precious, monosyllabic way and I was just beginning to relax into my new role of patient-who-has-jousted-with death when the heart consultant walked in.

The thing about Aud is that, whilst I have gone to hell in a hay-cart, the years have been bounteous to her. For me, it's her breasts, or rather it's that unique combination of weight and buoyancy that makes them jiggle so deliciously when she walks; perhaps for others it's the legs that go all the way up or the careless rotundity of her bottom; but for

## Dangerous Cocktail

me it's her breasts. Whatever, I have seen the admixture of breasts, legs and bottom – and a more than presentable phisog – all ripened and firmed by countless hours of physical exercise reduce veritable pillars of society to lolling tongues and eyeballs on stilts. Most amusing. The more so because Aud always seemed immune to such droolers, treating them all as she might our retriever, playful things with not much brains.

The consultant took one look at Aud and went into drool-induced-stupor. And she smiled at him. She smiled. Not a wifely 'I'm so concerned and trying to keep my end up' sort of smile, no, not that; it was a 'Well I wouldn't mind *you* in my knickers' smile, the kind she'd only ever bestowed on me before. The truth was as good as a second heart attack. I looked into a different kind of abyss. I knew, immediately and ineluctably, that I had lost her; that, if a fat indolent husband was tolerable, a fat, indolent, infirm husband was not.

The consultant was tall, greying, magisterial, slim. I didn't hate him – it would have been a damned fool idea in any case, seeing as I was rather dependent on his good offices – but I knew that he was the beginning of the end. The game was up.

I decided not to plead – that really would have been too demeaning. Instead I concocted an air of wounded forbearance which I put on every time she came home at two a.m. after yet another tryst. I lost count of how many there were; Aud lurched from monogamous wife to tart in one easy movement. I was appalled, at least as much with how little I knew of the true nature of the old bird as at her knickerless forays into the nobs' end of Nottingham society. Meantime, to add self-chastisement to a growing sense of self-loathing I gave up eating; I gave up drinking; I stopped smoking. I acquired a new retriever puppy to drive our moth-eaten ancient to distraction and, by way of getting my heart to put up or shut up, took to marching them both off on long forays into the surrounding countryside – the old one didn't last long: it slipped away one night, no doubt glad to be relieved of harassment at the hands of the newcomer and dreary route-marches alike.

# The Dauber

Aud left eventually, to move in with a life skills coach three years her junior, all suntan, gold-rimmed spectacles and teeth like tombstones. By that time I had lost all the weight I had put on since college days, and a bit more besides, I think. Problem was that my skin resolutely refused to notice that it now had less flesh to hold in place, and took to hanging off me like all-over jowls. It was so gloomily hideous that I couldn't bear to see myself in the mirror. And the possibility of eating my way back to contentment disappeared with Aud: her family dropped my like a red hot turd, and the presents and commissions went with them. Needless to say, now that there were no Northern upstarts to keep in their place, the mater's set retracted their attentions too. I found myself facing starvation.

I had never thought of myself as the kind of spineless modernist who suffers from depression; but, increasingly, I found myself suddenly sobbing for no immediate reason, or collapsing in black despair when I couldn't open a jar of instant coffee. I began to cease to notice the passing of days; or perhaps I should say that I began to regard daylight as the world's repeated and repeatedly failing attempts to make some inroads into the night. It all became as one.

The end came when, one slightly less than ghastly summer morning, driven by a kind of convulsion of the spirit, I took sketch pad and paints (watercolours!) down to the weir. I set myself up: portable easel, portable chair, little plastic pot of water, paints and brushes at the ready. And then nothing. I could not make a single mark. At first I thought This is preposterous, and forced my hand to dip a number eight into the water and slurp it around in Payne's Grey (a fine colour for a summer sky). It obeyed, if somewhat reluctantly, but then refused to make a single further movement. It would not take the brush anywhere near the paper.

If I had felt terror when my heart decided to have its little joke; if I felt a deeper terror when I realised I had lost Aud; then this was worse than either. If I could not paint what was there left? Nothing. Nothing. Nothing.

## Dangerous Cocktail

At first I was blankly stunned: at a stroke my eye had been eclipsed. And then my brain leapt into frenzied action, questioning, questioning, how had this happened, what did it mean, might it be permanent or was it just a little inner storm to be weathered. Could you die of an inability to paint?
Questioning.
Questioning.
Until it was getting near tea-time and there were no more questions.
I carefully stowed paints, brushes, water pot, paper and easel and then just sat looking at the weir. It happens so often: you get the answers when you stop thinking. It slowly came to me that it was not that I could not paint; rather it was that the world had nothing to say to me.
All those countless portraits and anonymous landscapes: I had thought that I was merely exercising my meagre talent, imposing *my* order, making *my* marks. But, sitting in the simmering half-silence by the weir, I realised that it wasn't really like that at all. And then the true vacuousness of Emma Rush-Butter's pictures hit me. I should have laughed out loud; it would have been the right and fitting thing to do. But I couldn't. I was consumed by such sorrow that I could only weep a little; and then I walked home, leaving all my painting gear to be found by whoever stumbled across it.

# Thirteen Minutes

## Peter Goodsall

"Yes, of course," I'd said.
"I'd be happy to," I'd said.
The cash was only a minor consideration. I'd be doing my bit, needed: required by society.

Inadequate strip-lights fail to haul the gloom from corners. Why paint a small room dark blue? To make it seem smaller? To introduce you to incarceration perhaps. Nothing is said, gazes avoided, the floor studied. After one of those interminable waits that lasts only minutes, we are called through and file down the still dingier corridor to the door, a beacon of brilliant white in a fog of deliberate shadows.

What if she chooses me? I swallow down the nagging fear, but the precursor of doubt remains. How could she? Don't be ridiculous! We don't even all look that alike. Well, we must look somewhat alike. Perhaps she only got a fleeting glimpse. Perhaps she only saw him from the side or back. Perhaps she's completely myopic.

Perhaps ... perhapses are smacked down by the demands of the events unfolding about me.

"Stand up, crouch down, number six do your jacket up."

Suddenly I'm back in the Air Force: a small gear turning only at the whim of others.

"Right, choose where you want to stand."

He's looking now. A nasty, evil, ferret of ... but he's not what I want him to be, what we all wish they were, those others, that different species that is one of us. A demon with the volcanic debris of a raging acne suppressed by a few days growth. Pale eyes wash over the line until the figure, with a smoker's hunch, too slight, too short, too ordinary, slots himself in, down the line to my right.

# Dangerous Cocktail

What if she chooses me? We all look so normal. Number three is the culprit. Number three fits in; do I? Choose number three. He's the one you want, not me. Nobody else, number three. Well, maybe one of the others, but number three, not me.

We're all wearing blue jackets. Now that my eyes are accustomed to the gloom I can see that the shades and styles of these garments vary more dramatically than I would have thought useful. But what do I know? I don't have anything like that required and have been given an ill-fitting hood-less anorak, musty and scratching. I shift the irritating collar that taunts my neck as if I'd just had a hair cut and the barber has been remiss with the wipes.

"Put your collar right back up number seven."

What if she chooses me? What does it matter if she does? They've literally pulled you in off the street. They can't possibly think that you had anything to do with whatever this is. You don't even know precisely what this is all about! What if they begin to suspect you because you've been identified? What if they investigate further; find that you were out at the time in question? What if you have no alibi?

What if ... what ifs are sunk by command.

"Stand up straight and face the front please gentlemen."

What if she chooses me? The lights dazzle. My eyes snap shut instinctively and they object, wincing, when I attempt to force them open again. The gloomy auditorium, filled with barely discernible seating, has been magicked away and I gawk at my own eyes. My stare travels up and down the reflect line expecting, hoping now, for clones but finding a variety that demands no surprise.

"Number seven look straight to the front please."

I wouldn't glance twice at any of them: no second thoughts, no quizzical frown would result. Isn't this what sentience is? An understanding of your own self? These faces would trigger not even a flicker of recognition. I am hoping for a lucent doppelganger but see merely a crowd.

## Thirteen Minutes

What if she chooses me? It's number three. *It's number three.* This is taking an eternity. What can be taking so long? Surely she either knows or she doesn't? Control breathing. Control breathing. Calm now. Calm.

"All turn to your left please. Hold your heads level," more militarism. "Turn to your right please ... turn back to face the front."

Pause. The pause is too long. Why is he keeping us here? A distant buzzer echoes.

"Numbers three and seven step forward please."

Dread words from deadpan bureaucrat.

Pause. Just the two of us now: me and other, clamped together in an embrace that vacuums all the air from between us. The pause is too long. Why is he keeping us here?

"Stand up straight."

The power of humanity is eviscerated by the scrutiny. Now I am little me, vulnerable before the anonymous glass. I can feel her eyes cutting away at the artificial layers of complacency, arrogance and certainty that we all use to shield ourselves. I can feel her trying to divine the truth: fact is born of supposition is born of allusion.

Small beads of moisture form on my temple. More is beginning to trickle down the back of my neck. Mustn't do this; it'll make you look guilty. Don't do this – she'll choose you. You never could act. You never could lie. Look at you: you're pathetic, sweating in case somebody makes an obvious mistake: debilitated while it's impossible for harm of any kind to come to you. Yes, but, what if she was adamant?

"Step back again. Thank you."

"Right, thank you for your time gentlemen, see the Desk Sergeant in a moment to return clothes and sign your attendance."

What if she has chosen me? I look at my watch. Thirteen minutes; unlucky for someone?

"Mister Jackson. Could you just come with me for a moment please? It's nothing to worry about, won't take a few moments."

## Dangerous Cocktail

"What about the coat?"
"That's ok, I'll take that. If you just follow me down this corridor then you can see the Desk Sergeant later."

# Café des Amis

## Patricia Golledge

There we are, just across the street, that's the place we are looking for – Café des Amis. Doesn't look anything special does it? The red paint is chipped and peeling, even down to the wood in places.

There is Monsieur le Patron. There, the little chubby man sweeping the step. I know, I know, if you asked a schoolboy to draw a typical Frenchman he'd draw Jacques there. All that is missing is a string of onions and a beret, although the latter is hanging on a peg just behind the kitchen door.

He likes to sweep the pavement outside his café every morning, not because it needs sweeping but so he can have a look at his neighbours. Le Clerc, the fishmonger on the right side is no problem, apart from the occasional smell. Although he has been rather cool towards Jacques since he started buying fish from an attractive widow down by the railway station. It's Le Clerc's own fault for charging Parisian prices for his coquilles.

Now the Romanas on the left – well, frankly, they scare the shit out of Jacques. Italians. Very shady. Come on, there is no way they could afford that new glossy green paint job on their Pizzeria on the custom they've had through the winter. But Monsieur Le Patron is at heart a pragmatist and Pizzeria Romana doesn't really pose any competition to his crepes and Ricard clientele; so he merely keeps a watchful eye.

Where has he gone now? Ah there he is in the Café, behind the little bar. That's where we'll find him later once the lunchtime trade is under way.

The spring sunshine is quite warm as the couple open the door of the Café des Amis. Jacques seems pleased to see them, doesn't he? He tries to usher them to the table in the window behind the geraniums

## Dangerous Cocktail

wintering there in their wind worn terracotta pots. Ah, no, how odd! They've chosen to sit at the little table under the newspaper rack at the back of the Café. Maybe they don't want to be seen. Jacques shrugs and flicks his tea towel over the table, as is his habit.

I wonder what they are ordering, perhaps the same as last time? You see they have been here before – four or five times now. Jacques is an expert on faces. You only have to step foot in the door twice and you're filed away in the card catalogue that is his brain. They must be in a hurry. They've only ordered a carafe of rose. Do you think it's a bit early for that? Remember this is La Belle France.

Jacques' got a real soft spot for these two. He's a real old romantic. Not that you'd believe that if you saw Helene, his wife. She's very scary. But that'll have to wait until later. Jacques believes in Un Grand Passion – with capitals. He thinks he sees that in these two. How marvellous it must be to have such a passion for each other that you look really miserable. Shall we take a closer look at them?

They could almost be French. Their clothes are immaculate, expensive but timeless. He is in slacks and sweater. She wears dark jeans with striped fitted shirt and contrasting scarf at her neck. Her auburn hair is sleek, shiny; simply cut. But it's her companion who is attracting the most attention in the Café. He's very dark, older than his first impression and muscular. He is definitely a man's man. Jacques looks round the café; all his other customers are watching this handsome virile specimen, who stares so intently into the green eyes of his companion, his hand gripping her wrist tightly.

Jacques fantasies that they are having an affair. No wedding bands. He checked the last time they paid the bill although they do glance furtively around every time the door opens. If they are having illicit afternoon romps they are incredibly discreet, unlike that pig Duvall. Mon Dieu, last year he had the nerve to parade his scantily dressed Romanian tart in this very café, pawing and slobbering over her, when six months earlier he had hosted his wife's sixtieth birthday party here.

## Café des Amis

He had even sidled up to Jacques, pushed twenty francs across the marble counter and whispered,
"Hey, mon ami, how about we use your Maman's old flat upstairs for half hour?"
Jacques had spluttered, chasing them out, just stopping short of taking the broom to the pair of them. He wasn't sure what offended him most, the disrespect to his poor dead mother's memory, the fact that Duvall only wanted it for half an hour; or that it was only a paltry twenty francs. Helene had been so furious when she heard. She called Duvall's wife immediately. On returning home he was met with an empty bank account and a whack on the head with a cast iron skillet.
The big dark man is looking around, watch, he's trying to get Jacques attention. But Jacques is picturing Duvall's wife and her skinny sister spending all that cochon's money at the racetrack at Deauville.
"Ah, monsieur?"
Did you see that? Jacques actually jumped off the stool then? The voice that called him is strong, deep, and thick. As he reaches the table Jacques is pretty sure that the man is not French. Yes, the accent is good but he is too broad, maybe too virile. He doesn't have the suave style of a true Frenchman. Jacques likes the look of him – up close Jacques is sure the couple are diplomats from over the border in Geneva. It is a good hour and a bit away and though thronged with tourists in the summer Annecy is quiet in spring. They wouldn't be seen here. Oh espionage -Jacques come on pull yourself together!
"La meme chose?"
They nod and Jacques gets another carafe of rose and sighs loudly, loudly enough for the rest of the Café to hear. The old regulars like Martin Parnet smile. That's the elderly chap sitting in the window, he's the man that made Jacques move his "crepes emporter" sign up the window a bit because it was obstructing his view of the street and canal. Helene had gone crazy because he's sat at the same table for thirty years you'd think he'd be fed up with the view. Jacques had said nothing but had moved the sign.

# Dangerous Cocktail

Now look I've gone off on a tangent again. We were examining the young foreigners. Oops I think she might be crying. What is he saying to her?

"Fucks sake, Cath. Will you pull yourself together?"

"I didn't think it would end like this Frank. Frank?"

He is staring over her head into the street, "What did you expect? You've done your job and can go. That's it."

"Are you sure, it's as easy as that Frank?" She runs a finger along the inside of his wrist.

His smile does not quite reach his eyes. He gently removes her hand from his arm.

"What did you have in mind, some mad passionate sex out there in the side alley? You're not that irresistible, you know."

She laughed coyly but stopped abruptly as two stocky men in dark suits approach the table.

Jacques seems confused, doesn't he, but he hangs back sensing that they are not here for the lunch-time specials. The girl seems angry now; her voice is raised.

"Frank, what is this? I thought you lot were lifting the leak today? I worked my arse off as your informer, and put my reputation on the line. Does this mean its not happening?"

Frank motions the men to sit at the next table, and imperceptibly waves Jacques away.

"No, its happening, but we know who was providing the information to the Syrians and it wasn't that poor Registry clerk, though God knows he must have been tempted considering the amount of debt he was in. It was someone with more sinister motives, someone who was playing a controlling game and who thought they'd got the better of us and the Security Services ... but you know that?"

Jacques is mesmerised by the change in atmosphere. Goodness, he is so entranced that he almost dropped the glass he was drying. Is that a siren outside, yes it's the Gendarmerie screeching to a halt outside.

## Café des Amis

Frank stands, taking Cathy by the arm,

"Cath, times up. Let's go."

Jacques approaches the man

"Eh monsieur?"

The man shrugs his shoulders and apologises for the disruption. As they head towards the door flanked by the Gendarmerie, Jacques picks up the empty carafe and glasses, quickly and follows them out of the Café.

Jacques stands on the street and watches the cars speed off in the direction of the motorway. He is dumbfounded. He was right. Espionage. That pretty young thing selling her country's secrets – *incroyable!* He could have sworn there had been passion in the air.

Martin Parnet beckons him over to his table, the only one now occupied. Jacques has a quick look to check that Helene hasn't sneaked in and goes over to his table. This time he's got an extra glass and the bottle of Ricard with him, and he flips over the sign on the door to Ferme.

So I think that's where we'll leave them, doing what they do best gossiping about the clientele but today they have something substantial to get their teeth into. Tomorrow may not be so exciting.

# Traitors!

## Alyson Heap

Only my hands hold the secret of my age;
Traitors.
My face is pampered and protected from the truth.
My hair is too long tinted
To remember its roots.
My legs can joyously pump up hills,
Protected by a fake tan preservation order.
(My feet are just glad of the exercise.)
My calcium enriched bones are far too strong
To give in under interrogation.
They hold up well under pressure.
My breasts can request support at any time.
Only my hands know the truth;
Traitors.
They have been gossiping with my neck.

# Crossing Point

## David Mills

The bridge dominated the landscape, its arches striding across the valley, giving shelter from the rain, shade from the sun and a home to thousands of creatures. Its strong back no longer did the work it was built for, the wagons of coal having stopped when the colliery was closed; the carriages filled with faces disappearing when Dr. Beeching brought down his axe. It no longer flexed under the weight of two trains speeding past each other, instead it just stood there stiff and unmoving, a monument to times past.

Today it had felt feet upon its back, no great weight for its shoulders, no pressure for it to withstand, just a feeling that something was crawling upon it. It welcomed visitors who would wonder at the vistas visible from its shoulders, marvel at the thin ribbon of silver water at its feet that they knew to be an un-fordable river and wonder at the ingenuity of the craftsmen that had bonded the millions of bricks so carefully into place.

But they normally came on foot, occasionally on wheels. Not like the wheels of the past, now they are soft wheels that mark its surface. The marks are only temporary: they are gone in not much more relative time than the marks left by the visitors' fingers upon each others skin. The last visitors though were different.

The report had come from a walker; exercising with a dog in the early morning half light. There appeared to be a body hanging from the old viaduct.

The viaduct used to be part of one of the many East-West rail links that had snaked their way across the country prior to the nineteen-

## Dangerous Cocktail

sixties, but now proved an irresistible draw to others. Although not officially part of any footpath network, it was now used, as it had been when the trains were there, as a shortcut between the villages of Longford and Easton, approximately twelve miles apart by road and less than two using the viaduct.

It was also well used by couples with nowhere else to go and thrill seekers who liked to attach ropes to the old structure and leap off it.

The old structure had felt all of these things and more in its long years standing sentinel over the landscape.

Today the viaduct could feel something different. There was weight, not a great weight, but a weight hanging beneath one of its great arches. It was like one of the people that came and jumped off, but this was different, this weight was not moving, there was no bounce. It just hung there, the only movement caused by the wind. Always there was wind. Many days and nights there was only the wind to keep it company, the wind and the animals that hid within the recesses of the structure, where the old bricks had crumbled and fallen to the valley floor below.

There was something wrong, it didn't know what, but things did not feel right.

They had come in the night. It knew it was night, because there were only the owls hooting their conversations through the woodland and foxes barking their presence across the valley. It knew they had come because it could feel their wheels marking it. It could hear the whispered voices, it could feel the rope being attached through a culvert and it felt itself give as the weight went over its parapet. Usually the visitors who came to jump off it visited in daylight. The viaduct felt something was wrong: the rope had no give and it felt the wheels leaving and something scrape its side, but the weight still hung from it.

All night it hung there. The viaduct couldn't understand; this had

## Crossing Point

never happened before. Then as the night leaked into day the visitors began to come, slowly at first but then more and more.

Today it had much company, many vehicles were on its back and crossing its shoulders but it was still strong. It carried the weight as if it was no more than an additional few of the bricks that created its arches. They clustered around its base peering up at the object that slowly twisted in its suspension. They searched through the undergrowth at its base, beating back bushes and brambles that clustered around its piers, finding only the detritus left by the many visitors. The weight was removed and its surface probed. The viaduct had not had this much attention since the day the first train passed across its back.

Then as slowly as they had come they dispersed, leaving behind only the stench from their vehicles and the measly scratches from their puny wheels. The viaduct was left alone once more, sentinel of the landscape. But there was a secret that it had not relinquished. There had been other visitors through the nights. These visitors had not climbed onto the broad shoulders, but had footled around at the base of its arches. They had removed some of the bricks and secreted things within the structure.

The viaduct could not tell this though, nor could it point to the place. Nor did it know that the hanged man was one of those that had hidden the items within its walls. All it knew was that some things had occurred here that weren't as they should be; all it could hope for was that somehow it would bear testimony to these events as it bore its silent witness to the past.

At first there were many more visitors, all of them wondering and peering over the parapets to try and work out if this was the place where 'it' had happened. But the numbers soon declined, cold wind and isolation soon overcame the curiosity that had brought them to this isolated spot; that and the fact that apart from the vistas from its parapet there was nothing to see. Until one night, when there had been

## Dangerous Cocktail

no visitors for over a week, in the depths of darkness someone was approaching the structure. It could feel the faintest of vibrations caused by their footfalls. It could feel the faint pressure from their hand upon its walls, the merest hint of heat permeating through to its massive heart.

It could feel the fingers probing its ancient pointing, grasping and groping for any brick that might have worked itself loose. The bridge knew which ones were loose, it knew where things were hidden but had no way to direct anyone to the spot and somehow it didn't think that it would show this one anyway. It got the feeling that this wasn't the best of people, after all it didn't get many night-time human visitors, and those that did come usually came on wheels, not feet.

The visitor left without finding what he was searching for. Once again the great bridge was alone.

Time passed: where once the structure was able to mark its passing by the wagons that crossed its back, now it could only count the passages of darkness and daylight, and as they passed so the fabric of the bridge slowly disappeared: mortar falling from the pointing, the bricks losing their texture as they slowly turned to dust. As water leeched through it added tiny stalactites to the underside of the arches and made the streaks on its columns ever larger.

Then they came again, in the darkness, but this time instead of climbing upon the structure's shoulders they dug at its feet, burying something there, and then, as they had arrived, so they left.

It wasn't long before once again the bridge had visitors milling around the base of its buttresses. Again they dug, but this time in daylight. Again tape was draped around the structure and across the landscape. The men that came leant against its columns and tilted their heads, losing themselves in the height of its arches. The bridge liked to think that people were still awestruck by its presence within the landscape, still marveling at the skill and ingenuity of its builders.

## Crossing Point

A large heavy object was dragged slowly from the ground, placed into one of the vehicles, which then slowly disappeared over the horizon followed by the others; once more leaving the marks of their passing as a stain on the landscape.

Again it happened, the curious and the morbid, meandering by many means to the old structure stretching across the valley. They came to gaze and gawp, to stand and stare at the places that they had seen the headlines. They came to see for themselves the hauntings that were being reported. And again as they came so they slowly dribbled to a stop.

The bridge, alone in its landscape, slowly felt itself melding once more into the ground from which it had grown all those years ago. Its bricks were becoming more friable and everyday the pile of reddish-brown dust grew imperceptibly thicker: the mortar holding its soldier courses in place was no longer proving to be the unbreakable bond that had been its strength over the centuries. Then for the bridge the unthinkable happened; the early spring sunshine was warming its shoulders as some early day-trippers exercised across them. The winter damp that every year penetrated deeper into the structure was just beginning to withdraw. One of the trippers leant upon the parapet to view the fuzzy colours of the spring flowers below that were sprouting forth like the fluff on an adolescent's face, when the stones gave way. The tripper and stones fell to the valley floor.

For a third time they flocked to the bridge, but this time they swarmed over and under it, they poked and prodded rather than teased and caressed. Then finally they strung wires that cut and scratched across its shoulders and placed notices on the giant legs and then, as they left, once more it felt alone with only the night creatures to keep it company, only the small things that dwelt within the holes and creases in its aging brickwork. Only the small things and several larger ones.

The wind did not make it sway, the rain trickled through its pores,

## Dangerous Cocktail

the sun baked it dry once more, yet still it stood sentinel over the valley, the men that had condemned it not returning. Day turned to night turned to day in a never ending cycle, the bridge no longer feeling useful. Then they came.

Over the horizon it appeared at first, a prehistoric machine with long neck and steel jaws, followed by its army of ant-like workers. The jaws bit into the bridge, tearing lumps from its once proud structure. The bridge let out a silent scream and as the drills began to pound into the legs that had supported it so faithfully for so long it knew the end was not far away.

When it came the end was swift, there was a loud noise, the bridge felt its ancient joints shatter and with a last exhalation of dusty breath all that remained of the magnificent crossing was a large dusty pile of broken bricks, mourned over only by the circling rooks cawing in their confusion, and a group of workman in yellow helmets who stared at the one final secret that sat glowing in its golden glory atop and amongst the pile.

# Sir Willoughby

## Peter Owen

Those familiar with the West Wallingford 'Gentlemen's Members Club' will be saddened to hear of the sudden mysterious passing of club treasurer Major General Sir Willoughby Theodore Jennifer Barking-Madd MC-DVD-IBS.

There are, according to Inspector Throbe of the local constabulary, 'some unfathomable mysteries' surrounding Sir Willoughby's final moments. The deceased had been discovered by his loyal butler 'Gribble' lying face down in the drawing room, a cigar shaped object, said by 'Gribble' to be making a "strange whirring noise", protruding from, and here I quote Inspector Throbe, a particular orifice currently being probed by Sergeant Gaylord of the 'Unusual Practices Division'. Apparently, and 1 again quote the Inspector, Sir Willoughby had of late been suffering 'severe bouts of peculiar goings on and utterances, bordering on lunacy', following the disclosure by club auditors of unaccountable discrepancies with regard to the Christmas drinks fund.

The lights burned long into the evening at Sir Willoughby's residence, the crumbling decadence that was Fa'hartingbells Manor, as family and friends gathered to pay their respects to Sir Willoughby, who had been laid out on a sequined cloth by the ever loyal 'Gribble'. Inspector Throbe had been summoned and on arrival he and his officers were requested by 'Gribble' to take off their uniforms as a mark of respect. 'Gribble' then joined the scantily clad officers in a slow march with truncheons reversed along the dimly lit corridors and up the oak-panelled stairway to the darkened room where Sir Willoughby lay with Nurse Simpkins who was trying to administer the kiss of life. An emotional Inspector Throbe led the officers in a subdued version of the hymn 'Jesus wants me for a sunbeam' as they stumbled around the

## Dangerous Cocktail

candle-lit room and back down the stairs to the east wing to reconsider their position.

Meanwhile 'Gribble' began embalming the immobile form of his master with perfumed oils and, in a touching display of devotion, was frantically attempting to make certain adjustments to Sir Willoughby's 'body language' before the onset of rigor mortis.

A memorial play-let was hastily penned by the eccentric bushy haired playwright Alphonse Mandolino to be acted out in the great hall on the eve of Sir Willoughby's funeral. A select group of thespians from the 'Gentlemen's Members Club' and the constabulary's light opera section were chosen. Inspector Throbe was offered a small part which he immediately dispatched for an autopsy before accepting the role of a 'trembling' policeman which he initially rejected on the grounds that the word 'trembling' could easily be misconstrued to be of a seductive nature. In the opening scene Lord Belshaft, playing the villainous knight Sir Esmond of Esmond, is seen striding across the stage, an implement of Amazonian proportion protruding from beneath his scant garb drawing gasps of disbelief from the small audience. A duel then takes place between Sir Esmond and an unwelcome interloper played by Sergeant Gaylord. The duo leap around the makeshift stage with great athleticism, brandishing their enormous weapons with an assured maturity to the accompaniment of ancient music provided by the 'Ernie Entwistle Ensemble' featuring 'Gribble' on first violin. The music rises to a crescendo as the interloper (Sgt. Gaylord) eventually stabs Sir Esmond (Lord BelShaft) who falls to the floor in a very contrived manner crying "thou hath done for me". The curtain is then lowered and the ensemble switches to a selection of mediaeval banquet music, while it remains clear to the audience from the aggressive movements of the curtain and occasional bumps and groans that the action continues unabated. When the curtain is hoisted once more the play has moved into the twentieth century and Inspector Throbe has taken centre stage as the 'trembling' policeman. A moment passes before a country yokel (Constable Tompkins) enters and attacks the 'trembling'

Sir Willoughby

policeman with a large stick at which point the curtain comes down once more to the sound of the ensemble playing out time with 'God Save the Queen' to which all were encouraged to join in.

The cast emerged from behind the curtain to great applause and calls of "go forth and prosper" – 'erectabli de superbo' and 'Sir Willoughby lives', the audience finally making their way to the drawing room to feast on hot pheromones, cheese bites and freshly gathered seaweed baps before retiring to their rooms describing the play variously as 'quite' – 'enormously enormous' and 'never before seen the like'.

In the early hours of the morning the guests were disturbed by the purring engine of a taxi parked at the manor gates and were surprised to see a hooded figure swathed in blankets being escorted by Nurse Simpkins and 'Gribble' to the waiting taxi which then drove off at great speed, the hooded figure clearly seen waving from behind the rear window.

The funeral service took place behind closed doors, those in attendance commenting on the apparent lightness of the coffin as it was borne by Nurse Simpkins and 'Gribble' to the family crematorium. The ancient dance of Saint Anguin was performed by all present and the traditional Celtic/Germano verse 'transvesty bachichmienadildoh' recited by those who could remember the words.

Television's favourite Reverend Mickey 'bojangles' Dell placed a garland of violets on the head of the loyal 'Gribble' who immediately collapsed and couldn't be aroused until Nurse Simpkins returned with a large brandy and a chocolate profiterole.

A séance was conducted in the evening at the behest of Lady Belshaft, who claimed to possess great psychic powers. A table and chairs were prepared and the small party of remaining guests, including Lord and Lady Belshaft, Nurse Simpkins, 'Gribble' and Inspector Throbe, sat together and linked hands in a bid to channel their combined energies towards the world of spirit, hoping for a link with Sir Willoughby.

## Dangerous Cocktail

Lady Belshaft's face began to contort in a frightening manner, her body teasing as if under great strain, strange unworldly noises heard escaping from deep within the bowels of her ample frame. 'Gribble' noticeably paled and shifted uncomfortably, claiming he could sense 'psychic breezes' drifting across from Lady Belshaft's direction engulfing him in an unpleasant odour that Lady Belshaft insisted proved beyond all doubt the presence of an ethereal substance. Nurse Simpkins suddenly sat bolt upright claiming to have made contact with a large barn owl called Remus who had been a Zulu warrior in a previous life, while Lord Belshaft broke down in tears accusing Lady Belshaft of exposing herself to the delivery driver from Waitrose.

Inspector Throbe emerged from his trance like state saying he'd just seen a mouse run across the floor towards Lady Belshaft but didn't know if there was any significance in that, because he'd seen a mouse before and hadn't been at all phased by it, though he would make 'certain enquiries' and if needed call in 'the lads from Rentokil'. Lady Belshaft then concluded it was time to close the circle because she could feel one of her funny turns coming on, stating that it was quite likely anyway that because of the distance involved and the possible shortage of celestial chariots Sir Willoughby hadn't yet arrived in the world of spirit.

Inspector Throbe sniffed and offered to make the cocoa.

# Enoch and Claude

## Martin Mickleburgh

A fter Mother died, I decided to go to Paris.

It wasn't much of a funeral, I knew she wouldn't want the fuss, just a few friends. So I invited Edgar and Simon. Edgar's never been the same since that run-in with a shunter; half scared him to death it did and he doesn't talk much any more, which is no great loss seeing as he didn't talk that much before. Anyway, he was taking the dog to be spayed so he couldn't make it. And Simon was giving a talk to the Coseley branch of the National League for the Defence of Steam Enthusiasts that evening and had to mug up his speech so he couldn't come either. I asked Mrs. Fearnihough, her from the corner shop, seeing as how she and Mother used to natter so much, but she had a bad leg. I thought of asking the doctor but I reckoned she might have been a bit uncomfortable at the funeral of one of her own patients – not exactly good for business, if you see what I mean. And of course our Sheila couldn't make it; doing some course in database design, so she said. It's always some course or a conference or a management meeting with our Sheila. Must be seven years since I've seen her. Wonder if she's got fat. So it was just the vicar and me in the end.

Of course I'd made far too many sandwiches; Mother always said I was half way to useless in the kitchen. They all sat there on their plates, turning up at the edges. The vicar didn't stay long: I think he managed one ham and one egg and cress. Didn't say much either, just kept looking around him at our living room and making this odd sucking noise on his teeth. In the end I was glad when he went.

## Dangerous Cocktail

I don't hold with this grieving nonsense they keep talking about on the telly but I wanted to be on my own, just to feel what it was like with Mother not there. The strangest thing was not hearing her voice, which is odd when you think about it because she didn't say much towards the end anyway. It's not like her voice suddenly stopped: it just sort of faded away. She didn't say a single word on the day she died; she was wide awake, right to the end, right 'til the last breath, but she just looked about her, staring at things as if she was seeing them for the first time, the way that babies do. But I don't think she was feeling like a baby, not surprise or wonder: I think she was terrified, too terrified to speak a single word. I know how she felt: when I used to hide from Father in the coal shed, I used to be terrified like that, like you just want everything to stop, you just want one more breath, just one more, before something terrible happens.

So I stood in the middle of the living room and just listened. At first I thought it was dead silent. But then I started noticing little clicks and wheezes and sort of faint grunting noises. The house, talking to itself. No, that's daft, that's fanciful. How Mother used to hate anything fanciful. Never read a novel in her whole life, hated the idea of going to the pictures – I can hear her now: 'What? Go and watch a bunch of stupid bloody Yanks prancing about and preening themselves? Over my dead body.' I'm not sure she knew the difference between Riverdance and Titanic. But she didn't hold it against me when I went to see a film every year or so, said I should indulge myself once in a while even if it was doing something daft. I remember thinking, standing there in the living room, that that's what I'd miss most: her keeping me in order, not letting me get too far above myself, not letting me go off on some mad adventure that could only end in tears.

It was like that with the trains.

I blame Edgar for it all. It started with him asking me if I'd help selling tickets on the Severn Valley, just in the ticket office at Bridgnorth. Well, I didn't know he had anything to do with the Severn Valley: right close is Edgar. Anyway I asked Mother and she went into

## Enoch & Claude

an A1 flap about it, making out Bridgnorth was only just this side of Siberia and what would happen if I fell under a train, who'd look after her and what would Mrs. Fernihough say about her being such a bad mother as to let such a thing happen to her only son. It took a day or so but I eventually calmed her down. Mind you, reminding her I was forty-three and quite capable of looking after myself proved to be a bit of a mistake. I remember her saying just as I was leaving the first time "Enoch", she said, "you'll regret this, you mark my words."

It was alright for the first couple of months. I spent most Sundays in the ticket office, at first with Edgar, but as soon as he reckoned I'd got the hang of it, on my own. Never did find out where he bunked off to. Always came back wearing a grin to shame the Cheshire cat. Anyway, I reckon it would have all been just fine if I hadn't met Simon. He was a driver, you see, trained up so he could actually drive the steam trains. He was the same age as me and lived with his mother too. We hit it off right away. Before I knew it, he had me on the footplate all the way to Stourport and back. Me! Riding in the cab of a steam engine! I was that made up. Edgar had never done the like of it and he was jealous as sin and threatened never to talk to me again; like I said, that would have been no great hardship, seeing as how little he talked anyway. But I knew Edgar of old; I knew he'd come round in time, and, sure enough, within six months he was grunting monosyllables at me again. Meantime Simon had got me a job in the sheds, cleaning the engines. And he taught me all about them.

I'd never been much interested, not really interested, in anything before. I was a dead loss at school; Father said I'd flunk breathing if there was an exam in it. And Sheila was always so good at everything: she could make me look stupid just by standing next to me. I reckon it was down to the interest. See, if you're not interested in a thing, how are you ever going to find the inclination to get good at it. And I was just never interested. Until Simon started telling me about steam locomotives. It was like a light going on in my head; not a piddly little light bulb, a bosting great searchlight, shining into all the corners that

## Dangerous Cocktail

had never seen the light of day. Within a few weeks I was immersed in valves and pistons and pressures and hammer-blow and bogies and drivers and God know what besides. I was that happy! Mother kept asking "What are you wearing that silly smirk for?" I knew better than to tell her.

Even then it would probably have turned out only mildly disastrous if it hadn't been for the King from Tyseley. They were bringing it over for a bit of a run: in Tyseley you can only go up and down the yard, quarter of a mile at most. Keeping a King like that is like keeping a tiger in a dog-kennel. Anyway, it was arriving mid-week, so as to keep the crowds down until they'd had it up and down the line a time or two and got the feel of everything. I had to see it arriving. I just had to. I had to be there so I could say afterwards "I was there the day the King came". Problem was it was a Tuesday. I lay await all the Monday night, fretting and thrashing about in the sheets, knowing what I was going to do the next day and knowing it was wicked and knowing I'd do it anyway. I did it. I took the day off work. Didn't say nothing, just didn't turn up.

Oh that King! That great and glorious King! Like poetry it was, poetry in steel, everything polished to perfection, gleaming and hissing as it sat in the siding waiting for its first run. I think it must have been love.

Mr. Timkin didn't think so. No matter how I tried to tell him what wonderful piece of engineering a King is, all he could see was how I'd missed a day's work and Lolly and Susan had had to work twice has hard and there'd been queues at the pumps and drivers getting agitated and how, much more of that, and he'd lose his job.

It was Simon that finally did for me. He said "Why don't you come for a ride on the footplate when we take the King out on Friday?" I tell you, Satan himself couldn't have whispered sweeter perdition. Off I went, and when I turned up at the garage on Saturday Mr. Timkin asked my why I was grinning and swooning like a silly tart, and then

## Enoch & Claude

he handed me my cards. No explanation, no goodbyes. I'd had that job for thirteen years.

Mother went into orbit. I took to the coal shed.

-oOo-

I never thought then that that would be my last job, but that's how it's turned out: living on the social ever since. All our little treats had to go: the bars of Twix on a Sunday from the paper shop, the Jersey gold-top on Fridays, new socks twice a year.

She never let me forget it. Her last day alive was the only single day in the fifteen years before she died when she didn't remind me of what a mess I'd made of it all and how useless I was and how she'd warned me it would happen. What could I say? She was right: I'd never shown much promise of amounting to anything much and now I'd just proved I was never going to amount to anything at all.

I never got used to it. You'd think you would, hearing the same thing over and over, day in, day out. I suppose the problem was that at least while I had the job, I didn't have to listen to her all day; afterwards there was just no getting away from her, except when I went to the social to pick up the benefits or to Tesco's to get the week's shopping. And before, I used to talk to our whippet, Goliath, but he died a year after the job went and then there was no-one.

Every Christmas I met up with Edgar and Simon for a re-union at the Stoat and Forceps. I saved ten pence a week all year round so I could afford to buy a pint or two; even then I couldn't afford a round: we bought our own. Mother would start her airating a good month before the event, telling me what a rotten conniving pair they were, dragging me off the straight and narrow and then leaving me to it. On and on she'd go. But seeing it was only once a year, I put up with it. She did have a point, after all. There was always the coal shed when things got really bad.

## Dangerous Cocktail

About a week after she died, I got a letter from a solicitor, asking me to attend the reading of Mother's will. I never knew she'd even made a will and I couldn't think what she could possibly have to leave to anyone anyway. Turned out to be five thousand pounds. Five thousand! You could have knocked me sideways with week old kipper. And she left it all to me. Sheila didn't turn up for the reading and she didn't get a penny. I have to say I did feel a bit guilty. When she phoned up about six weeks later and I told her about it she just laughed and said "Well you'll soon blow that and then you'll be back where you started", and put the phone down.

At first I couldn't think straight: so much money! I must have gone about in a daze for a month or more. And then I started to think of all the Twix bars and gold-top and new socks I'd had to do without and how embarrassing it was to have to buy your own drinks at a reunion and I started to feel just a bit hard done by. She could have used a bit of it at least. Five thousand pounds is twelve thousand Twix bars which is one a week for two hundred and forty years. But then, she'd left it all to me, as if she was trying to make up for something.

I spent days on end dreaming about all the things I could do with it. Simon soon put me straight about how much a King would cost and anyway where would I keep it. I thought of buying a new bicycle, but the old one was still going strong except for the gears so what good would a new one be?

And then Edgar said Why don't you do something really mad and go to Alaska? Well I was quite taken with the idea: I'd never done anything really mad in my whole life. But Alaska seemed a bit far, so I said What about Blackpool but Edgar said that was silly so we settled on Paris. You can get there by train, you see, none of this flying malarkey. I went to the local travel agent in Canal Street and they found me a nice little deal, five nights for three hundred pounds in a little hotel near the Arc Dee Triumph.

I'd never stayed in a hotel before but they were very kind and spoke an odd sort of English, bit like Geordie, so we got on just fine. They told

## Enoch & Claude

me all the places I'd want to see and where to find the metro and what to do if a John Darm waves at you to get out of the road. So there I was, a stranger in Paris in the Spring. I did the Sane and Verse Aye and the Eyefull Tower and Nottrer Dam and the Twee Lurry and Mon Martrer and Napolaynion's tomb and I walked around and had coffee on the pavement – can't ever see them doing *that* in Bilston – and even drank a glass or two of wine.

By the third day I'd done everything and I was at a loose end. Then the maid on the front desk at the hotel, who knew I liked trains, said why didn't I go to this museum, the Musay Dorsy that was converted from an old station. Well I jumped at the idea and off I trotted, map in hand so I could find it.

It wasn't much of a station, not like Snow Hill, but beggars can't be choosers so in I went. I thought that when she'd said museum she meant it would be full of railway stuff, but instead it was paintings, hundreds of the things, plastered over every bit of available wall space. I was that disappointed, I was all for turning round and walking out; but I'd paid my money so I thought the least I could do was wander around.

Paintings all look the same to me, so I pretty soon stopped looking at them and started watching the people instead. You can't do that in Bilston; folk get pretty upset pretty quickly if they think you're staring at them. But in the museum, no-one seemed to mind much. So I ended up in this one room, sitting on a wooden bench in the middle of the room watching all these Japanese tourists filing through, and just about every one of them stopped in front of these five paintings on the wall and took a picture with their digital cameras and then moved on. Didn't stop to look at the paintings, just snap, flash, and then on to the next one. Well I was a bit puzzled by this. Why come all the way from Japan to take a picture of a picture without looking at it? Seemed mad to me. But I sat and watched them for about an hour or two, until it was getting close to chucking out time and there was only me and an old woman sitting looking at these five paintings; I hadn't been able to

## Dangerous Cocktail

see them properly for all the tourists, but now I could see they were all of the same scene, the porch of a church. They looked sort of odd and washed out: all the shadows were blue instead of black. I looked at them for a while and then I stood up and walked over for a closer look.

And then the strangest thing happened. As I walked up to them, they sort of dissolved; I can't think of another way to put it. One minute there was a church, all solid stone and shadows and sun, and the next it was gone and there were just these little spots of colour, thousands and thousands of them, all different ones right next to each other. I backed away and the church came back, walked forward and it disappeared again. The old woman must have been watching me do this and she came over and said Say Clawed Monnay. Well I don't understand a word of French so I thought she was telling me not to be such a fool, but she smiled and pointed to the sign by the door: Claude Monet. It was the painter's name. I said 'Oh, ta,' or something like that and she must have realised I was English because she said 'It's the cathedral at Rouen.' He painted them all at the same time, moving from one to another as the light changed. I stepped back and then I could see it: they were done at different times of the day, you could tell by the light and the shadows. She smiled at me and then left me to it.

I just couldn't make it out: how could you make something real and solid out of those little dots of colour; and how had he painted them? When I looked really close there were more colours in a square inch than I could count; hundreds of them there were.

Backwards and forwards I went: colour, church, colour, church. I tried to see if there was an in between where it was neither one or the other; I tried standing close but half-closing my eyes; I tried looking sideways on, from the far side of the room, over my shoulder. I couldn't see it: I couldn't see how he'd joined all the dots up to make a building.

Eventually they came and chucked me out, but I went back first thing the next morning, before the tourists arrived and just sat and looked. Even when the place was awash with Japanese and Australians, I just sat and looked, catching a glimpse of the paintings every now

## Enoch & Claude

and then as they moved past. Sitting there, I found myself thinking of him as Claude, a bloke you might meet in the Stoat and Forceps, instead of Claude Monet the great painter. By the time they chucked me out at the end of the second day I still hadn't got it and there was only one day of my holiday left, so the next morning I was beginning to feel a bit desperate and I thought I'd try something different: I tried another painting.

It was a picture of water lilies. It was on the opposite wall of the room and it was so big that you couldn't really get far enough away from it to see the lilies for what they were: it was just a mass of colours. I had this daft imagine of Claude painting it with a brush fifty feet long. And then, as I stood looking at it, it suddenly came to me: I realised what was going on. He wasn't painting the flowers as flowers, he was painting the colours themselves, and the light and the shadow, and it was only because you *knew* it was a water lily that you saw it as one. If you hadn't known, if you'd never seen one before, you'd just see the colour and the light; and that's what he must have done when he was painting: he must have looked right through the thing, the flower, to what it was made up of. And now the pictures of the church made perfect sense: if you didn't see it as a church then you could just paint the colours and the church was bound to come out of it, made up of all those tiny spots.

I felt quite giddy. It was as if I'd seen something that was mind-bogglingly important and it had just been sitting right there in front of me for my whole life waiting to be noticed: you could look at things and see past their outsides, see into their real selves, like seeing into a secret.

As I walked back to the hotel, I kept my head down, just looking at the pavement in front of me; it sounds daft I know, but I was afraid of what I might see, afraid that I wouldn't be able to look at things straight again.

Well I got over that: the hotel was still the hotel and the next day the train was still just a train. But I had this feeling that I could do it

Dangerous Cocktail

myself, that I could look through things like Claude. All the way home I felt as excited as that Christmas when I was seven and got the Dinky car-transporter and the leather gauntlets from my Gran.

When I got back I went straight down to the Severn Valley to see if I was right. I went up the line to the sheds at Bridgnorth. There was a Hall there, on loan from Didcot and I sat myself down across the tracks from it on the wall by the coaler and I just looked. And it was like looking past it and underneath it and right through it all at the same time: I wasn't seeing a Hall, I was seeing light and shadow and lines and shape and colour. You'll think me daft; I started to cry. Me, a grown man of fifty-eight and in broad daylight. But I'd never seen anything so beautiful in all my life. I sat and I blubbered like an infant because it was more than I could bear and I couldn't tear myself away.

Well, of course, I did eventually. And when I went home, I made a decision. The next day I got the Gas Board to give me a quote for central heating and when they'd put it in, I knocked down the coal shed with a sledgehammer.

# A Love Story

## Sarah Maguire

"I'm pregnant!" I gasped, slightly out of breath, having run to tell my fiancé the incredible news. The bubble of excitement within threatened to explode. I watched as conflicting emotions assailed him. Shock, a fierce love for me, momentary anger and disbelief, compassion. I read them all in the lines and movement of his worn yet lovely face. Of course we both knew that the baby wasn't his. I looked into his eyes, saw a flicker of pain and for the first time experienced a stab of uncertainty. 'Oh please let it be alright.' I'm not explaining this well - I think I should start again, since it really all began with the angel.

There is nothing more satisfying than stepping into the cool of home after a journey of dust, glare and heat. As I blinked, allowing my eyes to adjust, there was a burst of sunshine and the words "Good morning!" resonated through my body. Water slopped from the stone jar I was carrying over my sandaled feet and I bent quickly to stand it on solid ground. Closing my eyes I fought a wave of nausea as the world tilted. I was going to faint. It was one thing to talk with God each day, quite another to have His messenger standing directly in front of me. The moment passed and I opened my eyes.

He was huge, towering above me, radiating light, making my parents' home seem rather shabby and dim. His wings beat rhythmically creating a breeze against my cheeks. His face in part human, kind eyes fastened steadily upon me. He was terrifying, he was magnificent ...... how do you describe someone from heaven in the words of earth? There was such a beauty about him that I wanted to cry.

## Dangerous Cocktail

Still trembling and with a mouth that was unnaturally dry, I forced myself to focus on his words. He was saying that *I* was beautiful as far as God was concerned! His melodious voice continued,

"You're beautiful inside and out. God has a surprise for you. You will have a son and you're to call him Jesus."

Now there was a delicious jumble of excitement and anticipation rising up in me. To choose me………wow! There was just one problem.

"I've never slept with anyone so can you explain how all this is going to happen?"

The angel looked down at me patiently.

"Through the power of God! God will hover over you so the son you have really will be His. You see absolutely nothing is impossible with God."

I did see. God was most definitely at work here and I had to trust him with my life.

"Fine, I'll serve God however He wants. Let it happen exactly as you've said." And that was it. He'd gone, leaving the whole place in gloom. Gosh this was incredible! I couldn't help but give a little twirl. God chose me, chose me, chose me. "Yes!" I shouted aloud. I was the most fortunate girl on earth. Wait until my friends found out, they'd never believe me. And that's when it finally hit me - they actually might not.

I spent the whole of the journey to my cousin Elizabeth's alternately overwhelmed with wonder then gripped with fear, not over what people might think but what they might do. More importantly how would Joseph react? It mattered it really did. Well, I'd said I'd trust God with my whole life hadn't I? I knew that what the angel had told me was the truth and that's all that mattered right now.

*\*\*\**

## A Love Story

That was a gratifying response. A believing Believer, how refreshing! I must warn Gabriel to curb his enthusiasm when bringing these messages from the Boss. Admittedly my fellow archangel did better than his earlier attempt where he rendered the priest Zechariah speechless. He maintains that this was a part of his instructions; I remain unconvinced that it wasn't simply a by-product of the terror he'd inflicted on the man. Their bodies are frail, he needs to remember that. I think he should try thinning down further next time.

Mary's guardian angel returned briefly to report her moment of anxiety on the journey to her cousin's. The Boss soon resolved that in their subsequent encounter. Elizabeth gave Mary much needed encouragement and confirmation that she would indeed be the mother of God's son. And so the plan continues to unfold. There He was right in the middle with them (although naturally they weren't fully aware of that). In fact so effusive was their praise that for a moment I was nervous that the Opposition might be alerted. For now all is quiet and after all I do trust the Boss implicitly.

We encountered potential difficulty in the case of Joseph. It is most peculiar since he is a Believer; nevertheless Gabriel simply remained invisible to him. Gabriel didn't find it amusing when I playfully suggested that he may have thinned down too much on this occasion. In fact it was no laughing matter as by this time Joseph was talking to Mary about divorce, albeit the quiet no fuss variety. Gabriel is nothing if not creative (we know from whom he gets that of course!) and decided on the dream option. He called in the angel Jerababel, a specialist in that field and hence managed to deliver the instructions. I'm pleased to report that Joseph is a humble, obedient man, as a result of which the marriage is back on and everything is running just as it should.

## Dangerous Cocktail

I'm off to choir practice now. We're rehearsing a new song ready for the shepherds. Hopefully this time Gabriel will get it right.

***

Millions of stars shimmered in the clear night sky. I stared captivated. There was something mesmerizing about the vast deep blue expanse. Some nights you could see a shooting star. I shivered pulling my cloak tighter about me.
"No lad, you can't be soft like them townie shepherds." Inwardly I groaned; I'd certainly heard *this* before. "Down in the warm they are. When they've counted the beasts in, just the one lays across the pen like to keep sheep safe. Simple. Here you have to be tough, vigilant lad, keepin' your eyes peeled, right? We don't want any of the silly beggars wanderin' off do we?"
I grunted assent. I knew all about hunting after a lost sheep............but that was another story.
"An' you watch out for the wolves".
So he said, but all I'd experienced was a false alarm. Not that I minded. In spite of myself I glanced at Matthew. You couldn't really see it now but in daylight there was an ugly mark running down his wrinkled face, a tussle with a wolf they said. You had to respect him; he really loved those sheep. The others said he gave them all names. I hadn't had the courage to ask in case it was all some huge joke at my expense. How did he know the difference between them? I had a lot to learn, I knew that. No adventures tonight anyway. There was our flock dotted over the landscape, the occasional shuffling sound, a bleat.

I turned to survey the stars once more. There it was! A shooting star and it was heading this way. Matthew's voice faltered as we stared in fascination at the object hurtling towards us. It was like a brilliant ball of fire. I wanted to run, to hide but somehow my body was paralyzed, my feet fixed. "What the - ?" There were gasps from men older and

## A Love Story

more experienced than myself. I looked at Matthew and swallowed a whimper. Tremendous thudding from my over-excited heart told me I hadn't yet stopped breathing.

"Angel, lad" hissed Matthew. Oh…………my…………goodness.

Out of the glorious heat, light and energy came a voice. "Don't be afraid". The words echoed over the hillside. They seemed to flow right through me. But I was. The threat of wild animals? It was nothing compared with this. Zaccheus and Simon were on their faces but Matthew was standing, leaning on his staff, muttering, "Glory to God. Praise be to God. That I should live to see this with my own eyes."

"Good news! A Saviour has been born today in Bethlehem. He is the Messiah. How will you know it's true? You'll find a baby lying in a manger."

The Messiah had arrived? In my lifetime? As the thoughts darted through my mind the angel seemed to multiply and the stars were blocked out. There were hundreds of angels as if heaven had been ripped open and they'd spilled out. I forced myself to look into their fiery brightness. It felt rather like looking into the sun, a golden glow which pulsated from time to time, out of which I could pick faces and wings. And the noise - it was like the music I've heard from streams but magnified so that it became a roar. They sang and it was more beautiful than anything I've ever heard, so sweet, so clear and pure. They were praising God and telling us about God's peace and I could feel it welling up. There was light and warmth right inside me and I felt that I was somehow being burnt up by the fire but I wasn't afraid any more. I was clean and very much alive.

For several moments there was complete silence as we remained transfixed, staring at a suddenly empty sky. I could feel my throat constricting, the world blurring momentarily. Then Matthew's gnarled hand gripped my shoulder as I blinked furiously.

## Dangerous Cocktail

"We have to go to Bethlehem," tears coursed freely down his weathered cheeks, "straight away." He gave me a reassuring pat. "Take the lantern and run as fast as you can, we'll be right behind you." This was the most important day of my life. The Messiah....the baby..........As I ran surefooted towards the town, the lantern swinging violently, I knew deep inside that the words the angel had spoken would be true. It would all be true.

\*\*\*

I relaxed with relief at being outside of time once more. How did they bear it? "That was a display of self-indulgent showing off wasn't it?" I fixed my colleague with a withering look. Gabriel's wing tip quivered. "Oh very well, you were simply over zealous - once again."

Those poor shepherds; I fully expected them to expire! At first sight they'd seemed to me inauspicious creatures, a rag tag bunch including a strip of a boy and a curmudgeonly old man. Nevertheless on witnessing their heartfelt response I could see something of the attraction they hold for the Boss. Off they'd scampered to find the baby, - such a painstaking means of travel as far as I'm concerned. In a manger, I ask you. The Son of God himself in an animal's feeding trough and a none-too-clean one at that! Surely something more sumptuous would have been appropriate?

The Boss is here. He's read my thoughts of course. One look from Him, no words are necessary, and I'm bowled over once more by such amazing love. All my fractious thoughts are ousted and I am reminded once again, He knows exactly what He is doing. More than that He really does love them extravagantly, passionately and is prepared to risk everything in order to win them back. It's an audacious plan - but He knows exactly what He is doing.

\*\*\*

## A Love Story

The strangest thing happened today. Joseph and I had travelled to Jerusalem with Jesus; we were off to the temple to present our first born son and offer a sacrifice. The lambs on sale were far too expensive for our purse so we settled for two doves. There were hordes of folks but as we walked across the outer courts an elderly man - I later learned his name was Simeon - came striding towards us. He gently took the baby from my arms and in a voice shaking with emotion pronounced, "I've seen him! I've seen the One. I've waited for so long and now here he is, a gift from God, a Saviour for all." I recognized in him the same excitement that I'd experienced when the angel visited.

I remember vividly the next moment as Simeon passed the baby back. I held him in my arms tightly and took in his face, the mop of dark hair, brown eyes. Jesus gazed back contentedly. I touched his cheek - such soft skin- and tiny fingers, perfectly formed, gripped mine. I was consumed by waves of love for him. He was mine, my son. Yet at the same time not mine but God's. God who made heaven and earth, who spoke and it came into being, embodied in a tiny baby, my child. I could only entertain the thought for a few moments before pushing it to the back of my mind. I looked up as Simeon addressed me alone.
"A sword will pierce your heart."
I flinched as I felt it, a shadow and a moment of anguish.
"Now I can die in peace," rasped the old man.
Death. I looked at the aged Simeon before me, at my older husband and at my baby son. Surely not? Yes, there was something of death hanging over him already. Yet there was tremendous life and hope too. Saviour......a rescue mission of some kind? I struggled to comprehend. I would treasure every word that had been spoken, hold deep within me everything which had happened. I held the babe more tightly, eyes only for him. I would love him with all my heart and one day I would finally understand.